Hidden Treasure

G·K
Hall
&C°

Also by Stephen Bly
in Large Print:

Fool's Gold
Miss Fontenot
Proud Quail of the San Joaquin
Red Dove of Monterey
Sweet Carolina
Last Swan in Sacramento
The Marquesa

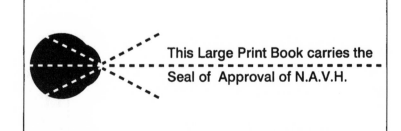

This Large Print Book carries the
Seal of Approval of N.A.V.H.

The Skinners of Goldfield

Hidden Treasure

Stephen Bly

G.K. Hall & Co. • Waterville, Maine

Published in 2001 by arrangement with Crossway Books,
a division of Good News Publishers.

G.K. Hall Large Print Western Series.

The text of this Large Print edition is unabridged.
Other aspects of the book may vary from the original edition.

Set in 16 pt. Plantin by Myrna S. Raven.

Printed in the United States on permanent paper.

Library of Congress Cataloging-in-Publication Data

Bly, Stephen A., 1944–
    Hidden treasure / Stephen Bly.
        p. cm. — (The Skinners of Goldfield : bk. 2)
    ISBN 0-7838-9609-3 (lg. print : hc : alk. paper)
    1. Gold mines and mining — Fiction.   2. Goldfield (Nev.) —
Fiction.   3. Nevada — Fiction.   4. Large type books.   I. Title.
PS3552.L93 H54 2001
    813'.54—dc21   2001039590

For the Wilsons and Halls

A good man
out of the good treasure of the heart
bringeth forth good things:
and an evil man
out of the evil treasure
bringeth forth evil things.
Matthew 12:35 KJV

Foreword

Dearest Punky,

I trust Myrtle has recovered sufficiently from her bout with the creeping crud. Harold says that she should eat dried peaches sprinkled with sulfur. I can't be too sure that isn't a joke. Give her my love.

It seems strange to see our story in print, doesn't it? Oh, that the others had lived to see the day. Wouldn't Mama be proud? And Rita Ann? My, my, my, she would have carried on! I imagine she would have purchased a hundred copies and sent them to every shirttail relative in California, Oklahoma, and Texas.

Oh, how I miss them all so.

But no more of that. I did not intend to be melancholy. At least, not today. I'm sending along some pages of the second book for your comments. Especially examine the scenes when Pop Brannon came to see us. I was so nervous at the time I probably did not remember much. I know you were too little to remember, but you did hear Rita Ann tell the story over and over.

I noticed in *Western Horseman* magazine that Colin Maddison III (with two d's) passed away in May at his ranch outside Winnemucca, Nevada. I'm rather glad I was smart enough as a young lady to decline his advances. I can't imagine more happiness than my Harold and I have had over the years.

The grapes are drying on the trays, so pray that it doesn't rain. Harold is thinking of pulling out the twenty acres of Thompsons on the old home place and planting oranges. I think it's too cold there, but what does a woman know?

Do you remember that peach tree Mama had in the whiskey barrel in Goldfield? Wasn't it a sight to watch her hover over it? I don't believe we ate a single peach, but we all cried when it died. It was like losing a member of the family. Do you remember the funeral service that Rita Ann organized for it? And Tommy-Blue built that long coffin out of barn boards. How we entertained ourselves in those days!

How would we know that in a few years it would be Tommy-Blue who was buried in Goldfield?

Oh, my, now I'm melancholy again.

Please let me know how you like the story. I believe he has captured our family quite well . . . but then I do have a bias in the matter.

Did I tell you our Sully died? We are both heartbroken. I don't think we'll get another dog. At our age it's just too painful to go through this again.

Tell Myrtle that sunshine and orange honey tea always help me.

Love, Sis
Corrie Lou (Skinner) Merced
September 7, 1971
Dinuba, California

One

Goldfield, Nevada, July 11, 1905

"I think someone is followin' us, Daddy."

O.T. glanced back over his shoulder and spied nothing but desert. "No one back there, darlin', but this is a public road. Anyone can use it."

Ten-year-old Corrie Skinner perched next to her father in the buckboard. Her fingers, still showing sticky streaks of strawberry jam, were laced together in her lap. "Tommy-Blue said that if we find any diggin's that look promisin', we should post it and file a claim," she reminded him.

O.T. glanced down at his youngest daughter. "We're just goin' for a ride out to the Wilkins brothers' mine — not stoppin' to look for color."

"I know. But he made me cross-my-heart-and-hope-to-die promise," Corrie explained as she pushed her hat back, letting her dark bangs flop down in her eyes.

"Sounds serious," O.T. remarked.

"Yes, I wanted everything in writing," Corrie informed him. "I told him I get a finder's fee, plus one percent of the gross for the first three years."

O.T. glanced across the barren, buckskin-colored desert floor. *My word, Lord, we have*

11

only been here for a month, and they all sound like mining speculators. "What did your brother say to that?"

Corrie's little, round lips carefully formed each word. "He tried to haggle me down to one percent of net, instead of gross, but I wouldn't go for it."

The heat off the desert floor swirled with the heat tumbling down from the sun, making O.T. feel as if he had just opened the door to a charcoal furnace. "Seems to me you ought to be playin' with dolls instead of speculatin' on gold mines."

Corrie licked her thumb and then slipped her hand into his arm. "Daddy! This is 1905. You act like it was the olden days and we were still back in Oklahoma."

He patted her dress-covered knee. "Darlin', don't you grow up too fast. One twenty-year-old daughter is enough."

Corrie clung to her father's white-shirt-clad arm. His collar was buttoned at the neck, but he wore no tie. The only pattern on the plain cotton shirt was the yellowish ring of sweat and alkali dust on the cuffs and collar. "Daddy, Rita Ann is only twelve!"

"That's what Mama keeps telling me, but I forget."

O.T. let the two brown horses slow down as they pulled the buckboard up the grade just north of the Montezuma Mountains.

Corrie licked the dust off her full lips. "Of course, she acts twenty . . . sometimes! Other times she can be quite annoying." She stared behind the wagon to the south. "I do believe he's following us."

"Who?" O.T. glanced back over his shoulder again and could see absolutely no movement in the shimmering heat reflections on the desert landscape.

"There's a man back there," she insisted.

"Well, he'll catch up with a slow buckboard soon enough." O.T. watched their shadow move ahead of them. "Now what's this about you being bothered by Rita Ann?"

"Rita Ann puts this crease in the covers and tells me to make sure I don't cross the line when I roll over. How am I suppose to know where that line is when I'm asleep?"

"I can see that's a real difficulty."

"You're lucky you get to sleep with Mama. She doesn't make you stay on your side of the bed, does she?"

"Eh . . . no . . . I don't recall she ever made a crease in the covers."

"See there!" Corrie held her little, round nose up in the air. "And Tommy-Blue never complains about Punky."

"Neither of your brothers would wake up if a firecracker went off under their bed, darlin'."

Corrie tried to brush a gravy stain off her brown dress. "Do you want to trade with me, Daddy?"

"Trade?"

"You sleep with Rita Ann, and I'll sleep with

13

Mama." Corrie tapped the toes of her dusty black lace-up boots against the floor of the buckboard.

"Eh, no. I think we'll keep it just like it is." *Ten years old is a wonderful age.*

"How about Mama sleepin' with Rita Ann, and I could —"

"No, darlin'. I'm rather partial to your Mama in that regard. So I'm afraid you will have to learn to get along with your sister."

"That's easy for you to say. Mama don't get out the ruler and measure how far you turn back the cotton sheet."

"I talked to Rita Ann about that. She's not supposed to measure your side of the bed anymore."

"I like Rita Ann, Daddy," Corrie announced.

"I'm very glad to hear that."

"You know, as long as I don't have to get too close to her."

O.T. put his arm around her shoulder and gave her a hug. "I reckon that would apply to lots of folks."

Corrie pointed across the barren desert floor. "Are those the Weepah Hills, Daddy?"

"Yep."

She stood up and steadied herself by holding onto his shoulder. "Can we see the Thomas Motor Mine yet?"

"Nope."

Corrie turned and glanced back down the dusty alkali road toward Goldfield. "I think it's

14

Mr. Rokker following us."

O.T. slowed the rig and turned to look back. "Looks like a man ridin' a big mule. He's too far away to tell who it is."

"It's Mr. Rokker," she insisted.

O.T. slapped the lines on the lead horse's rump. The buckboard lurched forward.

"Aren't we goin' to wait for Mr. Rokker?"

"Whoever it is will catch up soon enough, darlin'. Now you sit down. I don't want you to fall."

Corrie flopped down beside her father. "Danny Rokker said he knew a boy that fell out of a wagon, and the wheel ran right over the boy's head."

"That's exactly why you shouldn't stand when the buckboard's movin'."

"But the boy didn't get hurt! Isn't that a miracle?"

"Seems tough to believe."

"Danny said it didn't hurt the boy one bit! Except he talks kind of funny now."

"I imagine so."

She hugged his arm. "I sure do like gettin' to come with you."

"It was nice of Rita Ann to volunteer to do your chores at the café, wasn't it?"

"Daddy, is Mr. Tolavitch going to buy an auto truck? Rita Ann said he might buy one and let you drive it on your deliveries to the mines."

I believe you just ignored my question, young lady. "I haven't heard anything about it. I

15

wouldn't want to drive one anyway." O.T. tried rubbing a sharp cramp out of his left shoulder.

"Why, Daddy? Why don't you want to drive an auto truck?"

"They're just toys for rich men in the cities mainly — not for rough country like this."

Corrie danced her shoes against the buckboard floor. "Are you ever goin' to get our auto car fixed?"

"I wouldn't want to spoil you kids' fun playin' in it. It makes a nice toy to climb on."

Corrie turned and sat on her knees, holding his arm while she stared behind the wagon. "Mr. Rokker is getting closer. He might be turning off toward Coyote Springs. Aren't we goin' to stop and say hello?"

"Whoever it is might be in a hurry to get somewhere."

"It's Mr. Rokker," she declared. Then she waved her hand and shouted, "Hello, Mr. Rokker!" Corrie turned around and sat down. "He didn't hear me."

"Well, you tried to be friendly."

She brushed down her dress and folded her hands. "Yes. Everyone says I'm a very friendly person."

"Oh?"

"Mrs. Marsh says I'm the friendliest person she has ever met in her life, and she's really old and has met over 100 people."

O.T. hugged his daughter's shoulders. "You

are a friendly girl — that's true. Course, our whole family is sort of that way."

"Rita Ann's friendly with boys, especially Jared Rokker. I'm friendly with everyone. Boys can be a pain. I'm glad you're not a boy, Daddy."

O.T. rubbed the dust and sweat off the back of his neck. "Well, I was a boy once."

"Yes, but you grew up rather well."

"Thank you, Miss Skinner."

"You're welcome." She glanced back over her shoulder. "He's gaining on us. Hey, do you want to know a boy who is a real pill?"

"I surmise you will tell me."

"It's Colin Maddison, the third."

O.T. pulled out his bandanna and wiped the sweat and dust out of his eyes. "The third?"

"With two d's."

"What do you mean, with two d's?" he asked.

"He spells Maddison with two d's."

"He goes around saying that his name has two d's?"

"Yes. I saw him down in front of the Esmeralda Hotel, and he said, 'Hello. My name is Colin Maddison, the third, with two d's.' Isn't that a funny way to introduce yourself?"

"What did you say to him?"

"I said, 'I'm Corrie Skinner, with two n's, three r's, and one c.'"

"Was he amused?"

"No. His father is a banker. I don't think banker's kids are allowed to be amused."

"Are you glad you aren't a banker's child?"

17

"Oh, yes." She hugged O.T. "Me and Tommy-Blue think you and Mama are the most wonderful parents in the entire world."

"And Rita Ann? What does she think?"

Corrie shrugged. "She said she sees room for improvement."

"Yes, I imagine she does," O.T. laughed. "There's hardly a person on the face of the earth that big sister couldn't improve. Now who is this young Mr. Maddison, the third, with two d's?"

"His daddy is Colin Maddison, the second, president of the Ormsby State Bank up in Carson City. They own some mining stock down here. Colin says they are building the largest home in Nevada on the mountain west of Carson City."

"And how did you respond to that, darlin'?"

"I stuck my tongue out at him."

O.T. reached over and brushed her thick bangs off her forehead, which felt sweaty and sticky. "I believe that was an appropriate response."

"Hey, Skinner!" It was a deep male voice.

O.T. pulled the rig over to the side of the road as Elias Rokker rode up on a mule.

O.T. shoved his hat back. "Elias, you're a long way from town."

"Well, I was headin' to Coyote Springs and saw Rita Ann wave. Thought maybe she was signaling me," Rokker explained.

"I'm Corrie," she corrected him.

"Yep, that's what I meant."

O.T. leaned back, trying to stretch the cramps out of his back. "Sorry about that, Elias. She was bein' friendly — that's all. Didn't mean to divert you."

"I'm very friendly," Corrie mumbled without looking Mr. Rokker in the eyes.

Rokker's shirt collar was tight and drenched with sweat. "You deliverin' assay reports, Skinner?"

"I'm headed out to the Weepahs with an analysis for the Wilkins brothers."

"Wilkins brothers?" Rokker patted the butt plate of his Winchester '94. "I don't envy you none."

O.T. slid his boot back under the wagon seat to see if he had remembered to toss in the shotgun. "They've always treated me square." He felt the double barrels under his heel.

"Ever since you walked on that rock wall and got us all free water, ever'one in town treats you square, Skinner," Rokker replied.

"That was last month, Elias." O.T. smiled. "People forget those things soon enough."

"They ain't forgot about me walking across town drunk as a skunk in my cut-down long handles. I get razzed about it most ever' day."

"I reckon they'll even forget about that in time."

Rokker pulled a folded piece of yellowing paper out of his pocket. "They will when this plays its hand."

"What you got there?" O.T. asked.

Elias Rokker rode close to the wagon. "A fortune — that's what this is!" His voice was soft, and he glanced around as if a crowd was listening to every word. "Eh, Rita Ann, why don't you hike over to that there red rock so me and your daddy can talk in private."

"I'm Corrie," she mumbled. "Daddy, can I get some sample rocks over there for Tommy-Blue?" She pointed across the road.

"All right, darlin', but don't go past those red boulders."

Corrie scampered out of the buckboard and across the powdery yellow-red dirt.

O.T. dropped the lead lines over the hand brake and climbed down to face Rokker.

The huge man leaned over in the saddle until Skinner could smell garlic from his breath. "I got me the original map to the Don Fernando gold!" he sputtered.

"You do?"

Rokker rattled the paper. "Yep. It's right here."

"To tell you the gospel truth, Elias, I've never heard of the Don Fernando gold. Is it a mining district?"

"Better than that. It's refined gold. Over 500 pounds of it."

O.T. let out a whistle and then strolled up to adjust the rigging on the horses. Rokker dismounted and followed him. "You see, back when this country was still Mexican, this here fella Don Fernando had a gold mine on the east side of the Sierras. He had a whole crew of digger Indians

20

that dug it, crushed it, and, thanks to a barrel of mercury, separated it. Don Fernando waited until he had a whole ton of it. Then he started out in four groups to cross the desert for Santa Fe."

"Let me guess." O.T. rubbed the horse's neck. "One of this Don what's-his-name's crews never showed up in Santa Fe, and people have been lookin' for his gold ever since."

"So," Rokker boomed, "you *did* hear the story!"

"Not really." O.T. sauntered back to the buckboard. "I was jist guessin'."

"Well, this morning I was unloadin' a whole shipment of mining goods that came up from El Paso. The boys out at the July Extension bought a used millin' outfit down in Sonora. They had a couple of Mexicans who rode the train show 'em how it all went back together."

O.T. pointed to the paper in Rokker's hand. "And one of them had this map?"

"Don't that beat all? And he asks if I know where the place is on the map. I tell him I can't read the Mexican writin', but it sort of looks like the mountains out west of us."

O.T. stared off to the west toward the distant Sierra Nevadas. "I suppose a person could cross the desert around here about as well as anyplace . . . providin' they steered clear of Death Valley."

"That's what I'm thinkin'. Well, this here Mexican gets all excited and starts to make plans to ride west when the other one comes

21

along and says they have to go back to Mexico. They had a telegram waitin' for them at the hotel that ol' Pancho Villa is raidin' their village, and they better get back pronto."

"Don't tell me he offered to sell you such a valuable map?" O.T. probed.

"No, he just folded it and put it back in his pocket. But I tagged after him and made him an offer he couldn't refuse."

"What did you pay him for it?"

"I paid $100 cash."

"That's a lot of money, Elias. I didn't know your job paid so well."

"It don't, but today was payday, and Miller advanced me some from next week."

"You spent grocery money on a map?" O.T. challenged.

"Skinner, with this gold my family won't have to worry about groceries for the rest of their lives." Rokker unfolded the paper. "Take a look at this. It even has the seal of Mexico on the corner . . . see? You know it's got to be authentic."

O.T. Skinner held the map out in the sunlight and studied it. "Did you read these Spanish words, Elias?"

"No, sir, I don't read Mexican. But I can follow a map as well as the next guy. Here's the Montezumas . . . and the site is jist *uno* . . . *dos* . . . *tres* . . . *cuatro* miles away."

"Maybe that's four days," O.T. cautioned.

"Four days west? That would put it in the heart of the Sierra Nevadas. It ain't up there because he was headed out into the desert."

O.T. handed the map back to Rokker. "You might want to get someone to read those Spanish words to you."

"I ain't cuttin' no one in on this fortune. No, sir, it was my $100, and I'm — say, I take that back. You and Dola Mae took good care of us when we was down and out. And you nursed my Nellie back to health." Rokker's voice dropped to a whisper, and he glanced up and down the empty road. "For $25 cash I'll cut you in for 25 percent."

O.T. pulled himself back up into the buck-board. "I'll have to pass on it, Elias, but it's a mighty generous offer. First of all, if you go out there and don't find it, I'll have to —"

"It ain't a question of findin' it!" Rokker boomed as he mounted his mule. "It's a question of haulin' it to the bank — that's all. That much is heavy. I could use the help."

"Yes, well, if we didn't find it, I'd have a tough time lookin' my Dola Mae in the eyes and tellin' her I gambled away our money."

"I'm goin' to find it. Then you'll be sorry," Rokker insisted.

"I would be delighted to have very rich friends. Besides, if you find it, you deserve it all," O.T. replied. "I'll volunteer to bring out a wagon and help you haul it in."

Rokker stood up straight in the stirrups, and the mule shied back at the shift in weight. A slight grin crept across the big man's

23

unshaven face. "You might be right, Skinner. I do deserve it all. But I want you to know I don't forget them that shows my family kindness." Rokker sat down in the saddle. "I reckon I better get on this here trail. I want to get out there and mark the spot and get back to Goldfield before dark. Figure I'll rent a wagon and tote it to town. Don't know how I can keep it a secret. I'll figure out something."

"I assure you that I won't tell a soul."

"Especially don't tell my Nellie. I want to surprise her with the good news," Rokker insisted.

"I won't say a word."

"I know you won't. Wouldn't have showed it to no one on earth but the Wall Walker. You're the only man in this town that I'd trust with my family — or my treasure map."

"Good luck, Elias, and make sure you get back before dark. The desert can spin you around at night."

"Yep, Skinner, ain't that the truth?"

Corrie sprinted up to the buckboard from the other side. "Daddy, look at this rock. It has pretty turquoise in it. Can I keep it? Please, Daddy!"

"I thought you were going to take it to Tommy-Blue."

"I'll take him the red one. This one is so pretty."

"Bring 'em both," O.T. replied. "By the time we make it home, I have a feeling I'll have a buckboard full of rocks."

24

"Isn't this a pretty rock, Mr. Rokker?" she asked.

"Yes, Miss Rita Ann, it's a fine specimen." Rokker turned his mule. "Are you sure you don't want in on this, Skinner?" he called back.

O.T. pulled off his hat and wiped the sweat off his forehead. "Thanks, Elias, but I need to save up so we can get to Dinuba, California. Good luck to you just the same."

"A man don't need luck when he has a map. I ain't never met nobody so happy about bein' poor," Rokker mumbled.

Corrie dumped the rocks into the back of the buckboard and crawled up next to O.T. "We ain't poor, Mr. Rokker. I got me three dresses, and one of them is a readymade that nobody but me has ever wore."

Rokker tipped his hat and rode his mule south.

O.T. snapped the line on the lead horse, and the buckboard rumbled forward.

Corrie curled her lip and muttered under her breath, "And my name ain't Rita Ann!"

Dola Mae Skinner wiped her hands on the white cotton apron and brushed a strand of brown hair off her sweaty forehead. At 4:30 A.M. that morning her hair had been neatly pinned, but there was no air movement in the hot, stuffy kitchen.

"Rita Ann, take the butter out, please. Hurry back. No dawdling!"

"Mama, I did butter yesterday morning. It's Corrie's turn. Let me pour the coffee!"

"Corrie Lou went with Daddy out to the Wilkins brothers' mine. Hurry now."

" 'If there be nothing new, but that which is . . . hath been before, how are our brains beguiled.' " Rita Ann sighed and balanced butter bowls along her arm.

"Maybe your Mr. Shakespeare can help you serve butter," Omega LaPorte teased.

Rita Ann shoved her glasses up on her nose, snatched up more butter dishes, and marched toward the huge restaurant dining room. "Where's Tommy-Blue?" she called out.

Dola folded green peppers and onions into the eggs. "He and Danny Rokker found a new lot to prospect on."

Rita Ann rolled her eyes toward the ceiling. "And that means I'm the only one left to help!"

"It's the curse of the oldest child," Omega remarked from the stove where she was turning bacon with a long fork. "My sister Alpha used to complain the same way. Besides, your baby brother is out there helping."

Rita Ann paused at the doorway. "Punky's only two. What can he do?"

"He's entertaining the men until breakfast is ready," Dola answered. "That's why the men come early."

"Heavens, I thought they came early to see the cute serving girls," Omega teased.

"Only Lucky Jack," Rita Ann smirked. She backed the door open and scooted out of the kitchen.

26

Omega wiped the sweat off her black forehead. "She's growin' up, Mama, she's growin' up."

"In the month we've been in Goldfield, she's aged five years," Dola concurred.

"And if you and me keep feedin' seventy-five hungry men twice a day, we're going to age just as fast." Omega's grin revealed perfectly straight white teeth.

"Who would have thought the demand would be so great, what with all the other restaurants in town." Dola grabbed the mixing bowl and whipped another dozen eggs.

Omega stretched each piece of cooked bacon on the drip rack. "Well, we do sell a meal cheaper than anyone in town."

Dola glanced down at the sweat stains around the lace cuffs of her dress sleeves. *I wish I had the nerve to push them up to my elbows like Omega.* "A man ought to get a good hot breakfast for fifty cents. It's not a matter of what others charge, but what's fair."

"We could double our prices tomorrow and not lose a customer."

"Yes, but I couldn't justify that before the Lord someday."

"Dola Mae, you are like nobody I ever met. You enjoy being poor that much?"

"I've never been poor in my life," Dola snapped.

"How many dresses did you have when you came to town?"

27

"Eh . . . two."

"And one of them you never wore."

"I was saving it for special occasions."

"And how many dresses do you have now?"

"Three."

"And one of them you only wear to church."

Dola pulled a large tin bowl with handles off the shelf. "What's your point?"

Omega shook her head. "Nothin'. What can I say? If a woman don't think she's poor, then she ain't. That's all there is to it. Now me, I've been poor. I had to eat old turnips that someone else threw away and boil up spurge that most people consider weeds. And skin 'possums. I'll tell you right now, Dola Mae Skinner, I ain't never goin' back to that. Lucian and me even tried skinnin' a big, old, fat skunk one time. Oh boy, I ain't never goin' to do that again."

Dola separated a huge pan of steaming biscuits into napkin-lined baskets. "Is the bacon ready?"

The black woman peeked in at the warming pans in the big cast-iron stove. "Might as well start servin' before there's a riot in the dining hall. Sounds like they're clappin' for food."

Rita Ann buzzed back into the kitchen. "Wasco is playing his harmonica, and Lucky Jack has Punky dancing on the table."

"Omega and I will serve now. How about you pouring the coffee?"

" 'How can I return in happy plight, that am debarred the benefit of rest?' " Rita Ann intoned.

28

Dola rolled her eyes at Omega. "It's the summer when she memorizes the sonnets."

With biscuits, butter, and jam already on the tables, Dola ladled out the scrambled eggs. Omega LaPorte followed behind with the bacon, making sure each man got only five pieces. Rita Ann trailed them, refilling tin cups with steaming coffee. The roar of conversations diminished with each full plate of food.

The Miner's Delight Café dining room was sixty feet wide and forty-five feet deep. Behind it, the kitchen was a long, narrow fifteen by sixty feet. Inside the dining area were long tables and benches. The clientele varied from dirty, sweaty men coming off the graveyard shift to suit-and-tie men, ready for a busy day at one of Goldfield's several stock exchanges. Almost all the men had two things in common.

They were single.

They were hungry.

Dola had just emptied the first pan of scrambled eggs and turned toward the kitchen when she heard an angry voice behind her. A tall, thin man with dirty beard and faded denim coveralls shielded his plate from Omega's fork full of bacon.

"I didn't come in here to get food cooked by some Negress!" he roared.

Omega skipped the man and continued to serve the others.

Dola marched up to the complainer. "What did you say?"

"I don't want no dumb darkie touchin' my food!" he fumed.

Dola took a deep breath. *Help me, Lord.* She took the big ladle and banged it against the tin bowl until there was silence in the room.

From the other side of the room, she heard Punky squeal, "Uh oh!"

There was muted laughter.

"Boys," she shouted, "would you please escort this gentleman out to the street. He is no longer welcome at the Miner's Delight Café."

"Like Hades they will. I —"

"Lucky Jack, I wonder if you'd do the honors!" Dola called out.

From across the room the lanky, blond-headed man rose, half a dozen men by his side. "Our pleasure, Mrs. Skinner. Did he complain about too many peppers in the eggs?" Lucky Jack grinned as he strolled across the room.

"No, he used derogatory terms about the color of Omega's skin. I simply will not tolerate that for a moment in this café."

"Lucky Jack Gately?" the man with the dirty beard gulped.

The smile dropped off Lucky Jack's face. "Mister, you can walk out of here, you can run out of here, you can be thrown out of here, or you can be shot and dragged out of here. But anyway you look at it, you're leavin'," Lucky Jack announced.

The man jumped to his feet. "Wait a minute, boys! Maybe I was a little rash in judgment."

"I'm in favor of shootin' and draggin'," Wasco Delmar growled.

The man scurried toward the front door.

"Boys," Dola hollered so all could hear, "you can complain all you want about the food, but if I hear one word about Omega, you'll be tossed out on your ear. Is that understood?"

"Yes, ma'am," one of the men shouted.

"And if you make one inappropriate remark or action toward my daughter Rita Ann, you'll be shot on sight!"

"Mother!" Rita Ann gasped.

A wave of approval rolled across the room.

Dola and Omega returned to the kitchen to refill their pans.

"Thanks for stickin' up for me . . . again," Omega offered. "But I've been around jerks like that all my life. I just shrug it off."

"So have I, but this is one place where I don't have to tolerate it."

"You just lost a payin' customer," Omega pointed out.

"No, I didn't lose a thing. He just lost the best fifty-cent breakfast in the state of Nevada. It's his loss, not mine."

"What would you have done if Lucky Jack and them weren't here?"

"Then you and I would have tossed him out," Dola maintained. "I reckon we could have handled him, don't you?"

Omega's brown eyes danced. "I reckon we could, Dola Mae. . . . I reckon there ain't a

31

man in this town that the two of us couldn't dismiss with a thump if we set our minds to it. I ain't never known a woman as determined as you, unless it was me."

Rita Ann was breathless when she reentered the kitchen. "Mama, Lucky Jack said there's a mechanic in town who might be able to fix our auto car."

"I told you, that sounds like a very great waste of money."

Rita Ann refilled the coffee serving pitcher. "How do you know it will be expensive?"

"Ada and Ida are rested. Mule power is good enough for Skinners," Dola insisted as she hefted another bowl of scrambled eggs.

"She's afraid of auto cars," Rita Ann told Omega, who was loading up another pan of bacon.

"They are a noisy lot. But, oh, the rush of wind in your hair — I do like that." Omega wiped her hands on a flour sack towel.

"You've actually ridden in one — when it was moving?" Rita Ann exclaimed.

"Lucian and I went for a ride in New Orleans."

"Did it go fast?"

"Fast? It went over twenty-five miles an hour!" Omega declared.

"Were you scared?"

"Sort of."

"What do you mean, sort of?"

"Scared enough to clutch onto Lucian, but

not so scared that I wet my bloomers," Omega laughed.

Rita Ann's hand went over her mouth, and she blushed. "Oh . . ."

"I believe you two are needed in the dining room," Dola lectured.

"Your mama don't cotton to sluggard ways," Omega chuckled. She lifted the bacon-filled pan onto her shoulder.

Rita Ann carried the full coffee pitcher in front of her. " 'Being your slave, what should I do but tend upon the hours and times of your desire?' "

Dola scooped scrambled eggs into the large bowl. *Lord, You have been very good to us. We have a nice, huge room upstairs. Good meals everyday. And enough money to buy the children new shoes and clothes. And we've only been here a month.*

I like feeding these men. It's like taking care of family. I like the friends we've made . . . but I really do hate the desert. The heat, the flies, the wind, the dryness, the dust . . . Oh, how I hate the alkali dust.

Good thing we aren't going to stay here.

I can't grow a garden. Can't have an orchard. Can't plant roses . . . or grass . . . or anything. It's not a place to stay. A few more weeks . . . a few more months . . . perhaps next spring . . . after the children finish school.

Maybe we could save up a few dollars. Maybe the auto car could be repaired. We could roll into Pearl and Pegasus's place in grand style. Oh, wouldn't that be nobby?

Omega stuck her head through the doorway. "Lucky Jack is hollerin' for eggs."

"I'm on my way," Dola returned. *Lord, forgive me for such foolish dreams. That's why we must move. The whole emphasis in Goldfield is on accumulating wealth. Deliver me.*

The Thomas Motor Mine site followed a narrow arroyo west into the Weepah Hills. Several cabins built on pilings blocked the arroyo like a fort, with a closed gate between them.

"How come those cabins are up off the ground, Daddy? Is it to keep the snakes out?" Corrie pointed.

O.T. drove the team toward the gate. "It's for lettin' the water rush underneath them when it rains." The rough road jarred the wagon and O.T.'s back.

"When does it rain out here, Daddy? The ground's so dry it looks like it never rains. We've been here a month, and it hasn't rained one day."

"In the summer, darlin', it all comes down at once. It floods all these arroyos."

"Daddy, what's the difference between a gulch and an arroyo?"

"We call 'em gulches. In the southwest they're arroyos, and up in the northwest they call 'em coulees. I reckon they're mostly the same."

"Look! That sign says, Trespassers Will Be Shot! Does that mean us, Daddy?"

"Nope. We're invited guests."

O.T. stopped the buckboard in front of the gate.

"I'll open it, Daddy. Let me open the gate," she insisted.

"Okay, darlin'. Then close it behind me."

Corrie skipped over and opened the new wooden gate that was already starting to sag. A tall man with a mostly bald head appeared at the porch of one of the cabins, a carbine in his hand.

"What are you doin'?" he hollered.

Corrie shielded the hot desert sun out of her eyes. "Hi, Mr. Wilkins. I came out here with my daddy!" She smiled.

A wide grin broke across Ace Wilkins's face. "Corrie, darlin', you caught me by surprise!" Wilkins leaned the carbine against the porch post. "We haven't had tourists stop by and pester us. I didn't figure on seein' you." He stepped off the porch and helped her with the gate. "Howdy, O.T."

Skinner tipped his hat. "Howdy, Ace. Just bringin' your weekly assays."

"And you brought Corrie. She's the purdiest girl in camp."

Corrie folded her arms across her chest and scowled. "I'm the *only* girl in camp, Mr. Wilkins."

"Don't you go tormentin' me with the truth," he laughed.

The Thomas Motor Mine site resembled a small town. Besides the headworks of the mine shaft and several tin shop buildings, there were half a dozen cabins, a blacksmith shop, a warehouse, a barn, and a corral. All were made of new, unpainted lumber that had already faded gray in the heat and the wind.

O.T. pointed to a half-built concrete foundation. "The bunkhouse is coming along."

"Got to get it finished by September. We want twenty miners in here by then," Ace explained.

"Is Fergus here, Mr. Wilkins?" Corrie asked.

"That crazy, old Indian. We never know from one hour to the next if he's around or not. If he's here, he's at the cook's shack."

"Which one is that?" she asked.

"The one over there — with smoke in the stack."

"Can I go see Fergus, Daddy?"

"Yep, but don't get in anyone's way . . . and don't go beggin' for food. We didn't come out here to mooch a meal."

Ace leaned up against the side of the buckboard. "You and your kids can eat at our table any day. You know that, Skinner."

"Since Dola Mae opened that café, we've all been eatin' way too regular. We'll all be fat as hogs before long." O.T. reached into the back of the wagon and lifted out a large wooden crate. "Here's your samples and reports."

"How did it look?" Ace Wilkins quizzed.

O.T. shook his head. "We play this game ever' week, Ace."

"Just testin' you."

"I don't ever look at the reports. You know that for a fact."

"Skinner, Tolavitch was right in hirin' you. You got to be the only man in town that doesn't want to know how rich this claim is out here."

"I'm prayin' that it's rich enough to make you, Deuce, and Trey happy . . . and that it's meager enough to keep you from ruinin' your lives with wealth."

Ace Wilkins lowered his voice. "So far, Skinner, you jist about summed it up."

"Hey, Skinner!"

O.T. glanced up to see a tall, thin man with a dirty plaster cast on his right arm. "Howdy, Deuce."

Deuce Wilkins strolled over to where O.T. and Ace stood. "Did you bring me that cask of whiskey?"

"No, and I didn't bring any dancin' girls for Trey," O.T. laughed.

A wide grin broke across the tallest Wilkins brother's face. "You're kind of useless as a delivery man."

"I did bring the assay reports."

"How do they look?" Deuce grinned. "Silent O.T. Skinner. Might be the most important man in Esmeralda County."

"Might be the only one everybody can trust," Ace added. He opened the crate and pulled out a sheaf of papers.

"Daddy, can Fergus ride back to town with

us?" Corrie skipped out of the cook's shack, her arm laced in the arm of the white-haired, wrinkle-faced Paiute.

"Tomorrow is my birthday," Fergus announced. "I want to celebrate in town."

"How old are you going to be?" Corrie asked.

The old Indian shook his head. "I don't know. But it must be very old because I can't remember being young."

"If you can't remember," Deuce challenged, "how do you know for sure your birthday's tomorrow?"

"How do you know it's not?" the Indian countered.

"You can haul him off anytime, Skinner," Deuce added. "All he does is hang around here gettin' free meals."

"I'm merely lookin' after my investment."

"You didn't put one dime into this mine."

"Perhaps I should have left you to wander in the desert. You would still be plodding around out there."

"We was just takin' the long way — that's all," Trey explained.

Fergus started to climb into the buckboard and then stopped halfway, his shoulders bent forward. "I seem to be stuck," he said.

O.T. stepped over and gave him a shove.

"Thank you," Fergus said.

Skinner turned back to the Wilkins brothers. "You got any samples ready to take back?"

"Nope. We were waitin' for them results. You come back next week, and we'll load you down. Gettin' close to a rich lead," Ace announced.

Trey Wilkins swung down out of the shaft house and marched across the yard. "Skinner! Can you take a letter to town for me?" he called.

"Are you writing to your girlfriend, Mr. Wilkins?" Corrie called back.

He handed the smudged letter up to O.T. "No, Corrie, it's a letter to my mama. Say, are you goin' to run off without dancin' with me?"

Corrie clutched her father's arm. "I only dance with my daddy," she replied.

"You got smart kids, Skinner," Trey laughed.

"They take after their mama. See you boys next week."

"Say, O.T.," Ace interjected. "Had an old boy stop out here lookin' for that Thomas automobile of ours."

"It's parked in the alley behind the café if you need it."

"No, no, we was serious when we gave it to you. It belongs to you. But this old boy says he's a machinist and can fix it to run. I told him to look you up. His name is Frazier. I reckon it might cost more than it's worth though."

"If it costs a dollar, it's more than it's worth to me. The kids enjoy playin' in it, but they have a good time playing in a box or a hole in the ground."

Ace Wilkins closed the gate behind them as they pulled back out into the arroyo.

O.T. stuck the letter into his shirt pocket. *A letter to his mama? Kind of funny. Lord, reckless men like the Wilkins brothers . . . Well, I guess I forgot they have a mama someplace who thinks highly of them. Forgive me for failin' to see 'em clearly.* "Well, Mrs. Wilkins, your boys is settlin' down a little, and they jist might be rich real soon. I reckon they'll come home and paint your house and buy you a new winter coat."

A rattle in the back of the wagon caused him to spin around and see the old Paiute perched on the back of the buckboard.

"Fergus, you can sit up here with us," O.T. invited.

The Indian lay down on his back, his Springfield trapdoor carbine by his side. "I think I will take a nap."

"It's not very comfortable back there."

"It is better than sleeping on cactus."

"I reckon you're right about that."

"And it is better than sleeping in a snake den. And it is better than sleeping in a cold stream. It is better than sleeping in the snow, and it is better —"

"I get your point, Fergus," O.T. laughed. "Go to sleep."

"Thank you, Wall Walker. I intend to do that."

The sun was straight above them, and the day was so hot and dry that the sky was a pale pastel blue. Corrie retrieved her wide-brimmed straw hat from under the bench. "I hate this hat, but it's too hot not to wear one."

"It looks very pretty on you."

"Daddy, you would tell me that if I had a lard bucket on my head," she scolded.

"Well, it would be the truth."

"This makes me look old."

"Darlin', there isn't a piece of clothing in the world that could make you look old."

"I wouldn't mind being a little older."

"How old would you like to be?"

"Thirteen. Then I'd be older than Rita Ann, and Mama would let me read that book."

"What book?"

"*La Paloma Roja de Monterey — The Red Dove of Monterey.*"

"Is it too mature for you?"

"Daddy! If it was a mature book, Mama wouldn't let me read it ever! She said there are too many Spanish words, and it might be confusing. Everybody is a Don or a Doña. What is a Don, Daddy?"

"It's sort of like sayin' Lord and Lady, or somethin' like that, in Spanish."

"Mama says I have to be older to understand all those Spanish words."

"Don Fernando," O.T. mumbled.

"What did you say, Daddy?"

O.T. glanced back in the wagon. "Fergus, have you ever heard of Don Fernando's gold?"

Fergus sat straight up as if prodded with a hot poker. "The gold of Don Fernando! When I was young, my father showed me the place it was buried! Oh, yes . . . I know the place. I think."

41

Two

Tommy-Blue stormed across the bare hardwood floor of the upstairs living quarters, a turquoise-colored rock the size of a baseball in one hand and a reddish yellow one in the other. He held them up as if presenting an offering to the bare electric light bulb in the center of the ceiling. "You were supposed to label each sample," he fumed.

Corrie refused to look at her brother. She carefully hung her brown dress on the wooden hanger. "I did label them," she said. "There's a CLS on each one. I etched it with a horseshoe nail. Fergus helped me."

Tommy-Blue marched over to the bed covered with a denim-scrap quilt. A collection of similar rocks lay scattered beside it. "Each rock should be numbered, and then I need a correspondin' journal entry with the exact geological description of the physical site. What am I supposed to do with a bunch of rocks marked with your initials?" he demanded.

Dola sat at the table rubbing a cramp out of her left hand. "Tommy-Blue, quit haranguing your sister. She did the best she could." Dola stared down at her callused, bony fingers. *Too young for arthritis, much too young. But, oh, how they cramp up and hurt every evening.*

Tommy-Blue carefully placed the two rocks on the floor with the others and threw up his hands. "Amateurs! I'm surrounded by amateurs."

O.T. looked up from the pile of notes and papers scattered across the small table. "Tommy-Blue!"

The barefoot boy with duckings, suspenders, and a new but not very clean boiled shirt dropped his chin to his chest. "Sorry, Daddy."

Punky dragged a small red-and-black afghan across the floor and meandered over to Dola. He lifted his hands. "Mama, do!"

She reached down and plucked him up. A sharp pain shot up from her thigh to the base of her neck as she let him ride on her hip. "You get any heavier, darlin', and we'll start callin' you Chunky instead of Punky. Mr. Skinner, I do believe your children are eating well."

O.T. looked up. "A good number of men in this town are eating well too. From all these receipts, it looks like the café is doin' well."

"This one little man is going to bed." She toted Punky across the room. "About time for the rest of you to do the same."

Tommy-Blue plopped down on the floor next to the rock collection, his back against the bed, a big book on his lap. "Mama, I can't go to bed. I have to return Mr. Tolavitch's book to him tomorrow, and I haven't identified all the rock samples that somebody didn't label correctly."

Corrie stuck her tongue out at him and continued to brush the brown dress hanging on its peg.

Rita Ann carefully set her glasses back on her nose. "Mother, I am twelve years old, and it's terribly unfair that I have to go to bed at the same time as my two-year-old brother. Surely there must be some privilege in age and maturity."

"Certainly there is," Dola assured her. "You have the privilege of getting up at 4:30 to help serve breakfast. And you have the privilege of not needing to take a nap every afternoon. I think that's quite reasonable."

Rita Ann began to unfasten her long, dark hair. "May I please leave the light on and read?"

"As long as you're in bed." Dola squeezed the rag in the basin and washed the two-year-old's happy face. He giggled. *Silas Paul Skinner, you are the Lord's special surprise blessing for me!*

Tommy-Blue slipped his suspenders off his shoulders. "Can I take my sample rocks to bed with me so I can identify them?" he asked.

Dola wiped off Punky's dirty, chubby feet. "No, you may not. There will be plenty of time tomorrow."

Corrie, now wearing an old shirt of her father's for a nightshirt, strolled to her mother. "Are you and Daddy going to sit out on the balcony and talk real low?" she asked.

Dola pulled the comforter back, and Punky crawled under the covers, his hand still clutching the small black-and-red afghan. "Probably," she admitted. "It's the one time of day we get to relax alone."

Corrie leaned her head against her mother's arm. "Why can't I sit out there with Daddy and talk real low?" she murmured.

Dola gave her youngest daughter a squeeze. "Because you must get your sleep. We need you to help serve in the morning. We missed you being here this morning."

Rita Ann waltzed over to her bed with her big book in her hand. " 'When I do count the clock that tells the time, and see the brave day sunk in hideous night.' "

Dola rubbed the back of her neck as she strolled to the table where O.T. sat studying the café receipts. "Could you tuck them in and say prayers," she asked. "I need to go down and check the pantry."

He neatly stacked the receipts in an empty cigar box. "You're supposed to be through with work by now," he chided.

She sauntered toward the light-green-painted wooden door that led to the stairs. "I just need to review the supplies. I won't sleep well until I double-check to make sure we have enough for breakfast."

O.T. stood. "It's nine o'clock. If you don't have it now, it won't matter."

She reached over and straightened his sweaty shirt collar. "Mr. Wilson would open up his store for me," she told him.

He laid his hand on her cheek until the worry lines across her forehead melted. "Pop Wilson will be in bed by now."

She pulled his hand down and kissed his fingers. "Yes, but he'll open up for me if I need something."

"Are you two goin' to smooch or what?" Corrie called out from across the room.

O.T. dropped his hand to his side. "I'll tuck them in, Mama. You go on."

"And prayers?"

"Yes, we'll pray that Mama doesn't work herself sick."

She paused at the door. "Orion, we've worked hard in the fields of Oklahoma, and we've worked hard on the road just to survive, and we're both workin' hard here in a desert gold town. I don't reckon we will ever have a time that we aren't workin' hard."

O.T. watched his thin-shouldered, narrow-faced wife descend the steep stairway to the darkened dining room. She wore no makeup, no jewelry, no fancy dress. Just gray-streaked brown hair pinned up on her head, wrinkles at her eyes, and a wry smile across narrow, tight lips. *Lord, there goes the sweetest, most gentle woman You ever created. I can't really believe it was Your plan for her to marry a no-account like me. But, oh, Lord, how grateful I am.*

Tommy-Blue slept on his back, one hand flopped over the edge of the mattress toward the neat line of fourteen rock samples on the floor. Each was turned with the CLS etching facing the painted wooden floor.

Punky was on his stomach beside him. His knees were tucked under him, and his night-shirt-draped bottom pointed up to the bare electric light in the middle of the ceiling. His left hand clutched the afghan.

Corrie was sprawled on top of the worn remnant quilt, one arm under her open mouth, the other across the dreaded crease line that divided the bed between "yours" and "mine." Her thick, short hair sprang out in several directions as if trying to escape confinement.

Rita Ann lay on her back, the sheet folded exactly two inches down from her long, narrow neck. Though her round blue eyes were closed, her silver-framed glasses were still on her delicate upturned nose. Her beloved but slightly tattered *Complete Works of Wm. Shakespeare* straddled her thin chest.

O.T. surveyed the sight from the double doorway to the balcony. He stole over to Rita Ann's side, carefully removed her glasses, and hoisted the heavy book.

"Good night, Daddy," she whispered without opening her eyes.

"Good night, darlin'. I thought you were asleep."

She kept her eyes closed. " 'Is it thy will thy image should keep open my heavy eyelids to the weary night?' "

47

He laid his hand on her soft cheek. "Just whose image is keeping you awake, Princess?"

She squinted her closed eyes and wiggled her nose. "Jared Rokker."

O.T. rested his hands on his hips. "You want me to run him off so you can get to sleep?"

Rita Ann opened one eye and grinned. "No," she whispered. Then she closed her eye.

"Night, darlin'. I'll turn off the light now."

"Night, Daddy."

O.T. reclined on the covered balcony. Although the desert still radiated heat, there was some air movement. The breeze felt almost pleasant as it rolled along Columbia Street. Electric streetlights cast a muted glow over Goldfield. O.T. watched shadowy people dart in and out of the cafes and saloons that were still open.

He unfastened the top button on his shirt and felt the drift of air on the sweat-drenched collar. Reaching down, he tugged off his dusty boots and peeled off his socks. He stretched his long legs out in front of him and wiggled his toes under the star-filled sky. A wagonload of miners rode toward Columbia Mountain.

O.T. leaned his head back against the hard wood of the chair and closed his eyes. *Lord, what are we doin' in this desert town? We don't fit in. We're just farm people on our way to California. The weather here is harsh, unrelenting. Sin is glorified. Greed is rampant. Spiritual sensitivity is scarce. The kids here grow up with sand in their eyes and gold fever in their bones. The people are blunt, rough, wild.*

Some of the people anyway.

If it wasn't for the people, we'd move on to-morrow.

It's always the people.

That's why You haven't given up on this planet.

That's why You will never give up on a place like Goldfield.

The people.

The ones You created in Your image.

The ones You came to save.

The ones You called to Yourself.

I guess that's why You're here.

O.T. opened his eyes. Above the shadows of the city, the desert sky seemed suspended in time, waiting for some event below. He allowed his vision to race from one white twinkling cluster to another.

I just can't figure out why we're here. Give us a reason, Lord — something better than the fact that I'm too tired or too lazy to move on.

The voice was a soft, melodious whisper. "Orion?"

He sat straight up and glanced back into the darkened room. "Out on the balcony, darlin'."

Dola scooted into the chair next to his and began unlacing her high-top shoes.

He locked his fingers behind his head and leaned back in the chair. "You were down there a long time. I was about ready to come fetch you."

49

Dola rubbed her hot, sore toes. "I had another mouth to feed."

In the distance O.T. heard an explosion, followed by barking dogs. "The café's closed."

"Was that a gunshot?"

"Or a backfire from an auto car. Or half a stick of dynamite in an outhouse."

She plopped her boots next to his and leaned back in the chair. The barking stopped, leaving only the sounds of night in a gold town. "Fergus showed up at the back door," she explained. "It's his birthday. I had to feed him."

"He said he was having a birthday dinner with friends or relatives or something." With rough, callused fingers O.T. rubbed dirt out of the corners of his eyes.

The hard wooden chair cramped Dola's back. She fidgeted to find a more comfortable position. "He said his cousin and family weren't at home. He got tired of waiting for them."

"Did you invite him to sleep in the café?" O.T.'s voice was low, smooth, like a deep river coursing down a gradual slope.

"Yes, but he went back to their place. He's sure they will return." Dola closed her eyes. She could feel her forehead muscles relax.

"He has some money now. The Wilkins brothers do give him his share of the mine."

"Yes, he paid me for supper. Fergus was very hungry. He must not have eaten in a long time." It felt comfortable, soothing for her to speak in a whisper.

"He was eatin' at noon when Corrie Lou and I got there. Ace says all he does is hang around and eat."

"But he's so thin and tired-looking. I suppose it's just his age."

"And you, Mrs. Skinner, are a little thin and tired-lookin' yourself."

"And old-looking?"

"I didn't say that."

"Well, Omega and I are getting a little run down. It's been a rather hectic few weeks. Learning how to operate a café with this many hungry men waiting to be fed puts the pressure on."

"I studied the accounts. You need to put on two more girls to help you."

"We can't afford that if we're going to save anything to buy that twenty-acre parcel in California next to Pegasus and Pearl. Goldfield is not the cheapest place for supplies."

"I know your profits aren't much. You could charge seventy-five cents for breakfast and $1.50 for supper and still give the men a bargain."

"Orion, I told you from the beginning I wanted to give the men a good, hot fifty-cent breakfast." Her voice was still soft, yet determined.

"Some goals can't be met, darlin'. A fifty-cent breakfast in Guthrie is different from one in Goldfield in the middle of a gold rush."

"Well, I'm not changing my mind."

"That is obvious, Dola Mae Davis Skinner. You never change your mind."

She scowled at him through the night shadows. "Are you saying that I'm a stubborn woman, Mr. Skinner?"

"Yes, ma'am. And it's that stubbornness that has helped us survive some mighty lean times. Still, I don't want you to work yourself sick in the café."

"I'm not sick."

"But you're tired."

"So are you, Orion Tower Skinner."

"I've been tired for twenty years," he replied.

"Then it's my turn," she insisted. "A month ago you almost worked yourself into the grave carrying water so that we could have a week's supply of groceries. You said it before — there are some things a family's got to do. Look back in there. We have four healthy children with full stomachs, a roof over their heads, and soft beds. That's worth a whole lot to me."

"Dola Mae, everyone in there and out here could not survive if you took sick. We want you to take care of yourself."

"I appreciated you and Tommy-Blue helping wash the tables and sweep the café tonight."

"Are you trying to change the subject?"

"I suppose," she murmured. "Tell me again what the subject was."

The wind picked up a little. O.T. thought the stars in the west were getting cloud-shrouded.

"Why can't you raise prices a little?"

"Because of the Skinners of Oklahoma," she declared.

"You want to explain that?"

"Orion, I know that many people in this town can afford dollar breakfasts."

"A good number could afford ten-dollar breakfasts," he remarked.

"Yes, but there are some, like the Skinners of Guthrie, Oklahoma, who would be stretching their limits on a fifty-cent meal. Where are folks like that going to eat when they come to town?"

"At your café?"

"Exactly. Someone has to look out for ordinary folks like us. It's not about money, Orion. It's about feeding hungry people."

As the breeze stiffened, it felt almost cool on his bare feet. O.T. closed his eyes. "A good portion of your customers could afford more, like Lucky Jack Gately and gang. They don't need fifty-cent meals."

"I know," she replied. "They won't complain about paying more, but I can't charge one price for one man and a different price for another."

"Why not?" he challenged.

"Are you serious?"

"How about calling it the Newcomers' Café? For the first week, people get meals at the lower prices and after that, meals at the regular prices."

Dola unfastened the top two buttons on the

high collar of her blouse and fanned the material back and forth. "Newcomers' Café? I like that. But how could we tell if a man really was a newcomer or not?"

O.T. folded his hands across his stomach. He could feel his shoulders and neck relax even more. "The customers will know. They won't let anyone get a bargain meal if he's supposed to be paying full price."

"I could issue them a little card with my signature and the date on it. As long as they bring in the card, they get the half-price meal. But maybe we'd give them a month."

"A month? We might not even be here a whole month," he protested.

"Then two weeks."

"What's wrong with one week?" he challenged.

"Because it takes a couple weeks to decide if you're staying here or pushing on." She laid her hand on his hard, muscled arm. "Can you find me a sign painter tomorrow?"

"You're serious?"

"Yes, I want it to read: NEWCOMERS' CAFÉ, Half-price Meals for Your First Two Weeks in Town."

"When do you want to up the prices for the old-timers?"

Dola's voice quieted. "How about next Monday? That will give them a few days to get used to the idea. How does that sound?"

"I think it will be fine. When will you add a

couple of girls?" he pressed.

"Oh, not until the prices . . . you know . . ." Each word came out more slowly than the previous one. "Until we . . . change . . . prices." She pulled her arm back to the armrest of her chair.

"I think you better start lookin' right away." O.T. cracked his knuckles one at a time. "Even if you have to hire them a few days early. We can pull a little out of our Dinuba funds to pay them if we need to. It will take time to train them to your routine. I don't expect any will adapt as quickly as you and Omega. She and Lucian are just about the easiest folks to get along with I've ever met."

"Uh huh," she murmured.

"Reckon you could just put a Help Wanted sign out front and see what response you get. Don't know when you'd have time to interview them." O.T. opened his eyes when he heard two riders gallop down the street in front of the café. They disappeared into the shadows. He closed his eyes again. "And don't you start thinkin' about servin' lunch. You have to have some break."

Dola could hear O.T.'s voice. It sounded like a pleasant, distant wave lapping a shore — indistinguishable but constant, reassuring, restful. The drift of wind from the west partially cooled her face. It was still a warm wind, but it rolled over her sweaty dress in a cooling manner.

"Maybe the day will come when Omega takes breakfast chores and you do supper, or something like that," O.T. continued. "You two would have a little break that way, allowing the other to take charge."

As she sat on the dark balcony, streetlights glowing below, Dola thought about pushing the sleeves of her dress above her elbows.

"Of course, it really will depend on who you get to help. There must be some other gals who want to work. I was thinking of Nellie Rokker. But she'll need to look after the children, and she is such a frail woman. I don't think she'd keep up," O.T. intoned.

Dola thought about a soft ocean breeze off the Texas gulf coast, about lying on a blanket on white sand.

"You should hire some sturdy girls. Not fat, but sturdy," O.T. suggested.

Her thoughts drifted to Magdalena, New Mexico. O.T. had worked the stockyards for a week, and the manager had let the whole family sleep in the barn. They had put two blankets over the loose hay and slept on top of the blankets. After weeks of sleeping on the ground, it had felt like heaven.

O.T. watched an automobile roll up and park by a streetlight two blocks away. "Say, did I tell you that Ace said there's a machinist in the area who claims he can fix auto cars? He said we ought to check with the man about fixin' the Thomas. But I wouldn't want to drive it."

For the first time all day, Dola's feet stopped throbbing. She thought about pulling off her stockings. Her chin rested on her chest, and she could feel sweat in the folds of her neck.

"Would you have any objections to me askin' him to give an estimate on repair?" he queried.

He waited for a moment.

"Thanks. I didn't surmise you would. I won't spend a dime on it without us talkin' it through, of course. I guess I still wrestle with that idea of driving the automobile over to Pegasus and Pearl's. May the Lord deliver me from such arrogance and pride."

In the dark night Dola's head bobbed even lower on her chest. *I wonder whatever happened to Grandma Davis's burgundy satin pillow. Every time I stayed over there, she would let me sleep on it. It felt so cool. So smooth under my face. Of course, my face was a lot smoother then. I think maybe Aunt Bertha got the pillow . . . or Cousin Marjorie. Probably Marjorie.*

"One thing about Goldfield, it isn't boring. Ever' day seems to bring in unexpected people and circumstances. There's talk that somebody famous is comin' in on the train from Arizona in the next few days. Folks is tryin' to keep it secret, but my guess is that it's Wyatt Earp. What with his brother Virgil passin' on last month, folks think ol' Wyatt's comin' to town to gather up his brother's belongin's. In a way it's kind of excitin' bein' here. Just when ever'one figures there's no more gold rushes,

57

along comes Goldfield. I reckon someday there will be books written about this place."

O.T. reached over for Dola's hand.

"Too bad it's not a nicer climate. We could stay right here in Goldfield and ride out this gold rush."

When Dola did not take his hand, he pulled back. "Then someday Rita Ann could write a book about it. She'll be the one to do it too. Tommy-Blue will be too busy to write. Punky too little. And Corrie Lou . . . well, someday, Mama, that girl will latch onto some young man, and she'll love and adore him every day of his life, and he'll spend his days happy as a cat with warm milk, thinkin' he's the luckiest man on the face of the earth. But she won't want to write a book. What do you think?"

He leaned his head against the back of the chair, closed his eyes, and waited for a reply.

And waited.

And waited.

She's plumb worn out, Lord. But at least this time, she's her own boss, and she's makin' money for it. Sometimes that can be a good worn out. Refresh her in her sleep, Lord. She deserves to feel good in the mornin'.

Sometime after the streetlights were turned out and before the sun rose, O.T. Skinner woke up in the hard wooden chair on the balcony above the soon-to-be-named Newcomers' Café.

His back ached.

His head hurt.

His legs were cramped.

His left hand was tingling numb.

His bare toes were cold.

Dust swirled in his eyes as a stiff breeze bellowed over Malpais Mesa and down the streets of Goldfield.

The blanket of desert stars had faded from view. In the dark shadows he could see the empty chair next to him. O.T. plucked up his boots and slipped into the huge one-room apartment, closing the balcony doors behind him. As he walked barefoot across the wooden floor, he could feel a layer of dust and dirt that had blown in through the open doorway.

Their bed was empty.

The homemade quilt comforter had not been turned down nor the pillows disturbed. *Dola Mae, there is a reason you didn't wake me up. I just don't know the reason.*

Leaving the electric switch off, he scooted toward the door leading to the stairs down to the café. A light filtered out of the kitchen, making weird silhouettes out of the chairs and benches stacked on the tables.

As he approached the kitchen, he whistled "Good-bye, Ol' Paint." When he entered the kitchen, Dola was slipping a large pan into the oven.

"Orion Skinner, don't you go barging around whistling at this time of the morning. You'll wake up the children!" she scolded.

A sly grin crept across his narrow, unshaven face. "And if I snuck up behind you without you knowing it, what would have happened?"

"I probably would have screamed and hit you with a frying pan."

"That's why I whistle, darlin'. Now when are you coming to bed?"

"I've already slept some." She refused to look him in the eyes. "Thought I'd get an early start on breakfast."

"What time is it?"

"Almost 4:00 A.M."

"What time, Dola Mae Skinner?"

"3:35. It's closer to 4:00 than to 3:00," she insisted.

"What are you doin'?"

"Making some bear claws. I woke up thinking that the men are probably tired of baking soda biscuits every morning. Bear claws take a little more time, so I wanted to get started."

"Word gets around that you're making bear sign, and they'll be beatin' the door down. You have any coffee made yet?"

"What's left in that pot is from yesterday. But it's hot. Would you like to make me a pot? On second thought, please don't. Your coffee could derail a freight train," she laughed.

"It's blowin' in some kind of storm out there."

"Feels too hot to rain."

"It's blowin' a lot of dirt around," he added.

They were startled by a banging on the back door.

"When you said they'd be beating down my door, I thought it was a hyperbole."

O.T. swung open the alley door at the back of the kitchen. He was greeted by a man with a toothy smile, pigtails, and a crisp, wide-brimmed black felt hat. "Fergus!"

"You were expecting someone else?" the old Indian replied.

"Come in."

"Thank you. It's too windy to sleep outside."

"Why didn't you come in here to sleep?" O.T. quizzed.

"Thank you, I think I will."

Fergus tipped his hat. "Good morning, Mrs. Skinner."

"Good morning, Fergus. Would you like a cup of coffee?" Dola felt the moist dough squish between her fingers.

The old Paiute poured a tin cup full to the brim. "Just a small one," he declared with a sip.

Dola wiped her hands off and hovered near the stove. "Where were you sleeping?"

"In the backseat," he announced.

"Of the auto car?"

"Yes, it is very comfortable. Unless it is raining or windy. It is not raining." Fergus dragged a wooden stool closer to the cookstove and plopped down on it.

Dola brushed the hair off her forehead with

the back of her hand. "I'm making bear claws," she explained, "but they won't be ready for a while."

He pushed his hat back. "I will wait."

With a wooden spatula, Dola scraped the last of the dough out onto the flour-sprinkled butcher's block. "It might be quite a while before they're ready."

Fergus shrugged. "I have no other plans."

"It will be at least half an hour."

The Paiute's only expression was the gleam in his dark brown eyes. "Which goes by quite rapidly in the presence of good friends."

O.T. sat on the second stool and sipped from the tin cup. "What's this I hear about your cousin's house being empty when you got there?"

"It was not empty. The wrong people were there. I don't know what happened to my cousin and family," Fergus declared.

"Did they leave a message with anyone?"

Fergus nodded. "It is a mystery."

"The message?" O.T. queried.

"No, that my cousin moved without telling me. I was told the house was sold and the family had moved to Pyramid Lake."

"Where is that?"

"Many miles north of Reno. But they did not go there."

"How can you be sure?"

"It is not our band. They would never go there."

O.T. found a clean spot on a tea towel and wiped dirt out of the corners of his eyes. "So what's your explanation?"

"I think someone just wanted the house, and so they took it," Fergus declared.

Dola buzzed next to the men and snatched up her flour canister. "But someone can't come in and take a house away from someone else."

"It has happened to Paiutes quite often."

"That's not right!" O.T. declared.

"I think the old Navajos have it right," Fergus continued. "They live in remote dirt houses that nobody wants to take."

"Where do you think your cousin really went?" O.T. questioned.

"Maybe to Schurz. We have relatives there."

"Perhaps you could write to them and ask if they've seen your cousin," Dola offered.

"That is an idea, but it is very slow to write."

"Isn't there mail delivery to Schurz?" Dola pressed.

"I'm sure there is. But it will take me some years to learn how to write." He grinned and took another sip of coffee.

"I'll be happy to write a letter for you," Dola offered.

"That is good. Very good. I would like to write to President Roosevelt," Fergus announced.

"My goodness," Dola exclaimed, "what do you want to write to Mr. Roosevelt about?"

"About the misallocation of government assets pursuant to territorial claims by various Indian tribes as stated in the initial treaties ratified by Congress and subsequently misinterpreted by the bureaucrats of Washington, D.C."

O.T. stared at Dola and then back at Fergus.

"I said I couldn't write," Fergus explained. "I didn't say I couldn't speak."

"I'd be happy to write your letter to President Roosevelt," Dola added.

"Thank you. 'Dear President Roosevelt —' "

"I can't write it right now, Fergus," she protested. "I'm cooking bear claws. Remember?"

"My mind forgot, but my stomach remembered."

O.T. refilled his coffee cup and then emptied the pot into Fergus's cup. "It might be a little strong, partner. We're about down to the eggshells."

"*Partner* is an interesting word," Fergus mumbled. "I believe it means more than friend, but how much more I am not sure. Is President Roosevelt also your partner?"

"I never met the man."

"Well, I think I will invite him to come to Nevada." Fergus rubbed his wrinkled but clean-shaven chin. "He likes the outdoors."

"That's what I hear," O.T. concurred.

"Nevada has lots of outdoors."

"And sand and sage and —"

"Don't forget the dust," Fergus reminded him. "We have plenty of dust. I hear he likes to hunt. I will invite him on a camel hunt."

"Camel hunt? I never heard of camels in Nevada," O.T. challenged.

"You have to know where to look for them."

"I imagine so," O.T. laughed.

"I know where to hunt for them. I have walked over the entire state."

"I reckon if there's a camel in Nevada, you could find him," O.T. declared.

"Thank you."

The banging on the back door was light but persistent.

"Goodness, we have more company." Dola glanced down at her flour-covered hands.

"Perhaps they smell the bear claws," Fergus said.

O.T. pulled open the alley door to find a teenage boy, hat pulled down with stampede string, standing on the concrete step. "Jared, come in! It's windy out there."

"And dusty," the boy said.

Dola wiped her hands on her white apron and scooted toward them. "Jared, what are you doin' out at this hour?"

The boy pulled off his hat and stared down at the floor. "Mama's worried sick."

Dola put an arm around the boy's shoulder. "What is it, honey?"

"Daddy didn't come home," he mumbled.

"Oh, no." Dola squeezed his shoulder. "Don't tell me he started drinking again."

Jared Rokker curled the brim of his felt hat.

"I don't think so, Mrs. Skinner. He ain't touched a drop since Mama was in the hospital. Besides that, I've checked nearly ever' saloon in town. Even Mr. LaPorte hasn't seen him, and he knows the whereabouts of most ever'body."

O.T. leaned his backside against the butcher block and surveyed the boy. "What time did your daddy make it back from Coyote Springs?"

"From where?" Jared asked in surprise.

"I talked to him yesterday mornin' halfway out to the Wilkins brothers' mine. He was on a mule and said he was headed toward Coyote Springs and wanted to get home before dark."

Jared took a deep breath. "All I know is that yesterday was payday, and he didn't come home."

"Oh, my!" Dola exclaimed. "I'm sure there is a good explanation." *Lord, forgive me for that lie. I'm not at all sure there's a good explanation.*

"The man at the hardware store said Daddy drew his pay and an advance for next week and took the day off. I don't know what to do. I cain't go home and tell Mama that. It would crush her spirit."

"Orion?" Dola waited for her husband to respond.

"Eh, maybe he got a little too far out on the desert and needed to wait until morning to come home."

"Why was he out on the desert, Mr. Skinner?"

O.T. looked at Jared Rokker. *Lord, how can I tell a twelve-year-old that his daddy spent grocery money on some phony treasure map. I can't.*

"He went to visit Don Fernando," Fergus blurted out from the back of the kitchen.

Jared turned toward the old Indian. "Where is Don Fernando?"

Fergus took a long, slow sip of coffee. "To the west."

Jared brushed his wavy red hair back off his forehead. "How far to the west, Mr. Fergus?"

The Paiute drank down the rest of his coffee and then stared at the tin cup as if expecting more to appear. Finally he looked up. "Several days."

"Days?" O.T. questioned. "When I talked to him, Elias thought it was only a few hours."

Fergus licked around the lip of the cup and then grinned. "I think he was wrong."

Jared Rokker paced between O.T. and Dola. "You mean, Daddy will be gone for days?"

"I'm sure when he figured out he was going that far, he turned back," O.T. surmised. "But by then it would have been too late to make it back to town. He probably slept out on the desert."

"It's really windy and dusty out there," Jared remarked. "He could get lost."

"He was on a mule. Mules don't often get lost. They somehow always know their way home," O.T. encouraged him.

Jared stared into his eyes. "Mr. Skinner, why

67

did he go out there and not tell Mama?"

Lord, how can I answer the boy?

Dola searched O.T.'s eyes and then blurted out, "Well . . . maybe it had to do with a surprise, Jared!"

"We were supposed to buy groceries today," Jared mumbled.

"Yes, well," Dola said as she buzzed back over to the oven, "Jared, I've been wanting to have you all over for dinner, but the restaurant just ties me up. So why don't all of you come over for breakfast? It's our treat."

"Really?"

"You will have to make more bear claws," Fergus suggested.

"I will have plenty for the Rokker family and a certain ol' Paiute gentleman who eats like a horse," Dola scolded.

Fergus's wrinkled face brightened. "An ol' *handsome* Paiute gentleman."

Dola stared at Fergus. *Everything about that man looks ancient . . . except his eyes. His eyes dance like a young man's.* "Yes, for an elderly gentleman, quite handsome."

O.T. put his hand on the boy's shoulder. "Jared, tell your mama that I saw Elias out near Alkali, and he mentioned business at Coyote Springs. He's probably riding out this dust storm and will be in after daylight."

"And invite them all to breakfast!" Dola urged. "We'll be serving between 5:30 and 8:00 A.M. You can come over anytime."

Jared took a deep breath, sighed, and then jammed his hat back on his head. "Thank you, Mrs. Skinner, I'll tell her. Do I have to tell her about him gettin' next week's pay?"

"Not unless she asks," Dola counseled. "You can wait and let your father tell her that. Of course, if she asks, you must be honest."

"Yes, ma'am." Jared turned around before he got to the door. "Them bear claws surely do smell good."

"It is not good for children to eat more than one bear claw each," Fergus announced.

"Now just where did you come up with that?" Dola challenged.

Fergus folded his arms across his thin chest. "Everyone knows it is bad for their teeth."

"And you? Are bear claws bad for *your* teeth?"

"It does not matter. There is some benefit in being very old. There is no reason to save my teeth now," he grinned.

The collar on O.T.'s worn canvas coat was turned up and his hat jammed down to his ears as he entered the front door of the café right before noon. The dining room was empty, and the tables and chairs were lined up in perfect order for supper.

Rita Ann must have measured each one with a ruler. Lord, I love her dearly, but I'm not sure why You dropped such a perfect, exact little girl into such an inexact family.

69

Dola swept out of the kitchen with a worried look on her face, but she managed a smile. "You home for some lunch?" she called out.

"After my fill of bear claws, I don't reckon to be hungry for a week. Mr. Tolavitch gave me the rest of the day off. Said this dust storm is too severe to send a messenger out to the mines. What are you doing?"

Dola pulled a wet towel out of a bucket. "Trying to keep some of the dust out." She squeezed out the towel and lined the window sill with it.

O.T. took off his hat and slapped it against his ducking trousers. Dust fogged in a cloud around him. "Sure is bad. Everyone is just sitting around waiting for it to go away."

"You should see our place upstairs. Every item, including the children, is covered with yellowish red dust. And they've been inside all day."

O.T. tried to find a clean place on his bandanna to wipe his eyes. Finally he brushed his eyes with an almost clean spot. "I reckon they've been restless, all cooped up."

Dola dropped another rag into the bucket of water. "Someone talked them into playing school. They're working on the annual play."

O.T. helped her wring out towels and line the windows. "I see big sister has set out the chairs. I've seen many a barn that wasn't built as plumb as these tables and chairs."

"She's marked the floor."

"Really?"

"Yes, she has a little X where each chair leg should go."

"That will work until the mark wears off," O.T. observed. "Do you reckon this dust storm will cut down on the number of customers tonight?"

"That's what I've been trying to decide." Dola rubbed her soft chin with hard, callused fingers. "Perhaps more people will stay in town, and the crowd will be bigger. The miners will be here. There's no wind down where they work."

O.T. couldn't see the buildings across the street. "Did Elias Rokker ever make it back?"

Dola reached up and began to wash his eyes with a clean, damp rag. "I was going to ask you the same thing."

He lowered his head and closed his eyelids. "I would imagine he'll just hole up until this passes by."

"How long do you reckon this sandstorm will last?"

"Tolavitch said they never last more than three days."

"Three days! Three days of this, and all the dirt in Nevada will be in Utah!"

"He didn't say they all last that long. That's the longest they've lasted." He walked toward the front of the restaurant. "Think I'll lock this door just so it won't blow open."

Dola followed him and placed the last two wet towels on the floor to block the crack under the doors. "Did you get my sign ordered?" she queried.

"Yep. Jersey said it would be ready Friday."

"Is Mr. Jersey a good sign painter?"

"Jersey is a gal."

"A lady sign painter?"

"Yep. Tolavitch says she's the best in town."

"What did it cost?"

"Ten cash dollars."

"We can't afford that fancy a sign!"

"Tolavitch and his partner bought it for you. Said it comes with the rent. They keep the sign if we move on."

"I do believe Mr. Tolavitch plays favorites with us."

"And I reckon he knows a good meal when he tastes one."

"I hope he doesn't mind paying more for it."

"He told me he's happy you're raisin' prices. Said he was tired of going to bed feelin' guilty ever' night."

"The pork roast might be gritty tonight if the wind keeps blowing. It's amazing to me how walls can't keep out the wind and dirt."

O.T. trailed Dola to the kitchen. "I did order you another sign."

Dola wiped her fingers along the kitchen counter. "Look at this dust. I just wiped this clean before you came in. Orion, this is horrible!"

"It's worse outside. Talk is, the city will turn on the streetlights before long. Can't see fifty feet as it is."

"We've seen wind like this in Oklahoma."

O.T. snatched the lid off the coffeepot and stared inside. "I believe that was one of the reasons we left."

Dola wiped the counter. "Do you think it blows like this in Dinuba?"

"Nope." He tipped the coffeepot over a tin cup and waited for the dregs to drip out. "I hear the sun shines ever' day of the year. It's always pleasant, and it only rains a little at night just to keep the roses bloomin'."

Dola sauntered over and slipped her arms around O.T.'s narrow, muscled waist. "You are such a wonderful dreamer, Orion Tower Skinner. Wouldn't it be nice to have roses? I believe I would rather have roses than gold!"

He hugged her tight and kissed her cheek. "And you are the rose in ever' one of my dreams, Dola Mae Davis Skinner."

She pulled her head back but kept hugging him. "Well, I'd better be!" *Mr. Skinner, there are times when I wish you and I could run off by ourselves for a month with nothing to do.*

He pulled back. "Is that the door?"

"I didn't hear anything. Are you sure you're not saying that just to get out of kissing me?"

He grabbed her so fast she barely had time to catch her breath.

Her feet were off the floor.

Her eyes closed.

Her lips pressed against his.

She clutched his neck.

And heard a tap, tap, tap on the back door.

Dola pulled back and tried to flip a loose strand of hair back up into her comb. "I do believe there's someone at the door. Let poor Fergus in. Who else would be wandering around in a storm like this?"

Danny Rokker dashed in as soon as O.T. opened the door. His dirt-filled eyes squinted as he pulled off his felt hat.

"Did your daddy make it in yet?" O.T. quizzed.

Ten-year-old Danny shifted his weight from one foot to the other, as if waiting for a turn at the privy. "He ain't home, and Jared took off after him. Mama fretted herself into a tizzy!"

O.T. glanced at Dola's worried eyes. "Jared did what?"

Danny licked his dry, chapped lips. "He rented a mule and said he was going to Coyote Springs."

Dola hung the damp rag on a towel rack. "He went out in this dust storm?"

"Said he'd bring Daddy home. But now Mama's worried about both of them. She went to bed and pulled a pillow over her head and won't talk to us."

"Who's with her now?" Dola asked.

"Just Stella and Caitlynn."

O.T. fastened the top button on his shirt collar. "When did Jared leave?"

"About an hour ago."

"Orion, I can't believe a respectable liveryman would rent a mule to a twelve-year-old boy in this weather. Perhaps Jared is still in town looking for a mule to rent," Dola suggested.

O.T. pulled his hat low. "I'll go check out the liveries."

"What should I do?" Danny asked.

"Go home and help Stella take care of your mama and little Caitlynn," O.T. instructed. "I'll let you know what I find."

"And if you haven't heard from Mr. Skinner, come over around suppertime. I'll give you a dinner bucket to take home," Dola Mae added. "Your poor mama won't feel like cooking. Tell her it will be okay. We'll pray them both safely home. Mr. Skinner will find them." Dola searched O.T.'s eyes.

He sighed deeply and ran his fingers through his gritty hair. *Lord, I really don't want to go out in this storm. But I know I don't have any other choice. On my own there is no way I could find them. But I reckon that's the point of prayer — not bein' on our own.* "Go on, Danny. I'll start lookin' for Jared."

"Thanks, Mr. Skinner." Danny stuck out his hand.

O.T. ignored the hand and hugged the boy. "I'll find them, Danny. You know I will."

Tears cut through the dust on the boy's face as he hugged back. "Yes, sir. I know you will. I don't know what scares me most — having Daddy and Jared out in this storm or Mama in bed with the pillow over her face."

"The Lord will see us through, Danny," Dola encouraged him.

"Yes, ma'am, I reckon He will. But I surely wish He'd hurry."

Dola plucked up a flour sack from the counter and stuffed it inside another sack. "Provided you can get them home without too much dust, do you think you and the others would enjoy more bear claws? I have some extras here."

Danny's face lit up. "I reckon we could help you out." He clutched the sack as if it were gold.

O.T. walked the boy to the back door. "Go straight home, stay indoors, and whatever you do, don't go out looking for your daddy or brother. Your mama needs you there."

"Can you make it home by yourself?" Dola asked.

"Yes, ma'am. If I get lost, I'll just stop and eat a bear claw." He smiled.

"Straight home, Daniel Rokker," she ordered.

"Yes, ma'am."

O.T. shoved open the alley door and jumped straight back when he found Fergus with clenched fist, ready to knock.

"Go on, Danny. Try to hold your breath and not breathe in too much of that dust."

"You look happy to see me . . . partner," Fergus noted.

"Yes, I am," O.T. replied.

"Good, I am happy to be out of the dirt. I think I will stay in the kitchen until it blows over. I have spent too many days of my life eating dirt. Are there any bear claws left?"

"I just sent them home with Danny," Dola admitted.

The old Paiute rubbed his lips. "I suppose I could kill him."

"Fergus!" Dola snatched up a small basket of leftover biscuits and handed them to him.

He inspected each one as if to find a blemish, selecting the largest in the basket. "A small lump on the head, properly placed, would do the trick," he mumbled.

"You don't have time for that, partner," O.T. interjected.

"Partner? I am a partner now? I have a feeling you do not want to talk to me about bear claws."

"Fergus, Mr. Rokker is lost out on the desert in this storm, and young Jared is lookin' to rent a mule to go after him. We have to stop the boy and see if we can locate Rokker."

"We will be lucky to locate the hotel across the street in this storm."

"There isn't any hotel across the street," Dola pointed out.

"You see," he retorted, "you have lost it already. It is not a good day to get lost on."

"There is no good day to get lost on," Dola commented.

Fergus scratched his forehead. "Perhaps my cousin and family are lost too."

"You haven't seen any sign of them?"

"The new owners of the house chased me off the porch, waving my cousin's Winchester '94, 30-30."

"There are a lot of '94s in this town," O.T. said. "How do you know it was your cousin's gun?"

Fergus crammed a whole biscuit into his mouth. He chewed and swallowed it. "Because it is a special order half-round, half-octagon barrel, takedown, one-half magazine with a tang sight and a shotgun butt."

"Sounds like a very nice gun," O.T. observed.

"My cousin would not go anywhere in the desert without it."

"We will look for signs of him also."

"Her," Fergus corrected.

"What? This cousin you've been concerned about is a woman?" Dola gasped.

Fergus rubbed his chin. "Did I fail to mention that?"

Three

Tommy-Blue manned the front door, making sure it was quickly shut behind each customer. Corrie made the rounds up and down the crowded aisles between the chairs and benches with the large blue tin coffeepot. Rita Ann served the golden-crusted baking-powder biscuits in a covered pan, hoping to keep them clean at least until they landed on a waiting plate. And Punky laughed and played while wearing a red bandanna over his face like a highwayman, an oversized cowboy hat drooping well past his ears.

Dola looked around at the dining room full of hungry male customers and shook her head. *Lord, I'm not sure how I ended up cooking for such a room full of men, but it's nice to make them happy.* She toted a wooden-handled tray for gathering up the dirty dishes. Omega LaPorte trailed her with a bucket for the silverware.

Lucky Jack Gately snatched up Punky and bounced the little buckaroo on his knee. The half a dozen kerosene lanterns scattered around the dining room barely supplied enough light to recognize most faces.

"Another fine meal, Mrs. Skinner," Lucky Jack said. His curly blond hair drooped to his eyes, and his dimples winked with every smile.

"I'm surprised to have a full house tonight," she declared to Lucky Jack, Wasco, and Charlie Fred. *I wonder if my dimples still accent my smile like that. With all the wrinkles it's a wonder they even show anymore.*

Punky shoved Lucky Jack's hat back on his head, and the tall man brushed the hair out of his eyes. "Even dusty, dirty men need a tasty, hot supper, I reckon. You got the best eatin' house in town."

"She's got the cheapest eatin' house in town," Wasco roared.

"Yes, but when the electricity went out, I was afraid everyone would stay home," Dola admitted. "It's a horrible night to be walking about."

"The lanterns work just fine," Wasco observed. "Can't see the dust in my mashed potatoes. It's better than havin' a bright electric light."

"They make a romantic atmosphere," Charlie Fred laughed.

"You start feelin' romantic, Charlie Fred, and you'll get a bucket alongside the head!" Omega LaPorte declared.

Charlie Fred's smile widened. His white teeth caught the light of the lantern. "Now, Omega honey, admit it. You often regret not waitin' to see the handsomest member of the LaPorte family. If you wouldn't have been in such a hurry, look what you could have got."

"I married the hard-workin' one," she scolded with the flip of her hand. "Not some no-account drifter who still wears a gun on his hip like he was some Stuart Earp or Wyatt Brannon."

"I do believe you are a little confused," Charlie Fred prodded. "Remember, Omega honey, I am a one-third owner of a very productive gold lease!"

"Hah! That don't make no difference to me." She dumped another handful of dirty silverware into the bucket and moved down the table a few feet. She turned back and grinned. "Maybe only a little, teensy-tiny bit of difference."

"See!" Charlie Fred shouted. "I knew it!"

Omega stalked back toward the black cowboy-turned-mine-owner. "Behave yourself, Charlie Fred, or next time I write home, I'll tell your mama you spend ever' night down in the crib district."

Charlie Fred stiffened his back. "I don't do that!" he protested. "I don't go down there at all!"

Omega continued down the line of men. "Yeah, but your mama don't know that. She'll believe me."

Dola set her dishpan down on the table and wiped her hands on her slightly soiled apron. "Lucky Jack, would you quiet this crowd? I have an announcement to make."

The blond-headed man squared his wide shoulders and stood, holding Punky Skinner with his left arm. "I'm goin' to whistle real loud, partner, so close your ears."

Punky jammed a finger in each ear, closed

his eyes, and gritted his teeth.

Lucky Jack poked two fingers between his teeth. He blew a whistle that silenced everyone in the room and woke up every dog in the vicinity. Then he held Dola's hand as she stepped up on the bench beside the table.

She steadied herself by leaving her hand on Lucky Jack's shoulder. The howl of the wind racing through the cracks of the windows and doors required her to shout even though everyone was silent. "I have an announcement or two to make. I thought it would be good to do it now before you leave. You are welcome to stay awhile tonight. It's just horrible and dirty out there. You can stay here and drink coffee as long as it lasts. Please forgive the grit on the tables and floors. I just don't know what to do about it."

"Mrs. Skinner," someone toward the south wall called out, "your meals in a sandstorm are tastier than any others on a good day."

"Thank you, but I know the nicest feature about my meals is the price. And that's the second announcement. I will be hiring a couple more girls to help so we can better serve all of you. That means the prices of meals will rise on Monday. Breakfasts will be seventy-five cents, suppers $1.50. I'm sorry to have to raise prices."

"Are them girls going to be purdy?" another man shouted.

"I'm sure they'll be ugly, fat, and mean, Earl," Dola bantered.

"That would be an improvement over some,"

Charlie Fred called out.

Omega spun around and hollered, "Corrie Lou, pour Charlie Fred some hot coffee."

"You done took my cup!" he complained.

"I know," Omega replied.

Dola held up her hands to silence the laughter. "Let me finish. We're going to call this the Newcomers' Café from now on. The new sign will go up in a couple days or so. New people will get their meals for the old prices for the first two weeks in town. It's our way of welcomin' folks and giving them a good start. Now even if the electricity is down, we'll serve breakfast as usual in the mornin'."

"We havin' them bear claws again in the mornin'?" a big man shouted.

"Cletus, I don't want to spoil you, so we'll have fried cinnamon bread and ham and eggs — seasoned with dirt probably."

"You can spoil me anytime you want, Mrs. Skinner."

"You talking about food, Cletus?" Lucky Jack challenged.

"Yes, sir. Ain't that the subject at hand?"

A thin, young man sitting with his back toward Dola craned his neck as he turned around. "My li'l sis is needin' work. Can I send her by?"

"By all means, Jason. I'd like to hire two girls as soon as possible. But they have to be at least sixteen and healthy enough to do hard work. This is not a place for the weak."

"And they got to be purdy!"

"With yella hair."

"And upturned nose."

"And blue eyes."

"Green eyes," another shouted.

"They'll have dust in their eyes."

"If I'm goin' to have a chance, they better be blind!" a big man hooted.

"Forget the eyes. They gotta have a mature physique," a young man hollered.

Dola held up her hands and waited for them to settle down. "That's enough, or we'll have to clear you all out. Stay as long as you like, and take this sandstorm with you when you go. I'll see you for breakfast. Prices don't change until Monday."

She reached out a hand to Lucky Jack Gately, who assisted her back to the floor level. Punky reached out to her, and she grabbed him up. "Oh," she hollered, "one more thing."

Punky put his fingers in his ears.

The crowd's laughter muted quickly. "Mr. Skinner and Fergus are out in this horrible storm looking for a couple friends of ours. I'd appreciate your prayers for their safety."

"I ain't prayed in years, but I'll pray for you, Mrs. Skinner. Hope I remember how."

"Thank you, Howard. I'm sure the Lord remembers all about you."

"There's some of it I hope He forgets," Howard replied.

The crowd roared in agreement and then broke into individual conversations again as

Dola toted Punky back into the kitchen.

Rita Ann buzzed in with an empty biscuit pan. "The biscuits are all gone. What do you want me to do now?"

Dola felt her lower back cramp with pain. "How about you watchin' Punky while I clean the stove?"

Punky stretched out his hands. "Rita-Rita-Rita-Rita-Rita!" he squealed.

"Punky-Punky-Punky-Punky!" she responded. She sat him on the counter in front of her and gave him the wooden mashed potato spoon to lick. "Mama, isn't Lucky Jack a very handsome man?"

Dola raised her eyebrows. "Are you pining for an older man?"

"Oh, no, Mama, not me!" A shy smile crept across the twelve-year-old's face. "I was just thinking how handsome he looked next to you, helping you up on the bench and everything."

"Me?" Dola's mouth dropped open. "Rita Ann, don't you think such things!"

"What things, Mama? What things am I not supposed to think?"

Dola's back stiffened, as did the muscles in her neck and shoulders. "Never mind. I don't want you talking about Lucky Jack and . . . well, you know for a fact that I'm married to the most wonderful man in the world."

"I know, Mama." Rita Ann stood next to Punky and watched the toddler as she talked. "He's the best daddy in the whole world. But

. . . well, he might not be the most handsome."

"I have never in my life met a man who attracted me more," Dola snapped. "And that certainly includes the likes of Lucky Jack Gately!"

"Daddy's attractive, but not the most handsome."

"Young lady, I don't like the direction of this conversation. Your father is the only man I've ever thought about in my life," Dola admonished.

Rita Ann looked up with patient, yet pleading eyes. "Mama, I was just needing to figure something out."

Dola tried to smooth the wrinkles from her forehead by running her hand across them. "What's that?"

"That just because someone is the most handsome man in the world, that isn't enough reason to like him. The person I like someday should be wonderful. He should attract me like no other. And he must be the only one in my thoughts all the time."

Dola stepped over and put her arm on Rita Ann's shoulder. "You learned all of that from looking at Lucky Jack?"

"No, Mama." Rita's high-pitched, sweet voice rang out like a victory bell. "I learned all of that by watching you hump your back when I mentioned you and Lucky Jack."

O.T. had his hat tied under his chin with a

86

makeshift stampede string made out of a short piece of clothesline. His shirt collar was buttoned tight. He wore a cut-off long-handle shirt over his cotton shirt to keep the dust out. Fergus wore a faded woven-cotton poncho, and his hat was held down by a flour sack tied under his chin. He had on small green glass goggles when O.T. met him by the livery.

O.T. leaned into the howling dust storm and hollered, "Where'd you get them driving glasses?"

"They were in the tool box of the Thomas auto car." Fergus held up a second pair and grinned. "Some for you too!"

O.T. took them and tucked them into the front pocket of his ducking trousers. "McMasters at the livery said that Jared Rokker took out of here about an hour ago on a short black mule." O.T. studied the flour sack tied around the Paiute's chin and the goggles that made him look bug-eyed.

"Where was he going?" Fergus quizzed.

O.T. kept his back to the wind. "I told him I saw his daddy west of Alkali headed for Coyote Springs. I suppose he's going to try to find Alkali."

"In this storm he'll be lucky to find Columbia Mountain."

"It's a cinch there will be no trail to follow. This wind will erase it the moment it's imprinted," O.T. declared. "Have you ever been to

Alkali? I've just skirted around it."

"Yes, many times."

"I hear it's out in the middle of nowhere," O.T. added. "Why do you go there?"

"Because being in the middle of nowhere means that it is halfway to many somewheres," Fergus managed to say while barely opening his mouth due to the sandstorm. "Are we looking for just the boy or the father too?"

"Just the boy until this storm is over. I figure Elias has crawled into a cave somewhere and will ride out this storm." O.T. tightened the stampede string rope under his chin and then re-pulled the cinch on the saddle.

"I know every cave for a hundred miles."

"We might need a cave ourselves if this keeps up," O.T. cautioned.

Fergus leaned closer. "It is a good boy who will go look for his lost father."

And it's a poor father who wanders off without telling his family. "He should have waited until this storm was over."

"He must be very brave."

"Or very foolish!"

"Is there a particular reason we're riding mules?" Fergus brushed the neck of the animal in front of him and looked at his hand as if inspecting the top of the bookshelf for dust.

"These are the only two animals I own. Besides, Ida and Ada will work with blinders on. That's the only way we'll get any animal to ride into that dirt storm." O.T. pulled himself up onto the lighter brown mule.

Fergus handed his trapdoor .45-70 to O.T. and then struggled to get his foot in the stirrup. He yanked and kicked until he pulled himself into the saddle. He adjusted his hat and goggles. "When I was a young man, mules were much shorter," he shouted. "Who is to lead?"

The sand stung O.T.'s eyes. "Ada and Ida work best side by side. They got used to doing everything together."

"That is good. They are partners."

O.T. handed the carbine back to the old Indian. "You got any bullets for that?"

"Two. That is all we need. Did you bring a gun?"

"Nope." O.T. patted the saddlebags. "But I have leftover bacon, biscuits, and two canteens of water."

Fergus offered a closed-lip smile. "That is better than two bullets!"

Crossing town was simple with buildings lining the way and no one in the streets. By the time they reached the stock exchange, both men had bandannas over their mouths and noses. When they reached the west edge of town, O.T. stopped and pulled out the driving glasses.

"I knew you would wear them," Fergus shouted.

"Am I going to look as handsome as you?" O.T. laughed.

"With sickly white skin you will never look as handsome as a Paiute. But that is how you were created. I do not blame you."

O.T. could not see the twinkle in the old man's eyes, but he knew it was there. He adjusted the strap on the goggles, slipped them over his head, and then retied his hat. He found instant relief from the biting sand. The green tint made the storm even darker, but now he could see a few feet in front of the mule's head.

Fergus leaned over and handed him the end of a rope. "Tie this on the saddle horn. I will do the same. That way we won't get separated."

"I can see you okay, partner."

"Yes . . . partner . . . but the storm is going to get worse. Malpais Mesa keeps the worst part from hitting Goldfield. Tie it on. I do not want to have to find three white men."

After dallying the sisal rope to the saddle horn, O.T. kicked Ada's flank. The mule trudged forward. O.T. slumped his shoulders and leaned into the wind. The dirt stung his uncovered upper cheeks and where the goggles did not cover.

Lord, this seems like a mighty dumb thing to do. Only I know if it were my boy, I'd come out after him. So I reckon Jared is jist as important in Your eyes. But I don't know how we can find anything out here. You will have to lead us. I will try to hear Your voice and follow.

The sandstorm didn't let up.

But it didn't get worse.

The day didn't lighten.

Or darken.

And thanks to the driving goggles, O.T. never lost sight of Fergus.

However, he could see nothing but the hard dirt wagon ruts that had been there since some distant wet spring.

O.T. had no idea which trail they were following. But as long as he could see some faint markings, he knew they were headed somewhere. He knew very well that they might not find Jared or Elias Rokker. But his conscience demanded that he be out in the storm looking.

Sand ground inside his socks, in the crooks of his shirt-clad arms, and between his backside and the saddle. His ears were caked with dirt. The bandanna over his mouth and nose had lost all of its red color. His lips were chapped like bark on a ponderosa pine. His mouth was gritty. His bandanna-covered nose was almost plugged.

After what seemed like a couple of hours, O.T. reined up close to Fergus. Every wrinkle in the old Indian's face was caulked with dirt and sand.

"You havin' fun, partner?" O.T. hollered into the storm.

"I would have more fun being dragged behind a wild stallion through a snake den!" Fergus yelled.

"You reckon this is the trail to Alkali?"

"This is it."

O.T. stared down at the barely visible old wagon rut. "How can you tell?"

"Two years ago a dead-axe wagon loaded with freight started out from Goldfield to Alkali. A thunderstorm struck, and the wagon began to sink low in the mud. That's what made these deep ruts."

"So this will lead us right to Alkali?"

"No."

"But you said —"

"The wagon did not make it to Alkali. It bogged down a few miles from here. They had to abandon the wagon until the ground dried and they could pull it out. The drivers rode back to town on the draft horses to wait out the storm. But when they returned, the wagons were much lighter."

"Everything got stolen?"

"Many things are abandoned in the desert. It is difficult to say how much is abandoned and how much is stolen."

"How much ended up at your house?" O.T. challenged.

"Merely the coffee, beans, flour, and sugar. It was not good to leave them in a storm. They could have been ruined."

"Nice of you to help them out."

There was no way to see the Indian's eyes. "Thank you."

"So you're saying this trail will end soon."

"Yes."

"Then how do we find our way on to Alkali?"

"I have been giving that much thought," Fergus replied.

"What did you decide?"

"The road across the desert to Alkali is a straight line from here. We should keep the mules plodding ahead and pray they know how to walk a straight line."

"Are you sayin' you're a prayin' man, Fergus?"

"Everyone prays, but not all admit it."

"Who do you pray to?"

"The God of the Wall Walker."

"Sometime when the dirt is not blowing in my mouth, let me tell you about Him."

"I have heard much about Jesus. First from the Spanish, then the Mexicans, from the Mormons . . . and then from the missionaries at Walker Lake. They tell different stories. I had heard of Him for most of my life, but I had never seen Him work until I met the Wall Walker and Mrs. Skinner."

"I'm afraid I ain't a very good example."

"You will do until a better one comes along."

"You need a drink?"

"Yes, but it will only make mud in my mouth. Perhaps I need one of the biscuits also."

"Won't that be difficult to swallow?"

"Yes, but it will make my mouth happy," the Indian declared.

The swig of water cooled O.T.'s tongue and mouth. As it quickly dried, his lips felt more drawn, chapped, and raw. Even though double-sacked, the biscuits too now had a brownish red tint.

"Will we make it to Alkali by dark?" he asked Fergus.

"It depends on the mules. We will make it somewhere by dark."

"If we can find Alkali, we'll see if the boy made it that far. If he went on, so will we. If he hasn't showed, we will wait for him."

When the wagon ruts ended, O.T. kicked his heels into Ada's flanks so the mule would not slow. He knew the mules would drift to the east as the dust storm pushed them that way.

The worst that could happen would be to wander over to the Tonopah road. At least we would know where we are.

All his exposed skin surface was raw as O.T. tried to keep his hat down to shield his goggle-covered eyes. Normally Ada and Ida would cover about four miles an hour. Now they were doing about two miles per hour. That meant it would be seven hours to Alkali, well after dark.

When the dust storm finally darkened, they tethered the horses even closer. Their stirrups and boots occasionally touched.

Lord, this seems so futile. Jared could have been ten feet away from us at any moment, and we would not have seen or heard him. Keep him safe, Lord. He is important to that family. They count on him for the stability that neither Mama nor Daddy seem to muster. It don't seem right for a twelve-year-old boy to have to look after a family, but he doesn't shirk from it. Fergus is right. A boy that looks after his mama and daddy has got to be doin' somethin' right. Keep him safe. Keep us all safe. Please lead us to him.

I don't reckon they have dust storms like this in California. Just rows and rows of peach trees and oranges and walnuts and vineyards. I hear there are tomatoes growing in straight rows and strawberries as far as the eye can see. And plums and apricots and figs and lettuce and carrots and black-eyed peas — crops so big you have to haul them to market in auto trucks. California is the land of tomorrow. It feels like I'm stuck in yesterday.

At least, today it seems that way.

If we had kept goin', we'd be in Dinuba by now.

But we didn't keep goin'.

Maybe California is a dream, a myth, a pretty story to keep me deceived. Maybe life is just a dust storm, and our lot is to wander around until life's end.

This storm is like a transition. Like the way I figure death is. A blurry passage between two worlds. It's like a dream. Or a nightmare. I trust it's one I won't remember.

The mules began to drift north. No amount of coaxing would get them to turn back into the wind. Coming from the left side now, the dust found new crevices to fill. O.T. felt sweat inside his goggles, sometimes burning his eyes. But the goggles did keep the dirt out. He could keep his eyes open, though there was nothing to see. Neither he nor Fergus tried to talk anymore. The only noise was the roar of the storm.

But even that sound was muted. O.T. had

ripped off a corner of the food sack and made four little squares of cloth. He and Fergus stuffed these into their ears to keep them from filling completely with dirt.

With darkness overtaking them and vision at zero, O.T. allowed his eyes to stay shut. His cracked and slightly bleeding lips were clamped shut. He struggled to keep the bandanna over his nose, filtering out some of the dirt.

O.T. was slumped low in the saddle when Fergus reached over and grabbed his arm. He stood straight up in the stirrups. An avalanche of dirt shifted down his body.

"The mules have stopped!" Fergus shouted.

How long have the mules been stopped? Have we been standing out here for minutes? Hours? Did I fall asleep? O.T. leaned toward the Paiute that he could not see. "I guess I should check on what's up there!"

"Yes, you check. You are already up," Fergus replied.

How did he know I was standing in the stirrups? The old man can't see me any better than I can see him.

With Fergus tied close to the right side, O.T. dismounted from the off side of the mule. *Ada, I wouldn't risk this with a pony, but you and me have gone through a lot. I know you don't mind which side I dismount from . . . just so I dismount.*

O.T. had just reached the ground and pulled his left foot out of the stirrup when he bumped right into an empty saddle.

Still strapped on a standing horse.

He backed up quickly into his own saddle. Ada shied to the east, and so did Ida.

"What are you doing?" Fergus shouted.

"There's a horse over here!" O.T. hollered back.

"Can we steal it?" Fergus yelled.

O.T. reached up and felt the empty saddle. *He's joking. Anyway, I think he's joking. Maybe this is Jared's horse. Then he must be here. No, he was on a short mule.*

His left hand clutching the horse's neck, his right on Ada, O.T. marched straight forward. Something slammed into his stomach right above the belt. He collapsed to the ground, gasping for breath.

Someone clobbered me with a two-by-four. I don't know where the hooves are! Ada will stay calm, but the horse could . . .

O.T. struggled to his feet, the bandanna pulled down to his neck, the goggles riding high on his forehead, the hat pushed back as far as the clothesline stampede string would allow. He reached straight out into the darkness and cracked his knuckles on a solid piece of wood.

A hitching rail? What is a hitching rail doing in the middle of the desert?

"Wall Walker, what happened?" Fergus bellowed.

"It's a hitching rail!" O.T. screamed into the roar of the wind and dirt.

97

"Good," Fergus replied. "We are at Alkali!"

We rode though the dust storm right up to the rail at Alkali? There's absolutely no way we could have found Alkali in this storm. It must be someone's barn or home . . . but there aren't any out here.

O.T. ducked under the hitching rail, took one step, cracked his shins on something immovable, and fell face first into a raised boardwalk. His hands stung as they slapped onto the unseen rough wood to break his fall. He struggled to his hands and knees.

Suddenly, like a new idea in a groggy mind, a thin vertical strip of light appeared in front of him. He squinted through the dust and caught sight of the barrel of a .405 Winchester '95 poked out a doorway.

"Who's out there?"

"Just a couple of pilgrims tryin' to find Alkali," O.T. shouted.

"It's blowin' right past you," the voice bellowed.

O.T. struggled to his feet. "The town of Alkali?"

"Town? Shoot, this is it, mister. Just one building."

O.T. attempted to rub splinters out of his hands. "You got room for two more to get out of this storm?"

"We're crowded, but we won't turn you away." The man looked tall, but with the dirt blowing into O.T.'s eyes, he couldn't tell. "There's two of you out there?"

O.T. glanced back into the dark night but couldn't see the mules, let alone the Paiute. "Yeah, me and Fergus."

"What's that on your forehead?"

O.T. reached up to the little, round glass cups. "Driving goggles."

"You got an auto car out in this storm?"

"Nope, just the goggles."

"Ain't a bad idee on a night like this. Come on in. Ever'one's hollerin' at me to close the door."

The door swung open a foot. O.T. and Fergus slipped in, and the door slammed behind them. For the first time in hours, there was no stinging sand plastering their faces, no dirt blowing up their noses.

O.T. glanced around the thirty-foot-square room that served as a hotel, café, store, saloon, card room, and pool hall. At least twenty men camped around the room on tables, on chairs, on the floor, and on the pool table.

"What's your excuse for being out on a night like this?" a big man challenged from behind the bar as everyone stared at them.

"A boy wandered out this way lookin' for his daddy. We're lookin' for him or the father," O.T. explained.

"What's the name?"

O.T. pulled off his hat and the goggles. "The dad is Elias Rokker."

"Ain't never heard of him," the bartender replied.

"The boy's only twelve," O.T. continued. "His name is Jared."

"No boys have been by all day." The bartender kept his eyes on Fergus.

A short, old man with a long beard pointed at O.T. "Say, you look familiar."

"We all look familiar — all covered with the same dust," a man in the back hooted. "Cain't tell one man from the next in a storm like this."

The man with a long beard stepped closer. "I recognize them eyes. Ain't you that there Goldfield Wall Walker?"

"That was last month, boys." O.T. tried brushing his hat on his duckings, but he stopped when it fogged up the already dusty room. "Now I work for the Assay Office."

"I heard you stood down the Wilkins brothers and Lucky Jack Gately and that bunch all at the same time. Took guts to do that," some man from the back hollered.

"Or just stupidity," O.T. admitted as he pulled the cloth squares out of his ears.

A man holding a deck of cards and wearing a bow tie called out, "Who you sidin' with now — the Wilkinses or Gately?"

"That feud's over, boys."

"You didn't answer me," the man insisted.

"I get along with both sides. All of them are friends of my family."

"You cain't be friends with both sides," the old man challenged.

Fergus untied the dirty towel under his chin

and pulled off his black felt hat. His dark pig-tails dropped down his back. "That is why he is still called the Wall Walker." Fergus's deep voice filled the room. "He can tread ground that no others dare try."

"Hey, you're an Indian!" the bartender shouted.

"That has always been my belief," Fergus contended.

"What are you doin', bringin' a digger in here?" another man demanded.

O.T. glanced around the room, studying the dimly illuminated faces. "Fergus is a friend. He's helpin' me find the lost boy."

"He cain't stay in here. I don't give free room to no digger." The bartender strolled out from behind the bar, toting a short-barreled shotgun. "In fact, he looks an awful lot like the digger that stole my pocket watch and pearl-handled sneak gun."

Fergus didn't flinch. He continued to brush the dirt off his hat and shirt. "It wasn't me. I do not need a locket on my wrist to tell the time of day. Nor do I need to sneak up on anyone. Perhaps I could have stolen your boots, your beans, your pony, or your wife. Those are things I sometimes need."

At the mention of his wife, the bartender threw the shotgun to his shoulder and cocked both barrels. "Ain't no dumb Indian goin' to insult my wife."

O.T. Skinner stepped in front of Fergus. "He

101

didn't mean it personally. He was just makin' a point."

"I'll shoot both of ya!" the man screamed, as the others scurried out of the way.

"You cain't shoot the Wall Walker," one of the men blurted out.

As he got closer, O.T. noticed the bartender chewing on a very short unlit cigar. "Who says I can't. Just watch me, boys."

O.T. set his jaw and held his breath as the big man stormed toward him, the shotgun barrel just two feet from his head.

"How long do you think you'd have until Gately and them team up with the Wilkinses and come after you?" the old man cautioned. "It could be worse than when the Earps cleaned out Curley Bill and that gang. What do you think, gambler?"

"I'll bet Isaac wouldn't last twenty-four hours once the news gets to Goldfield," the man with the deck of cards declared. "They'd gut-shoot him and leave him to the coyotes."

Suddenly the big man stepped to the side and aimed the shotgun at Fergus. "That Indian insulted my wife!"

Again O.T. slid over in front of the gun.

"Dadgumit, Isaac," the old man hollered, "ever'body knows your wife ran off to Bisbee with an Arizona Ranger. You been callin' her ever' name in the book for almost a year."

"That don't give no dumb Indian the right to insult her too. I ain't havin' no digger Indian stay in my place."

Skinner motioned Fergus toward the door. Both men backed up slowly. "We're leavin'," O.T. announced.

"You don't have to go, Wall Walker. He jist said the Indian," the old man proclaimed.

O.T. surveyed the room. "Why would I want to stay here?"

"To get out of the storm." The gambler shrugged.

O.T. paused by the door. "I won't stay with any man that don't like my friends."

Three more steps, and the men were on the porch.

Sand and dirt blasted their faces.

The wind roared.

Darkness blinded them.

O.T. pulled on his goggles and could see nothing.

But he felt ten times more refreshed than he had inside the building. He reached over for Fergus's arm.

"Can you see anything, partner?"

"I can see a brave man."

"I can't see a thing."

"That is because you are only looking with your eyes. They want to treat us like diggers. Then we will act like diggers."

"I ain't doin' nothin' illegal," O.T. hollered.

"I didn't mean that. I meant we will camp under their noses, and they will never know it."

In the darkness they found the rail and their

mules. O.T. followed Fergus by hanging onto Ida's tail. When they reached the east side of the building, they huddled close to the wall. The wind whipped past them on both sides, leaving a small triangle in the middle almost calm.

They dropped down on the desert floor, their backs against Alkali's only building. Ida's reins were tethered to Fergus's foot. Ada was tied to O.T.'s. In between the men were two canteens and a sack with grimy biscuits and dust-covered fried bacon.

Fergus leaned over. "Many a time I camped out undiscovered against a white man's cabin or barn."

"It ain't half bad right here, partner," O.T. admitted.

"The wind is tolerable," Fergus mumbled through a bite of gritty bacon.

"And the company is better than inside," O.T. added.

"As is the food," Fergus replied.

Minutes later O.T. leaned his head against the unpainted clapboard siding. He gulped down a couple of swigs of tepid water. Then he soaked his bandanna and clamped it between his lips.

Fergus leaned his shoulder against O.T.'s. "Now I know what the word *partner* really means. It means stepping in front of a loaded shotgun for another person when you don't have to."

"Mama, when is my daddy coming home?" Corrie whined as she tore an old newspaper into half-inch squares.

Dola was re-soaking all the rags and replacing them at the sills of the windows and door of the apartment. "He and Fergus want to find Jared. So I imagine they haven't found him yet."

"I'm sure Daddy will find him," Rita Ann announced as she pushed her glasses up and paced around the room, the thick book clutched to her chest. " 'Then let not winter's ragged hand deface in thee thy summer, ere thou be distilled . . .' "

Tommy-Blue made a face as he helped Corrie tear newspaper. "What does that mean, Rita Ann?" he demanded.

"I haven't the least idea," she replied, holding her nose high as she paced.

"You're worried about Daddy, aren't you?" Corrie observed. "When you get really, really worried, you start saying all sorts of strange things."

"I most certainly do not, my dear Muggins!" Rita Ann quipped. "Rabbit stew should never be served with white gravy."

"She's worried," Corrie retorted to her mother.

"We're all worried a little. It's a dangerous sandstorm," Dola commented.

"Mommy, look!" Punky called out as he

105

clomped across the room on all fours, wearing Dola's lace-up boots on his feet and Corrie's smaller but identical ones on his hands. "Look, I'm crocodilly!"

"Well," Dola grinned, "perhaps not all of us are worried. You're a dilly, all right." She scooped Punky up out of the boots. "Let's try to get a little of this dirt off you and get you ready for bed."

Rita Ann scooted across the big room bare-footed. "Mama, you simply must do something. This floor is gritty."

"Yes, it is. The floor is gritty. The furniture is gritty. The beds are gritty. We are gritty. The air is gritty. And there isn't anything in the world I can do about it. I'm sorry, darlin' — that's just the way it is."

"Mama, someone's knocking at the back door," Tommy-Blue called out.

Everyone in the room paused to listen.

Everyone except one. "I'm a crocodilly!" Punky squealed.

"Shhh, Punky . . . listen!" Corrie and Dola cautioned at the same time.

There was a distant rap and a muted voice.

"Maybe it's my daddy!" Corrie shouted.

"He's daddy of all of us," Rita Ann corrected. "I don't know why you insist on calling him 'my daddy.' "

Corrie was out the doorway and running down the stairs before Rita Ann finished her sentence. Toting Punky on her hip, Dola trailed the others down the stairs into the darkened room. Tommy-Blue carried a lantern into the kitchen. The only light in the restaurant dining room was a dim glow of reflected light. Dola found the children huddled at the back door with the Rokker children.

"Danny, what is it?" Dola called out.

Caitlynn Rokker ran to hug Dola.

Danny smeared tears across his dirty face and wiped his nose on the back of his hand. "The roof done blowed off our house, Mrs. Skinner. Half our stuff blowed clean across the state of Nevada!"

"The whole roof?" Dola gasped. She put her hand on Caitlynn's emaciated shoulders and held the little girl against her hip.

Danny jammed his hands in his back pockets. "It surely does seem like it."

Dola stared down at Stella's frightened eyes. "Did anyone get hurt, darlin'?"

The girl's lower lip quivered. "No, but Mama won't leave her bed."

"She what?"

Caitlynn tugged on Dola's dress. "Mama's in bed and won't leave," she whimpered.

"She's in bed with the covers over her head and said she won't come out until Jared comes home," Danny reported. "I begged and pleaded. What am I goin' to do, Mrs. Skinner? I surely do wish Jared was here. He'd know what to do."

Elias Rokker, you are never at home when you

are needed! They don't need a twelve-year-old brother. They need a father! "You are all going to stay with us until your roof is fixed. Corrie Lou, you get out the bag of lemons. Tommy-Blue and Danny, you help her squeeze lemons and make a large pitcher of lemonade. Rita-Ann, have Stella help you get out the big skillet and make popcorn. There are still some hot coals in the stove, I know. There may be a horrible dust storm outside, but we can have a little party in here."

"But what about Mama?" Danny protested.

"I'm going to go get her." Dola Skinner rubbed her pointed chin and her thin neck as she stared at the back door.

"She won't come," Stella protested. "She said she won't come out of the covers until Jared comes back."

"She can't lay out in the open in a dust storm. So I reckon I'll just have to hog-tie her, toss her over my shoulder, and carry her back here."

Caitlynn's eyes grew wide. "Really?"

"Honey, when she hears we're having lemonade and popcorn, she'll want to come." Dola laid her hand on Caitlynn's dirty cheek. "Wouldn't you if you were her?"

Caitlynn smiled and nodded her head up and down.

"Mama, don't you want me to go with you?" Tommy-Blue asked.

"You stay and help here, darlin'," she instructed.

"But it's dark, and there's a dust storm, and a lady shouldn't have to go out on a night like this," the nine-year-old protested.

Tommy-Blue already sounds just like his daddy. Orion Skinner, you are here even when you aren't here. "Darlin', there are emergencies, and this is one." She sat Punky on the butcher block and handed him a tin pan and wooden spoon. "Make Mama some cookies, little darlin'."

"Do you want to take the shotgun?" Tommy-Blue asked as she tied on her old calico bonnet. "Daddy left the shotgun for you."

"Heavens, no. I will be perfectly fine. The Lord will take good care of me. Caitlynn, will you play with Punky until the popcorn's ready?"

She buttoned her dress collar high under her chin and pulled on O.T.'s worn, long canvas duster.

"You look funny, Mama," Corrie said.

"Then it's a good thing it's so dark out there. No one can see me. You all behave. Rita Ann's the oldest. She's in charge."

"Hurry back, Mama," Tommy-Blue urged.

"Don't worry, I'll only be a few minutes."

Dola slipped out the back door, closing it quickly behind her.

The wind roared.

The dirt and sand blasted past her.

She couldn't see anything.

How on earth did the Rokker children find their way to our place? This is impossible. I can't even cross the street. I will just feel my way down the alley and out to the street.

Her hands out in front of her, Dola felt her way along the alley edge of the brick building.

There is a wood bin back here. Where is the wood? . . . Here it is. Okay. . . . I will circle around it. There should be nothing now between me and the . . .

It felt as if someone had slammed an axe handle into both knees at once. The pain shot up her legs, into her back, and then cramped her shoulders. She staggered to the right and fell face first into the alley.

The auto car! I walked right into the auto car!

She rolled over and reached down to rub her knees. The wind caught her skirt and blew it halfway over her head.

Thank You, Lord, for darkness.

She struggled to her feet. Her legs were shaky, but she hobbled around the auto car and followed the building wall out to the street. Up on the boardwalk she walked slowly west. The occasional lantern light from the businesses provided enough light to keep her from falling again. She kept her bonnet pulled down and her chin on her chest.

Suddenly a glow of light flickered out from a doorway. A worn pair of boots blocked her way. Squinting into the dirt and wind, she raised her head and stared at an unshaven man with a flat-brimmed hat jammed down to his ears. Even in the storm the stench of whiskey and sweat rolled off the man. "Little lady, whar do you think yore goin'?"

She dropped her chin back to her chest. "I have a friend who needs me," she muttered. "I must hurry."

"Well . . . what if I need you?" He reached over and grabbed her chin with sticky, dirty, callused fingers.

Lord Jesus, please send an angel of protection!

Her left hand slammed his hand away. She reached with her right to slap his face, but he lunged at her. Instead of a slap, her finger caught his eyeball.

The man jumped back and screamed, "You tryin' to blind me, lady!" He clutched his eye with one hand and pulled his revolver with the other.

The saloon door swung open again. "Mrs. Skinner, is that you?"

"Lucky Jack! How did you know it was me? I can't see anything in this storm." *I asked for an angel, Lord, and You sent Lucky Jack Gately. I've never been so glad to see a man . . . a friend in my life!*

"I heard your voice. Is this hombre harassing you?"

"Lucky Jack Gately?" The drunk quickly shoved his revolver back into his holster. "She liked to scratch my eye out. I didn't know she was your woman!"

Lucky Jack's upper cut caught the bearded man by the chin, driving teeth into his lip. He staggered back and collapsed against the building, squatting on the boardwalk. Even in the darkness of the dust storm, Dola saw blood drip down into his beard.

"I will not have you insult the most righteous woman in this town. She is not my woman but my friend. Her husband is the Wall Walker."

The man tried wiping the blood off his chin and pulled himself to his feet. "I ain't never heard of no Wall Walker."

"I can remedy that." Lucky Jack grabbed the man by the collar and dragged him over to the saloon door. He kicked the door open and shouted, "Boys, this hombre was out here harassin' the Wall Walker's wife. Could you explain the situation to him?" He shoved the bearded man into the room and closed the door behind him. Then he turned to Dola. "They'll school him."

Dola stared at the closed saloon door. "But I don't want . . ."

"You do believe folks need to learn lessons, don't you?"

"Well, yes, but . . ."

Lucky Jack pulled his bowler low and leaned toward her. "And sometimes the most important lessons we learn are painful at the time?"

Dola didn't back away. "Yes, however, I —"

Gately pointed a thumb back at the saloon. "That old boy will learn a lesson that will help him be a better man. Thanks to you, he will

112

probably never harass another lady the rest of his short, miserable life."

She caught a drift of spice tonic water on Lucky Jack's clean-shaven face. "I do hope it's not too short," she added.

There was just enough light from the saloon to see Lucky Jack's stare but not enough to see his eyes. "Now, Mrs. Skinner," Lucky Jack had to lean close so as not to shout above the roar of the wind, "just why are you out in this storm?"

She held her hands to the side of her face to keep the dirt from blowing directly into her eyes. "It's Nellie Rokker. The roof blew off their house, but she won't leave."

"Where do they live?" Lucky Jack's voice reflected concern.

"The old Oliver house. Do you know it?"

"Yeah. That ain't nothin' but tarpaper and shingles," he declared.

"I'm afraid there's even less now."

Lucky Jack pulled off his leather belt.

"What are you doing?" she demanded.

"Making a tether." He stuck one end out toward her. "Wrap that around your wrist and hang on."

"Why on earth should I do that?"

"Because I'm goin' with you, and I don't want us to get separated, and I make it a habit not to walk arm in arm with married ladies!" he shouted.

She grabbed onto the two-inch-wide leather belt. *Lord, You did send me an angel.*

Four

The sand and grit still peppered Dola's face, but she found it easy to follow Lucky Jack's lead. He tugged the belt through the darkness and waited with a helping hand whenever she needed to step down and cross a street.

She didn't even lift her head to look for him but just held out her hand. He was always there. She calculated they had made a turn to the north, then a turn to the west, and another turn to the north. Finally the tugging stopped. Even in the howling wind and darkness, she could sense Lucky Jack next to her.

Very close.

She knew his cupped hand was just inches from her ear. "This is the Oliver house or what's left of it," he called out.

She cupped her hand and called back. "I can't see anything."

This time his voice was softer, closer. "From what I can tell, only the door and framing is left. The shingles must have blown off the roof. The tarpaper walls are shredded."

Dola peered straight ahead at nothing. "How will we find Mrs. Rokker in the dark?"

Lucky Jack's voice sounded calm, like he did this sort of thing all the time. "Do you know the house?"

"There are only two rooms. The bedroom is in the back."

He nudged her forward. "You lead this time. Just tug on the belt."

Dola flinched. Then she reached out and felt the cold brass door handle. The blowing sand stung her fingers. When she shoved the door open, it caught on something before it had moved two inches. She used both hands and shoved on the door. "It seems to be stuck!"

"Over here . . . the wall's gone. We can walk through here," he called out as he tugged on the belt tether.

Dola held onto the rough-cut two-by-four framing studs and pulled herself into what had once been the Rokker living room, kitchen, pantry, and children's sleeping quarters. In the pitch-black of the storm, she turned and yanked the belt hard toward her. The belt was taut, then slack. Then she heard a yell. Then the belt was taut again.

She stepped back toward the wall. "Mr. Gately, are you all right?"

There was a clamor of motion and the smell of tonic water shaving lotion. "You just jerked my nose into a two-by-four," he hollered into the storm.

"This isn't working well," she said. "I can't see, and the way is scattered with obstacles."

"That's okay, Mrs. Skinner. You didn't break anything . . . yet."

Dola took a long, slow breath and bit her lip.

Then she let her breath out slowly. "Mr. Gately, I'm going to turn my back toward you. I want you to put your hands on my shoulders."

"What did you say?" His voice sounded truly surprised.

I don't believe I'll have the nerve to say that again. Dola turned around and waited.

Two strong hands rested lightly on her thin, coat-covered shoulders. She clutched the leather belt with both hands as she inched across the room. Her knees and already bruised shins shoved debris aside. When the object was big, she reached down and shoved it to one side or the other.

The hands stayed on her shoulders.

Dola felt for an interior wall but found only two-by-four studs. She scooted to the left and found the doorway. She had just taken two steps into the back room when her shins bumped against an iron bed frame. Her knees rubbed against a crumpled, dirt-covered comforter.

"Nellie!" she called out. "It's me — Dola Mae!"

The hands dropped off her shoulders.

There was a muffled response.

Dola lowered to her knees beside the bed. She tugged at the covers and jumped when a cold, sweaty hand grabbed her wrist. Every dusty hair on the back of her neck stood on edge.

"Nellie?" she blurted out.

"Is Jared with you?" came the weak reply.

Dola leaned over the bed and patted the hand that clutched her so tightly. "Mr. Skinner and Fergus went to get your Jared for you. They'll bring him home. You come to our place. Your roof is gone. You can't stay here, Nellie. When the storm is over, we'll repair your roof."

"Where's Jared?" The voice was anxious, terrified.

Dola rubbed the woman's arm. "He went looking for your husband, but Orion will find him. You can count on him, Nellie."

"I want Jared here right now!" the woman screamed as she yanked on Dola's arm.

"Nellie, you're scared. That's all right. This is a bad storm. But let's get you over to our place. Danny, Stella, and Caitlynn are already there."

Holding onto Dola's arm, Nellie Rokker pulled herself up on one elbow. "I won't go without Jared. He'll come back here. He'll need me."

Dola slipped her hands over and gripped Mrs. Rokker's shoulders. "Nellie, the others need you too. We'll have to trust Jared to the Lord and Mr. Skinner. Between the two of them, I guarantee everything will be all right. I want you to come with us right now!"

"Who's with you?" the voice was weak, almost a whine. "I can't see anyone."

"None of us can see anything, Nellie. Mr.

Gately is with me. You remember Mr. Gately and friends who let us camp on their lot when we first got to town?"

Mrs. Rokker's shoulders stiffened. "Why is he here?"

Lucky Jack leaned over Dola's shoulder. His voice boomed above the noise of the storm like a wave breaking on rocks. "Because two married ladies should have an escort on a night like this. Your husbands, bein' friends of mine and both bein' out of town, I figured it was my duty."

"I can't leave without my boy." Nellie's voice was now just pleading.

"Nellie," Dola countered, "I'm sure Mr. Skinner will bring your Jared to our place first."

"Why?"

"Because we live above a café. Jared will be hungry. You know how hungry a young boy can get. So naturally Orion will want to fill his belly before he brings him home to you."

"Perhaps I should get up," Nellie said.

"Do you still have on your dress?" Dola asked.

"Yes."

"And your shoes?"

"Yes, but there's a draft in here," Nellie remarked.

"A draft? Half the desert is inside your house," Lucky Jack roared.

"Mr. Gately, so nice of you to visit. Can I boil you some tea?" Nellie Rokker offered.

118

Dola grabbed her arm and attempted to pull her to her feet. "Nellie, you are coming over to my place. Remember? That's where we can have tea."

"Oh, I couldn't possibly leave until Jared comes home. I wonder what is keeping that boy?"

"Jared and Mr. Skinner are coming to my place. He'll be very disappointed if his mother isn't there."

"But I can't leave the house in such a mess. What will the neighbors think?"

Your house is all over the neighborhood. All over town. Oh, Lord, she's so frail. Her mind's so troubled. I don't even know what to say or do for her. She has so many needs, I don't know where to begin. "Nellie, Mr. Gately will help us back to my place."

"You go on. I'll wait for Jared. He and I will be over shortly," Mrs. Rokker insisted.

Dola tugged the woman to her feet, still shouting above the roar of the wind. "Come on, Nellie, it's time to —"

From out of the darkness the open hand slapped her face with such force that Dola staggered back. Two strong arms caught her and gently propped her back on her feet.

"Nellie Rokker! I've had about all I can take," Dola cried out through the dirt and tears. She grabbed the shorter woman by the shoulder and shouted, "This house is uninhabitable. My dear husband and Fergus are risking

119

their very lives searching for your son and your husband. Your other three darling but neglected children are over at our place worried sick about you. How dare you slap me in the face for helping you! You should be ashamed. Now you will either come along quietly, or Lucky Jack and I will roll you in a comforter and tote you across town screaming and yelling. At this point it really doesn't matter to me at all!"

There was no reply.

No movement except the sand and dirt in the air.

The wind howled like a choir of hungry, vicious wolves.

Finally from Nellie came a weak, almost distant whine. "Did you say that Danny, Stella, and Caitlynn are there?"

Dola felt her shoulders relax. The tightness in her neck lessened. Her voice softened. "Yes, they are. They are drinking lemonade and eating popcorn. Doesn't that sound nice?"

"I like lemonade."

"I think we better join them before it's all gone."

"Will they save us some?"

"I'm sure they will."

"Did they pop the corn in lard or in butter?" Nellie asked.

"I'm sure Rita Ann used butter." *That's a lie, Lord. I really have no idea what she used. She could have used olive oil for all I know . . . forgive me.*

"I like it best when it's in butter."

"Well, if we don't like it, we'll make our own."

"Yes, let me get my hat," Nellie Rokker shouted into the wind.

Your hat? Nellie, we are lucky to get out of this building with our lives. There is no way we can find your hat!

"Is this it?" Lucky Jack thrust something over Dola's shoulder.

"Yes, thank you, Mr. Gately!" Nellie hollered.

"Where did you find that?" Dola quizzed the unseen Gately.

"I was standing on it," he replied.

"Hold onto my hand," Dola cautioned. "We have to be really careful getting out of the house. Lucky Jack, take my other hand and lead us out to the yard."

A strong, masculine hand tugged her forward. A weak, feminine one pulled her back.

When they reached the yard, Lucky Jack huddled them close together. "Mrs. Skinner, how do you want to work this going back across town? I only have one belt!"

"Nellie," Dola called out, "keep your head down and your eyes closed. Mr. Gately will lead us there. You clutch onto his right arm, and I shall clutch onto his left. Don't turn loose for anything!"

"I'm a married woman!" Nellie wailed.

"So am I. But Mr. Gately is a perfect gentleman. Right, Mr. Gately?"

"I reckon it won't damage my reputation to be a perfect gentleman, at least until I get you to the café," he replied. "Mrs. Rokker, I promise to mind, because Dola Mae Skinner will beat me to a pulp if I don't!"

Dola clutched Lucky Jack's left arm with both hands, closed her eyes, and turned her back to the wind. *For such a tall, thin man, his arms are much thicker and stronger than I imagined.*

Not that it matters.

When O.T. woke up, he didn't bother opening his eyes.

The dirty bandanna still covered his mouth and nose.

The auto goggles still protected his eyes.

His felt hat was tied under his chin.

His back ached.

He could feel the sand between his socks and boot-clad toes.

He could feel sand everywhere.

And he could feel someone or something tugging on his ankle.

That's when he opened his eyes. A mule was yanking at the lead rope tied to his foot.

Ada, where do you think you're going?

O.T. shoved the goggles to his forehead and stared out at a star-filled night. *It blew on by! The storm is gone! Lord, how can it be gone just like that?*

Miles and miles of stars shone down on the sandy landscape, like a room swept clean with no traces of previous activity.

Ada yanked the rope out toward the desert floor.

O.T. pulled himself to his feet. His back ached. His legs cramped. All the loose sand inside his clothing shifted lower. He untied the lead rope, opened the blinders, and stroked the mule's neck. His voice was low, hoarse, raspy. "What's the matter, girl? You want to go back to your barn now?"

She continued to tug on the lead rope.

O.T. kicked lightly at Fergus's boots.

The old Paiute leaped to his feet.

"The storm's over, pard," O.T. said.

Fergus pushed the driving goggles to his forehead and stared at the heavens. "You woke me from a dream about a beautiful young Paiute maiden just to say the storm is over?"

O.T. laughed. "You're too old to dream of young maidens."

"I was not old in my dream." O.T. could see the white teeth of Fergus's smile.

O.T. pointed to the north. "Ada thinks she wants to go out there."

"It might be well to leave." Fergus unfastened Ida's lead rope from his ankle. "If those inside sober up, they will need a trip to the privy. I believe I will be gone before they see me."

They loaded the mules and re-set the saddles.

This time when they mounted up, there were no bandannas over their mouths.

No driving goggles over their eyes.

No homemade stampede strings on their hats.

No dirt and sand blowing in their face.

This time they could see for several hundred yards across the desert floor. But there were absolutely no tracks, no wagon ruts, no game trails to follow. Only virgin sand and alkali that had never been trodden by mankind.

"Which direction are we going?" Fergus asked as they plodded north, Ada in the lead.

"Toward Coyote Springs, I reckon. Young Rokker must have bypassed Alkali."

"If so, he is wiser than us. We are headed in the wrong direction. Coyote Springs is west of here. You are going north."

"I know. . . . We'll circle back. I'm giving Ada some rein. Maybe she smells water."

"There is no water north of here until Tonopah. And all their water comes from California," Fergus declared.

"We'll jist go a mile or so. Got to keep my ladies happy. Ada, Ida, and I have been through a lot."

The black sky turned to charcoal gray, then to light gray. The stars disappeared, and a cloudless sky emerged. The air was fresh, with a hint of coolness. O.T. and Fergus coughed and blew dirt out of their mouths and noses and wiped it out of their ears, eyes, and any other accessible location.

When they reached the top of a barren desert swell, O.T. stopped and glanced back. The sky was now a pale blue. The sand and dirt was a yellow-tinted buckskin. There were no trees in sight, not even a Joshua tree. No sage. No trails, no tracks. He saw in the distance, like an island, the one building and corrals at Alkali.

"I reckon they'll see our sign and know where we bunked for the night," O.T. offered.

"They could follow us, but I do not think they will consider us worth the effort," Fergus added.

They had ridden on for about half an hour when Fergus piped up, "Is it time for breakfast yet?"

"All we have are a couple of dirty, rock-hard biscuits."

"Thank you," the Indian replied.

O.T. handed him the food sack. "They're all yours, partner." He stared north. "We'll ride to where the mountain rises out of the desert floor. Then we'll turn back. No reason to start up into the hills."

"Perhaps we will turn around by that mule."

O.T. stood in the stirrups. "What mule? I can't see anything but sage and one Joshua tree."

"The tree is tethered. It keeps moving back and forth. It is a mule," Fergus declared. Then he dug out a biscuit that was the exact color as the desert sand.

"Partner, you got dust in your eyes. That's a tree!" O.T. watched carefully. "A tree that just moved over a couple feet!"

"It is a mule."

"How do you know that?"

"Because your mules are wanting to go investigate. Do you think they would do that for a horse?"

"Not these two." O.T. sat back down in the saddle. "They hate horses. Young Jared Rokker was on a mule."

"From the same stable as yours."

"You sayin' these ol' gals smell a friend out there?"

Fergus stretched his arms. "It is a nice morning for fresh smells."

O.T. stared again. "I don't see anyone around the animal."

Fergus chomped into a biscuit. "Perhaps they got separated." Crumbs sprayed out as he talked.

Skinner kicked Ada's flanks. Both mules trudged north. The sand was loose and progress slow until they started up the slope of the mountain.

"What's the little mule tethered to?" O.T. quizzed.

"Looks like a stick in the sand or perhaps a saddle horn." Fergus turned his attention to the second biscuit. "Perhaps it is a biscuit that it is tied to. This one looks as if it could be used for a tent peg."

O.T. glanced over at Fergus. "You don't have to eat that thing."

"My eyes tell me not to eat it, but my stomach insists."

"You think there's a saddle buried under the dirt?"

"Half buried," Fergus mumbled through the bone-dry biscuit.

"The mule didn't take the saddle off. Jared must have done that," Skinner added. "He's got to be around here someplace."

Fergus studied the second half of the biscuit as Socrates might have contemplated a cup of hemlock. "He could have walked off into the storm. The wind can make a person crazy like that." The Paiute jammed the piece of biscuit into his mouth.

"We've got to find him, Fergus. We have to find him alive. I can't go back to his mama with a dead boy."

The old Paiute chewed and then swallowed hard. "Life and death are in the hands of the Almighty."

"Are you preachin' at me, ol' man?"

Fergus sat up straight and pushed his hat back. "Yes! It is time I returned the compliment."

"You're right. Life and death are in the Lord's hands. And I'm prayin' Jared is safe."

The little mule pranced from side to side. Ada and Ida called out greetings as they approached. O.T. patted Ada's neck. "You were

127

right, ol' girl. You had a buddy out here, didn't you?" He turned to Fergus. "Jared must have tethered the mule in the storm and then gone looking for something."

"Not necessarily," Fergus responded. "A mule can drag a saddle a long ways, but this one didn't even start toward us when we came in view."

"What are you sayin'?"

"I once knew a man who rode out a sandstorm by hiding in a badger hole and pulling the saddle blanket over his head. He held the reins in his hands until morning."

"Just what man was that?"

"Stuart Brannon . . . in *The Last Raid on Fort Greener.*"

"Well, Brannon maybe, but no twelve-year-old kid. Besides, there aren't any badger holes out here."

"Perhaps. We will soon find out."

O.T. handed Fergus the reins, stepped down to the sand, and squatted. "I'll dig out the saddle. We'll see if we can find any clues about young Jared."

"I'm down here, Mr. Skinner, and I'm stuck!" a mumbled, muted voice replied.

O.T. jumped back, tripped over his boots, and sprawled in the loose desert dirt. Ada brayed, and Fergus laughed. "Must be one of those talking saddles, Wall Walker!" he hooted.

Skinner crawled over and stared at the saddle horn. "Jared, what are you doin' down there?"

"Nothin'. . . . I'm stuck."

"Keep your eyes and mouth closed. I'll dig you out."

The sand was loose around the base of the mostly covered saddle. O.T. unlaced the reins from the small mule and handed them up to the still-mounted Fergus. He tugged at the saddle.

"Ouch!" Jared called out.

"Turn loose of the saddle, Jared," O.T. hollered.

"I cain't. I have the cinch looped under my arms so the mule wouldn't drag it away."

"He's a very thorough boy." Fergus grinned.

"Jared, I'm going to try to pull you and the saddle up at the same time," O.T. called down. "Try to kick yourself free."

"Yes, sir."

O.T. looped his arms under the saddle and lifted up slowly. He got it high enough to see Jared Rokker's dusty hat and dirty face. "Come on, Jared, kick yourself free now."

"I cain't, Mr. Skinner. My foot is stuck good."

"Let me unfasten the cinch. Then I can pull on your arms. Can you get your arms free?"

"Yes, sir, I think I can. Did it stop blowin'?"

"Yep. It's peaceful and still." O.T. unbuckled the cinch from under the saddle. "How'd you get yourself in such a fix?"

"I got lost in the storm." Jared coughed out dirt with every word. "Could hardly open my eyes."

Fergus sat with both legs drooped over the left side of the mule, the trapdoor rifle still in his lap, the reins in his hands. "How'd you find that hole?" he asked.

"My mule stumbled in it and bucked me off. I felt around and figured it was as good a place as any to try to hide from the storm."

O.T. scooped away dirt with his hands. "How did you know to hole up like this?"

"I read about it in a book called *Last Raid at Fort Greener*," he replied.

O.T. glanced back up at Fergus. "What can I say? The boy has a good eye for books."

Jared was now free from his waist up.

O.T. shoved the saddle and blanket aside and stooped low next to the boy. "Jared, put your arms around my neck and hold on. I'll grab you under the arms and yank. Tell me if I'm hurting you."

O.T. grabbed Jared's back. The boy's thin arms clamped around O.T.'s neck, and O.T. pulled. But Jared's legs were still anchored in the hole. The boy slipped up an inch or two but was still held tight.

"Whatever it is, it ain't too big. My right boot's caught!"

"Let your foot slip out of your boot. We'll reach back down for it," O.T. suggested.

"These are my new boots," Jared complained.

"Let's get you out first. Then we'll worry about the boot."

"The Wall Walker's right," Fergus called down. "The snake won't wait forever."

"What snake?" Jared asked.

"That is not a skunk hole. It is not a badger hole. It is the hole of a rattlesnake," Fergus announced.

Jared Rokker's eyes grew wide. "A rattlesnake?"

"A large one, no doubt."

This time when O.T. yanked, Jared Rokker popped out of the hole like a cork in a champagne bottle on New Year's eve.

Minus his boot.

Both he and O.T. tumbled to the ground and then struggled to their feet.

All three mules brayed.

"So you mules think this is funny?" O.T. snorted.

Fergus shrugged. "Mules have a good eye for humor."

Jared stared back down at the hole. "Is that really a snake hole?"

Fergus dropped the mule's reins straight down and dismounted Ida from the off side. He left the rifle balanced on the saddle, strolled over to the hole, and peered in. "Yes, it is a snake hole, and the snake is still in it."

O.T. gawked over the Paiute's shoulder. "How do you know that?"

"Because no respectable snake would have been out on a night like last night. He would have been curled up asleep in his home. Snakes

131

are not as dumb as the Wall Walker and his partner."

"You mean I could have got bit last night," Jared gasped.

Fergus studied the top of the boot. "He must be quite large. Your boot cut off his entrance. He would have nothing to strike except the sole of your boot. Move the mules back. I will retrieve the boot." Fergus lay on the dirt, reached into the hole, and waited. "I expect he will be a little grumpy."

O.T. backed the mules and Jared another ten feet away from the hole. "He will be downright hostile. Do you reckon we will need your .45-70?"

Still lying on his stomach, the Paiute turned back. The tint of dirt on his clothing helped him to blend into the desert. "For a snake? That would be a waste of a bullet. I will dispatch him soon enough if he doesn't behave himself," Fergus assured them.

O.T. and Jared watched the old Paiute from a distance as he slid his upper body down into the funnel-like opening.

"Careful, Fergus," O.T. called out.

The Paiute stuck a gnarled finger into the side boot loop, yanked the boot out, and backed quickly out of the hole. He jammed his left hand into Jared's boot and with his right hand snatched a long hunting knife from his own boot.

The head of the rattler was as big as O.T.'s

fist. Its body was as fat as his arm. It slithered straight up out of the hole, rattles sounding like a dozen castanets.

"Good grief," Jared gasped. "That's the biggest snake I ever seen in my life!"

O.T. grabbed the trapdoor rifle off Fergus's saddle and checked the chamber. "Where's your bullets?" he shouted.

"Put the gun back. I have this under control." Fergus lay in the dirt not more than ten feet from the now-coiled snake. With rattles sounding, the snake stared at Fergus.

"Are you kiddin'? That snake is lookin' for someone to bite!" O.T. hollered.

"Distract him," Fergus called out.

"Distract him?" O.T. gulped.

"Walk close and get his attention."

O.T. swallowed hard. "Are you crazy?"

"This is no time to debate my sanity. Run by him so he will strike at you."

"I can't believe this." O.T. dashed in front of the hole.

The big snake lunged and missed.

Fergus dove at the snake's head. The boot-clad left hand clamped down on the snake just behind its head. The knife in his right hand sliced through the snake as if it were made of soft wax.

"Good gravy!" Jared yelped. "He done beheaded that snake jist as quick as you please! I ain't never seen anything like that!"

Using Jared's boot, Fergus pushed the snake

head back into the hole and stood up, holding the body of the seven-foot snake.

"This will make a fancy belt and a nice breakfast," Fergus announced.

"We goin' to eat it raw?" Jared gasped.

"What kind of barbarian do you think I am?" Fergus grinned. "If we can find anything that will burn, we will roast it over a sage fire."

There was one last lantern lit in the upstairs apartment. Dola reached out for it and surveyed the room full of people. Tommy-Blue and Danny Rokker slept on pallets on the still dusty floor, surrounded by a covey of rock specimens. None sported the initials CLS.

In Tommy-Blue's bed were Stella Rokker and Corrie, both with stomachs full of lemonade and popcorn and oblivious to the world.

Punky, with little, round bottom poked high, had his head toward the foot of Rita Ann's bed. His big sister had laid the complete works of Shakespeare between them. With face scrubbed clean and hands folded on her stomach, she had a smile or a smirch. Dola couldn't decide which.

Sound asleep in Dola and O.T.'s bed were Nellie Rokker and Caitlynn. Nellie still wore her dress, but Dola was able to coax her out of her shoes. Thanks to Rita Ann's persistence, Caitlynn's face was scrubbed clean.

With a thick, worn patchwork quilt over her shoulder, Dola slowly descended the gritty stairs to the darkened restaurant. She eased down on the next-to-the-bottom step and set the lantern beside her. Streaks of dim light crept across the room until swallowed up by tables stacked with chairs and benches.

Dola smelled the lingering aroma of pork roast from last night and the sweat of hard-working men. But, mostly, she smelled the alkali dust that hung in the air. Her face, also scrubbed clean, still burned from the blast of sand and dirt. Her shoulders shuddered as she pulled the quilt tighter and stared out at the empty, shadowy dining hall.

Lord, there are so many things I don't understand in this world. How I look forward to being at home with You where mysteries will be revealed and tears will be no more. Nellie is the most fragile woman I've ever known. And yet the path You have given her is so difficult — a husband who seldom takes care of her . . . a frail body that can barely stay ahead of disease . . . a temperament so easily crushed.

I know You don't make mistakes, but it is so difficult to understand sometimes. Morning will reveal that the only house in town that was completely ruined by this storm is Nellie's.

You could have done something about that, but You didn't. You let the roof blow off, the walls rip apart, and their meager belongings scatter clear across Nevada.

Why, Lord? Why did You do that? I don't understand.

How can I explain it to her? To the children?

Dola turned the lantern off. Gloom washed across her like a wave. She clutched the quilt and leaned against the stair railing. *It's too hectic here, Lord. I don't even have time to think. I just scurry from one meal and one crisis to the next. I'm so tired, Lord. Orion's tired too. I see it in his eyes. I've seen it for years. He's burning himself out. He looks closer to sixty than forty.*

Hot tears streaked her face. She didn't bother wiping them off. Droplets formed on her narrow chin and cascaded to her blouse.

All I ever wanted was to take care of my Orion . . . and my children. I only want to cook suppers for them. I want to wash their faces and tuck them in their own beds with clean sheets. I want to sit by the fire in the winter with knitting in my lap and Orion by my side.

I want to hold his hand. Oh, Lord, how I love holding that man's hand.

I don't want to be a widow. I don't want to be alone. I need him real bad. I need him right now. Lord, it's very difficult to hold everything together when I'm breaking apart inside. It's this town. Like the grit that hangs in the air, there's heaviness in my heart. It is the neediest place I've ever been. At every turn there's a new crisis. Not one week has gone by that Orion hasn't risked his life and health for someone else.

Why should he be out in this storm?
I know, he had to go.
Lord, when I think about it, I get so scared. If I

lost him, I would be no better off than that fright-
ened woman in my bed right now.

She reached down, unlaced her shoes, and
pulled them off. Then she pulled down her
stockings and rubbed her toes, her feet, her an-
kles. She wiped her eyes on the dusty sleeve of
her thick cotton dress.

Sometimes, Lord, I am such a whiner. Being tired
is no excuse for such self-pity. I sound so ungrateful.
I remember when there was no roof over our head,
no food in the larder, and no prospects for to-
morrow. Every good and perfect gift comes down
from above. Scattered across the room up there are
four of the most wonderful treasures You ever made.
And I have the great privilege to be called Mama
by them. And out in the middle of this dust storm is
a gray-haired, muscled, ruggedly handsome, simple
man who thinks I am the center of the universe.

She leaned forward and rested her head on
her arms that bridged her knees. For several
minutes only her deep sighs could fight off the
tears.

I don't want to be this way, Lord. I want to be
the Dola Mae Skinner everyone thinks I am. I
want to be strong. I want to be decisive. I want to
be gracious. I want Your praise to always be on my
lips. I want to buzz through the dining room like
the queen of Goldfield.

Dola was shocked when deep laughter exploded out of her.

Queen? Never in my life have I been queen of
anything. The queen of plain-looking women. The

137

*queen of average intelligence. The queen of medi-
ocre talent. The queen of pork potpie. No fancy
French entrees. No seasoned Mexican dishes. No
deluxe Danish pastries.*

Pork potpie. That's me.

Forgive me, Lord, for wanting more.

Forgive me, Lord, for whining.

Forgive me, Lord, for doubting Your will.

Forgive me, Lord, for a selfish spirit.

*Forgive me, Lord, for such puny faith. I must be
a very pitiful child.*

For a moment she sat, silent, listening to the
whistle of the wind through the building. She
let it mask all other noise, all other thoughts.

*And, Lord, forgive me for clutching to Lucky
Jack's arm much tighter than I needed to.*

I want my Orion.

I want him right now.

*I want him to hold me, kiss me, and look into my
plain eyes and tell me I'm the most beautiful
woman on the face of the earth. I want him to rock
me in his arms, and I want to go to sleep listening
to his heartbeat.*

Dola could feel her shoulders, her neck, her
back relax. She dropped off to sleep. Then the
wind outside jogged her awake. Soon, like a
door closing slowly, she began to doze again.

*Lord, I'm so tired of this storm. Haven't You
gotten Your full use out of it yet? In the name of
Jesus . . . I just want this wind . . . to stop.*

Her arm felt like a soft pillow, the wooden
steps like a feather mattress. The quilt at her

shoulders couldn't have felt better if it had been satin sheets. She wasn't tired . . . wasn't frightened . . . wasn't bitter . . . wasn't worried . . . wasn't questioning.

Just asleep.

Wonderfully asleep.

She had no idea the wind had stopped.

The dust was settling.

And like luminescent wildflowers, a field of stars now blanketed the southern Nevada sky.

Jared Rokker took a gulp of water and handed the canteen back to O.T. "That's the first time I ever ate snake meat," he noted. "It's a lot better than I thought it would be."

"I didn't figure we would be havin' a hot breakfast," O.T. added. He took a long drink from the leather-wrapped steel container.

Fergus reached for the canteen. "It would have been much better with Tabasco." He took a long drink. "And coffee . . . and a couple of bear claws . . . perhaps some scrambled eggs . . . with Tabasco."

"Isn't that stomach of yours ever full?" O.T. laughed.

"Only once."

"When was that?"

"When I discovered a patch of watermelons. I must have eaten a dozen one moonlit night."

"Where did you find those?" Jared quizzed.

"In Tonopah in the mayor's backyard," Fergus confessed.

"Mr. Skinner, are we going to go look for my daddy now?" Jared pressed.

O.T. glanced over at the filthy-faced boy. "I've been ponderin' that. I think it would be best to swing west of Alkali and go back to Goldfield."

"But I need to find him for Mama," Jared protested.

"First off, how do we know he didn't already make it home? If he woke up in some cave and saw that the storm has stopped, don't you think he would have hurried back to you and your mama?"

Jared brushed his dirt-caked hair back out of his eyes. "I reckon so."

Skinner pointed to the mountain range on the southern horizon. "If he was in the Montezuma Mountains, he would be home by now."

"But what if he ain't?" Jared pulled his stick out of the fire and slid a hot chunk of charcoal-covered white meat into his mouth.

"Maybe after we check on things in town, we can get the wagon out and a few supplies and go look for him. I've got to get some time off from Mr. Tolavitch though. He's going to wonder where I am this mornin'. We need to report in with ever'one. You went off without clearin' it with your mama, and she's worried sick."

"Sometimes there are things a man just has to do," Jared retorted.

O.T. stared at the shallow eyes of the twelve-year-old and then over at the old Paiute.

"The young man is right, Wall Walker . . . and you know it," Fergus declared. "And I must do what I must do."

"What's that?" Jared asked.

Fergus stood up. "I must go out to my gold mine and check on my 10 percent."

"You wouldn't be plannin' on gettin' there about lunchtime?" O.T. guessed.

"I must admit, the thought had crossed my mind. I believe I can walk there by noon."

"I'd offer you Ida, but she won't leave Ada's side. They're kind of pals that way."

"I am a very good walker. I do not walk the walls like some, but I am a very good walker even so."

"Take my mule, Mr. Fergus," Jared offered.

"He's right. Young Rokker can ride Ida back with me."

The Paiute stepped over to Jared's mule. "It is a small mule."

Skinner slapped Fergus on the back. "It will be easier to mount when you get your belly all loaded down with biscuits at the gold mine."

Fergus nodded at Jared Rokker. "The Wall Walker makes a very fine point. I will take the small mule. I think I can make it for mid-morning coffee . . . and maybe some leftover biscuits. It is not too far west of here."

"I'll tell McMasters at the livery to put the rent for the little mule on my tab. You can settle up with me later," O.T. declared.

"Yes, we will declare dividends at the end of the week," Fergus announced. "I will need to deposit another nice sum in my account at Mr. Cook's bank."

O.T. studied the leather-tough, wrinkled brown face of the Paiute. He wore new boots, dirty white duckings, and a soiled wool poncho over a battered blue flannel shirt. His felt hat was tipped sideways, the feather bent back into the band. *Lord, this is a crazy land and crazy times. An ol' Indian like Fergus, who's at home wearing moccasins and pulling rattlesnakes out of holes for breakfast, is going to sit at a meeting and declare himself a healthy dividend from his gold mine holdings. I've got to shake my head. The world's going by too fast. I can't even keep up.*

Fergus left camp first. Then O.T. and Jared mounted the long-legged mules and headed south. They had gone only a mile before Jared pointed down the shallow, barren valley. "What's that down there?"

"That's the town of Alkali."

"Looks like only one building."

"That's about it."

"Are we going there?"

"Nope, we'll swing west just to see if we can sight your daddy."

They rode side by side, leaving a new trail in the desert floor. Jared pushed his hat back. "Mr. Skinner, I'm glad you came out after me. I reckon it was dumb to go lookin' for Daddy, dumb to go out in a sandstorm, and dumb to get caught in a snake hole."

"Jared, we have to make our best decision when the time comes. There's no reason to go back and second-guess."

"I cain't believe you found me, bein's I was down in that hole."

O.T. gazed across the alkali valley that looked so narrow today but had felt so wide the previous night. "Jared, did you think I wouldn't go out in a storm lookin' for you?"

"I guess if anybody would, it would be you. But I ain't your kid or nothin'. We ain't even related . . . yet."

"Yet?" O.T. choked. "You and Rita Ann have some plans I don't know about?"

"Oh, no, sir. I'm too embarrassed to talk to Rita Ann about that stuff. But a man does like to dream."

You will not dream about my twelve-year-old daughter, young man! "You're still a boy, Jared."

"I'll be thirteen on August 22nd."

"Well, Mr. Jared Rokker, I don't intend to have this conversation for a few more years. Is that understood?"

"Yes, sir, it is."

O.T. cleared his throat. "The fact remains, I did come out lookin', and the Lord led Ada right over to you. You're safe. That's an answer to many prayers."

Jared laced the reins between his dirt-caked fingers. "But we ain't found Daddy yet."

143

O.T. snatched off his hat. He combed his hair with his fingers. "Maybe the Lord don't want to spoil us and answer all our prayers at the same time."

The rest of the trip into Goldfield was slow, uneventful. They watered the mules and re-filled their canteens at Yukon Springs and then followed fresh wagon tracks down to the Tonopah road. Traffic was still light on the dirt roadway. Crews were busy with horse-drawn scrapers, trying to remove the drifts of sand to open it up to wagons, stages, and auto cars.

The sun was high above them when they reached the outskirts of Goldfield. It was not as hot as on the days before the dust storm. The air tasted fresh and new. Most people were out-side shoveling and scraping embankments of sand stacked against the west side of every house and business.

"Where did all that sand come from, Mr. Skinner?"

"Right off the desert floor, I reckon."

"Must be a terrible big hole somewhere to the west." Jared pointed to one house where the sand made a rampart up to the windowsill.

"That's one of the reasons why no one can grow any lawns or flowers in this town," O.T. murmured. "There's a lot of weight stacked against some of those buildings. It's a wonder they didn't collapse."

"Our house ain't got nothin' but tarpaper

walls. It couldn't hold the sand back," Jared said.

"Maybe over a block or two it isn't this bad. Your house is up there on the other side of that new one they're building."

"What new house? Nobody's building a new house around us."

"Right up there. See the one with framing studs, trusses, and no roof? Looks like they're about ready to roof it." O.T. stared at the shell of a house. Goods were scattered in the yard, the road, and the vacant lot across the street.

"That's my house!" Jared yelled. He kicked the startled mule and galloped up to what was left of the front step.

He's right, Lord. . . . It blew away like the little piggy's house of straw! The children . . . what about the children? And Mrs. Rokker? It's like an Oklahoma twister with sand instead of rain!

Jared leaped from the mule and ran though the open studs into the debris that composed the living room. "Mama!" he screamed. "Mama, where are you?"

"Careful, son," O.T. called out as he dismounted. "The whole house looks like it's ready to collapse."

"Where's Mama? And Danny? And Stella? And Caitlynn? Where are they? Here's Mama's locket," Jared sobbed as he plucked up a gold and abalone shell cameo. "It's got a picture of Mama and Daddy on their weddin' day. She wouldn't go off without it." He ran to the back-room while O.T. stood next to the front door. "Mama! It's me — Jared!" he screamed.

"Come on, son, let's go find your mother. Let's go to the café." *Lord, I've never seen anything like this.*

"They could have blowed away. My whole family might have blowed away!" Jared wailed.

O.T. shuffled through the debris in the living room and took Jared's arm. "Come on, son."

Jared jerked his arm away. "I — I've got — I've got to clean it up . . . and fix the roof and gather up our —"

"Jared, the most important thing is seein' that your mama is safe. Now we can't find that out here."

"But what about our belongings?"

"We'll come back with the wagon and start loading up everything salvageable."

"But — but I —"

O.T. grabbed the boy's arm again. "Jared, your mama needs you. Come on! This will wait. It can't possibly get any worse than it is now."

"No!" He violently jerked out of O.T.'s grasp. But the boy's momentum caused him to stumble and crash into the doorjamb leading to the bedroom. A two-by-four broke. It sounded like an axe handle on a boulder. The ceiling trusses began to sag and sway.

"Come on, Jared," O.T. yelled, "the ceiling is about to collapse!"

The terrified young man didn't move. He

stared above at the trusses. "Help me," he cried. "I — I . . ."

O.T. grabbed Jared and threw him across his shoulder as he ran to the front yard. He stumbled over a wooden chair, and they tumbled to the ground. O.T. whipped around to see one truss after another collapse into the former living room.

"The whole house is falling down!" Jared cried. "I'm sorry. I didn't mean to do it!"

What was left of the roof collapsed and broke through the flooring and foundation timbers.

"No," Jared sobbed. "No!"

There was a rumble from deep in the earth. It sounded like a blast from one of the mineshafts. The ground in front of O.T. and Jared began to crack open.

Ada and Ida bolted down the street.

Like growling jaws of death, the dirt opened up in front of them.

O.T. and Jared leaped up and sprinted across the street. The yawning crevice of dirt seemed to chase them until there was a loud roar like a dozen black powder anvils blasting away on the Fourth of July. A thick cloud of yellow-brown dust shot up out of the ground like an ugly encore of the previous night's storm.

"What happened?" Jared clutched O.T.'s arm. "What happened?"

"I think things just got worse," O.T. murmured.

A whole lot worse!

Five

"My oh my, Dola Mae. Ain't you a sight?"

The voice had an effect somewhere between that of a feather under the nose and a sharp poke in the ribs. Dola stood straight up. The quilt dropped to the stairway. The electric lights blasted her eyes. She felt a pain in her lower back, and her left leg was asleep.

She covered her eyes with her left hand and peeked out slowly. "Omega, what are you doing here?"

The black woman in a green cotton dress sashayed over to the foot of the stairs. "What am I doin' here? Honey, it's 4:00 in the morning, and it's time to start cookin' breakfast for a room full of hungry men who want a few more days of fifty-cent meals. I work here — remember?"

Dola let her hand drop and squinted at the large, empty dining room. "When did the electricity come back on?" she mumbled.

Omega picked up the discarded quilt and began to fold it. "About thirty minutes after the dust storm quit."

Dola stared out the front windows. She could see lights in the grocery store. "It quit blowing?"

"Sometime between midnight and 2:00 A.M."

148

Omega plunked the folded quilt at the foot of the steps. "So Lucian says. I was asleep and dreamin' of an ocean-view house in Carpenteria at the time."

Dola tried to rub the stiffness out of her neck. "That was about the time I went to sleep."

"You always sleep on the stairs?" Omega flashed a wide grin. "Or is that something you don't want to talk about?"

"What?"

"Never mind, honey. If you don't know, it don't matter. What are you doin' on the stairs?"

Dola glanced back up the long staircase. "The Rokkers' roof blew away in the storm about midnight. We bunked them upstairs."

"Blew away?" Omega folded her arms and shook her head. "Honey, there was only shingles and tarpaper on that house. It's a wonder it stayed up at all. Never could figure out how they kept the kids from walkin' through a wall. Nobody should have to live in that kind of place."

"Yes, well . . ." Dola attempted to pin her hair up without the help of a mirror. "I suppose it was better than the tent."

Omega batted Dola's hands down and began to do the pinning. "Did O.T. get back yet?"

Dola's hands dropped to her sides. She slumped forward as Omega LaPorte fussed with her hair. "No, I don't think he did. I'm sure he didn't. He would have woke me."

"I let myself in with my key. I saw all the lights on, but I couldn't get you to open the back door." Omega stepped back and stared at Dola. "There! Your hair's pinned, but you still look like you slept on the stairs."

"I'll go wake the children. We'll have to try to clean some before we serve. I need to wash my face. Not that I can improve things much. You get to have all the looks!"

"Oh, sure." Omega's dark eyes danced. "They all want to tease me and call me their 'bronze darlin', but ever' one of them is hopin' to meet and marry someone just like Dola Mae Skinner."

"Now that's a lie, Omega LaPorte!"

Omega shook a long, narrow black finger at Dola. "Honey, don't you be callin' me a liar. You jist ask 'em. You ask your Lucky Jack . . . or Earl . . . or young Jason . . . or any of them."

Dola threw up her hands and grinned. "Okay, okay. Go fire up the stoves and get some eggs cracked," she instructed.

She clutched the folded quilt and scurried up the stairs. Then she crept across the room by the light shining in from a bare bulb in the hallway. In the shadowy room filled with sleeping bodies, she washed her face in the basin and then unpinned her hair and combed it out.

They all want to marry someone like Dola Mae? No, they all want to hire a cook and housekeeper like Dola Mae. They want to marry someone who

150

can dance and play the piano and fill out a satin dress. I'll never do any of that. I'll never even own a satin dress.

I'm not complaining, Lord.

I'm plain.

That's all I've ever been. That's all I will ever be.

You made some fancy . . . like Omega. You made some plain . . . like me.

Now You made Rita Ann fancy. I'm glad. She would not be happy to be plain. On the other hand, there's Corrie Lou. . . . Lord, You created her happy no matter what anyone does or says. She looks an awful lot like her mama, but she won't be melancholy about it. Life is too much fun for her.

Lord, O.T. is out there somewhere, and I'm glad the storm is over. Bring him back home. Bring them all back home.

I surely don't know what to do with the Rokkers. Maybe O.T. and some of the others can roof their house.

But I don't have time to worry about that. I have breakfast to cook. A dining room to clean. Eggs to break. Bread to slice. Meat to fry. Coffee to boil.

Plain Dola Mae Skinner. Everyone's favorite cheap cook.

I do like being needed.

With her hair piled on top of her head, she strolled back out to the middle of the dimly lit room. *Perhaps not needed quite this much . . . but needed.*

151

"Mama, is it time to get up?" a high-pitched voice whispered.

"Mornin', Rita Ann. I suppose so. The storm stopped, and we can clean the dining room."

"You want me to wake the others?"

"You come on down when you're ready. We'll let the others sleep a little."

Dola scooted back down the stairs, pleased that the pain in her back had eased, and thanks mainly to clean, dry stockings, her feet no longer hurt. She was surprised to see a blonde-haired young woman in a long brown dress sitting on a stool next to Omega.

"Good morning," the blue-eyed girl beamed.

"Well, good morning to you," Dola replied. She glanced over at Omega who was cracking eggs into a huge ceramic mixing bowl. "I didn't expect company at this hour."

Omega kept working but nodded at the young woman. "Dola, this is Haylee Cox. She's young Jason's sister and heard that we are hirin'. I told her to just wait here, and you'd interview her."

"Oh, my, well, that was a quick reply. I just mentioned something at supper." Dola strolled a little closer and surveyed the girl on the kitchen stool. "Well, Haylee Cox, I do believe you will pass the men's 'cuteness' test."

Haylee slid down off the stool. "I really want the job, Mrs. Skinner."

Dola noticed that the girl was about her height. "How old are you?"

Haylee chewed her tongue and rocked back on her heels. "I'm nineteen."

Omega rolled her eyes at the ceiling.

"You look a little younger," Dola replied.

Haylee stared at her lace-up, brown high-top shoes that peeked out from under her ankle-length dress. "I'll be nineteen on Friday."

Dola opened a cupboard and began searching for a pan. "Haylee, have you worked in a restaurant before?"

"No, ma'am. I've been cleanin' houses for ladies around Tonopah, but it's always temporary. I know they'll give me a recommendation. Mrs. Hamilton, Mrs. Cooke, Mrs. Sinclair, and Mrs. Edwards. Young Mrs. Edwards. . . . You couldn't pay me enough to work for old Mrs. Edwards, but I don't want to talk about that. Anyway, I'm lookin' for something permanent. My brother and me want to rent a house here in Goldfield, but I need to pay my share."

Dola picked up a large wooden spoon and waved it. "I need someone who will show up on time every day, work hard at whatever I ask her to do without complainin', and not fraternize with the patrons."

"Not do what?" Haylee gasped.

"Fraternize," Omega grinned. "You ain't one of those girls that fraternizes right out in public, are you?"

Haylee's eyes grew big. "I don't . . . I don't rightly know. But if it's sinful, I don't do it!" Haylee gulped. "I'm a good girl."

Omega burst out laughing.

Haylee took a deep breath. "What did I say?"

"Ain't nothin', honey. Fraternize just means wastin' valuable time flirtin' with the men customers."

"Oh! No." Haylee shook her head. The wavy blonde hair danced from side to side. "I wouldn't do that, Mrs. Skinner — honest."

"Can I count on you tellin' the truth?" Dola asked.

"Yes, ma'am." Haylee took a deep breath and pinched her lips shut.

"How old are you really, Haylee Cox?"

She dropped her chin toward a well-rounded chest. "I'm sixteen, Mrs. Skinner," she murmured. "I'll be seventeen on Friday. I really, really want this job. I'm sorry I lied to you. Please forgive me."

"You're hired, Haylee."

The blonde's head jerked up, and her eyes widened. "Really?"

"Because you told me the truth." Dola waved the big wooden spoon at her again. "If you had kept saying you were nineteen, I wouldn't have hired you."

"Thank you, Mrs. Skinner!" Haylee scooted over and squeezed Dola's hand. "I won't disappoint you. Everybody's always tellin' me I look nineteen, so I thought it would help. Thanks for forgiving me."

"Haylee, most of your body looks nineteen. I'll grant you that."

"And I guarantee you, honey, the men who come in here will treat you like you're nineteen," Omega added.

Dola pulled several bowls off the shelf and wiped the dust out of them with a clean white cotton towel. "But to a mama who has daughters like I do, your eyes give you away. There's a wonderful wide-eyed innocence about being sixteen that you just can't cover up."

Haylee followed her down the narrow kitchen. "Sometimes I wish I looked older."

"My oh my, Haylee Cox, most every woman in Goldfield will wish she looks like you," Omega called out. "Honey, enjoy every day of it. You'll get wrinkles and sags soon enough. Ain't that right, Dola Mae?"

"True enough. We all get old. Of course some of us have more wrinkles and sags than others," Dola replied.

"Now don't you get personal." Omega waved an eggshell at Dola.

"When would you like me to come to work, Mrs. Skinner?"

"How about right now?"

"Are you serious?"

"Yes, I am. We have some aprons on that peg by the door. Try to find one that isn't covered with dust. I'm going to have hungry men in here in a little over an hour, and that dining room is filthy from the dust storm. I need you to start cleaning. Take some hot water and rags and clean the tables and then the benches and chairs. When my daughter Rita Ann comes down, the two of you can do the floors. We just might have time to clean this place before the crowd comes in."

Haylee began tying on the apron. "How old's your daughter, Mrs. Skinner?"

"She's twelve, but she also thinks she's nineteen!"

Dola Mae was frying ham when a neatly dressed Rita Ann scurried into the kitchen. "Mama, who's that girl in the dining room?" she asked.

Dola glanced up. "That's Jason's sister Haylee."

Rita Ann ran her finger along the kitchen counter as she walked. "What's she doing?" Then she checked her finger for dust.

"She's cleaning up. I need you to bring down the newspaper we shredded and show her how to wet them, spread them on the floor, and use them to sweep the dust out of here. I hired her this morning."

What little color she had seemed to flood out of Rita Ann's face. "To work permanent?"

"Yes, I certainly hope so." Dola watched as her oldest daughter's eyes teared up.

"Mother, how could you?" Rita Ann sobbed.

Dola glanced over at Omega, who shook her head slowly. "I think you better explain yourself, young lady," Dola demanded.

"But, Mother," Rita Ann moaned, "when I stand next to her, I'll look like a little boy!"

"Don't be ridiculous. Go up and get that bucket full of torn newspaper. Then I'll introduce you and help you get started."

Rita Ann left the kitchen in a sulk.

Omega looked up from her bowl of cracked eggs. "She's right, Dola Mae. The difference is quite marked. I'm sure Haylee will get all the attention now."

Dola rubbed the back of her hand across her forehead and then began to carve thick slices of ham. "Thank You, Jesus!" she murmured. "Thank You, Jesus!"

It was past eleven when they finished cleaning up after breakfast, scrubbing the kitchen and mopping the dining room for the second time. Omega, Dola, Rita Ann, Haylee, and Punky collapsed in chairs at the table near the kitchen.

Punky crawled up on the table and clapped his hands and danced.

Dola hiked up her apron and wiped sweat off her forehead.

"Is it this busy every day?" Haylee asked.

"Every day but Sundays," Omega replied.

"Are Sundays slow?"

"We close on Sundays," Dola reported. "The day belongs to the Lord. Even in a place like Goldfield."

"My mama goes to church," Haylee volunteered.

"You're invited to go with us," Dola offered.

Then she saw Rita Ann's frown.

"Maybe I'll just do that. Right now, I think I'll go to my room and take a nap. I'm not really used to getting up this early. Boy, no wonder you don't serve lunch," Haylee declared.

Dola unfastened the top button on her high collar and fanned her neck with her hand.

"You're only halfway through as it is. It's still a long day," Omega declared. "I'm goin' home. One good thing about a man that works most the night — he's at home at noon! See you all at 3:00. You need any supplies for tonight?"

"I need some hot peppers. You think they'll have any yet?"

"I heard they're still working to open the roads to the north. But one of the roads from the south is open. They might have fresh supplies. I'll bring peppers back with me if they do," Omega offered.

Dola looked over at the young blonde, her blouse sleeves rolled up to her elbows. *The day will come, I suppose, when even old ladies expose their arms. Not in my lifetime, I trust.* "Haylee, you have time off until 3:00 also."

"Good. I can tell Jason about my new job. Thanks again, Mrs. Skinner, for hiring me."

"You worked steady and did everything I told you. That's all I ask. You did a good job, Haylee," Dola commended her.

Punky took a flying leap into Dola's arms. "Haylee's a girl!" he declared.

"You got that right, darlin'," Omega laughed. "How old is this boy?"

Rita Ann slumped back in her chair. "Yes, 'when I consider everything that grows . . . holds perfection but a little moment . . .' "

"Is that Shakespeare?" Haylee quizzed.

"Yes, I'm memorizing the sonnets this summer," Rita Ann explained.

Haylee rested her elbows on the table, her chin on her hands. "I envy you, Rita Ann."

Rita Ann sat straight up. "You envy me?"

Haylee stared steadily into her eyes. "Yes. Look at all those wonderful lines you have memorized. When I was your age, I was working for a rich lady with a big library in Denver and didn't memorize anything."

" 'Some glory in their birth, some in their skill, some in their wealth, some in their body's force,' " Rita Ann intoned. "I guess I'll just glory in the words I've memorized."

"I will expect a full recitation while we serve dinner," Haylee insisted.

"You don't know what you're asking," Dola cautioned.

"Mrs. Skinner, I didn't have much school in my life, but I'm not dumb. I know I have to get lessons wherever I can find them. We'll trade, Rita Ann. How about you telling me about Shakespeare, and I'll tell you about . . . about —"

"Boys!" Rita Ann blurted out. She immediately dropped her chin onto her chest.

Haylee leaned back in the chair. "Oh, my, I don't know very much about them."

"You're goin' to learn in a hurry around here," Omega chided. "The boys were buzzin' around you like hibernatin' bears lookin' for spring honey."

"Yes, but that's only because they like . . . they want to look at . . . well, you know."

"We know!" Omega laughed. "Oh, man, I can't even remember what it's like to be sixteen. Do you remember, Dola?"

"I never in my life looked like Haylee. Not even in my dreams," Dola grinned.

"You are embarrassing me." Haylee blushed. "I really don't know much about boys . . . yet."

"You were married when you were sixteen, Mama," Rita Ann said.

"Mommy's a girl," Punky declared as he crawled back up on the table.

"I'm glad you were able to recognize that, little darlin'. Yes, I didn't have much experience at being sixteen."

"Well, then, it looks like I got me two girls to school," Omega declared. "Now come on, Haylee girl, I'll walk you home and give you your first lesson."

"How about me?" Rita Ann complained.

"You, darlin'," Omega declared, "are way past lesson one."

"I am?"

"Trust me, honey."

Omega and Haylee sashayed out the front door together.

Dola held out her arms, and Punky leaped into them. "Well, li'l Punky, I think you and Mommy need a nap."

"I'm hungry," he announced.

"You are always hungry!" Rita Ann chided. "You should be called Mr. Hungry."

"I'm Punky! I'm a boy!"

The front door of the café swung open. Danny and Stella Rokker preceded Tommy-Blue into the café.

Dola stood up. "What did you find over at your house?"

"It done blew away, Mrs. Skinner!" Danny reported. "All our goods is gone."

"There's nothin' left but the wood-frame skeleton," Tommy-Blue reported.

"How's your mother doing?" Dola probed.

"Mama just kept shaking her head and saying, 'The Lord giveth, and the Lord taketh away,' " Stella reported.

"Where is she?"

"Some of the neighbor ladies were helpin' her scour the neighborhood for our belongings. She said we should come back here 'cause it made her cry to have us see it," Stella reported.

"Caitlynn stayed with Mama," Danny added.

Dola set Punky on the floor. "I should have gone with her, but I couldn't get away before now. Perhaps I should go over there."

"I'll go with you, Mama," Rita Ann replied.

"I need you to watch Punky, honey. That's way too far for him to walk, and heaven knows I can't carry him that far."

"Rita Ann can carry me!" Punky suggested.

"Oh, no," Rita Ann protested. "You aren't a little boy anymore. I can't carry you that far either."

"I'm medium!" Punky announced.

"Mama, let Corrie stay with Punky. I want to go over and see Jared's house. I'm the only one who hasn't seen it."

Dola took a deep breath. "Well, I assure you, I didn't see much last night." As she let her breath out, every joint ached.

"Ain't nothin' to see," Tommy-Blue declared. "Just some old two-by-fours holding up ceiling trusses and stuff blown all over the neighborhood."

"Where is Corrie?" Dola asked as she cut off Punky's path toward the front door.

"She stopped by the hotel to tell Mrs. Marsh all about Danny's house," Tommy-Blue announced.

Dola folded her arms across her thin chest. "Does she intend to walk home by herself?"

Tommy-Blue shrugged. "She said there's a boy staying at the hotel who wants to walk her home."

"What boy is going to walk her home?" Dola pressed.

Tommy-Blue looped his thumbs in his suspenders. "Colin Maddison, the third."

"With two d's?" Rita Ann asked.

Tommy-Blue stuck his finger in his ear and scratched. "Yep."

Dola paced across the restaurant. "Well, you just go right back down there and walk her home yourself, Mr. Tommy-Blue Skinner. That's what a brother is for. My ten-year-old daughter does not need a boy to walk her home no matter how many d's he has in his name."

"Do I have to?" Tommy-Blue fussed.

There was not an ounce of flexibility in the reply. "Yes, you do."

"I'll go with you," Danny offered.

"And we could crawl under the boardwalk at the Columbia Hotel and get an ore sample!" Tommy-Blue suggested.

Dola pointed her finger at her oldest son. "What you are going to do is walk your sister home!"

"If Corrie is still visitin', and we have to wait around anyway, can we get an ore sample under the boardwalk at the hotel?" Tommy-Blue pressed.

"I suppose so, as long as you don't bother anyone or get in anyone's way."

The two boys almost ran into a broad-shouldered man who pushed his way into the café just as they left.

"Excuse me. Are you Mrs. Skinner?" the young man asked.

"Yes. Can I help you?"

"Mr. Gately sent me over."

"Are you a friend of Lucky Jack's?" Dola inquired.

"Actually I just met him. He told me to check with you about meals and —"

Dola waved her arms at the empty tables. "Surely, he told you we only serve breakfast and supper."

The man pulled his cap off his thick blond hair. "Yes, ma'am, I heard that. I just wanted to talk to you or your husband about that Thomas auto car in the alley."

"It doesn't work, you know."

"Yes, ma'am, I'm a mechanic. I can fix it for you."

"You don't look all that old."

"I'm older than that auto car. I've been doin' this for five years. Ain't many in Nevada who can claim that."

"Well, you do need to talk to my husband. I'm not at all sure we could afford to have it fixed. It was given to us. We've never driven one in our lives."

The man glanced down at his shoe tops. "What I was hopin', ma'am, was to make a trade."

Dola thought she heard his stomach growl. "What kind of trade?"

"You see, I'm new to these parts. And I want to open a shop and do mechanic work, but I don't have a penny to my name. I was wantin' to fix the car in trade for meals."

"Just how many meals would that be?"

"I don't reckon I know. I was hopin' to trade an hour's worth of work for a meal. That way I wouldn't starve to death, and you'd get your car fixed . . . sooner or later. If I get other jobs, I'll stop and do theirs and then come back to the Thomas — providin' that's acceptable."

"I think we can do that, Mr. —"

"Hudson Frazier, ma'am. Most folks call me Hud."

"Have you eaten anything today, Hud?"

He stared down at his worn boots. "Eh, no, ma'am. I haven't eaten in a few days, but I ain't complainin'. I been travelin' down from Carson City."

Dola turned toward the kitchen. "Rita Ann . . ."

"I'll get out the leftover ham and some biscuits and maybe fry some mashed potato cakes." Rita Ann scurried toward the back of the restaurant.

"Mr. Frazier, my Rita Ann will fix you up something. This meal is on the house."

"I'm willin' to work it off."

"Hud, this is a way to welcome new folks to the café. You get this one free. The rest you will have to work for."

"Thank you, Mrs. Skinner. Mr. Gately said you was the nicest lady in town."

"Well, that indeed is a very flattering compliment, since Mr. Gately seems to know personally every woman in the state of Nevada, if not the entire West. However, I believe he was probably just courting an extra serving of pie tonight. But it won't do him any good. I'm not that easily bribed. Now you go on in there. Rita Ann will fix you up."

He shoved his cap back on. "Thank you, Mrs. Skinner. I'll get the auto car running for you. I know I can. I appreciate your gracious hospitality." He scooted into the kitchen.

Yes, and it seemed to me that a twelve-year-old was much more hospitable than I've ever known.

She glanced up in time to see Punky toddle out the front door. "Wait a minute, young man!" she hollered as she ran after him.

"Hi!" he called to someone approaching.

The door swung open. Caitlynn Rokker scooted in, holding Punky's hand. Nellie Rokker followed them.

"Nellie, oh, dear Nellie! Danny told me about the house!"

The shorter, extremely thin woman shrugged her bony shoulders. " 'The Lord giveth, and the Lord taketh away,' " she murmured.

" 'Blessed be the name of the Lord,' " Dola added.

"I don't reckon I got that far yet." Nellie Rokker plopped down in the nearest chair and folded her hands on her lap.

"Were you able to salvage anything?"

"We boxed up some things. I left them over at a neighbor's. As soon as Elias returns, we'll . . ."

Nellie Rokker looked at Dola and then brushed back tears. This time her voice was much less confident. "I don't suppose Mr. Rokker has come by here?"

Dola looked straight into Nellie's weak, pleading eyes. "No."

"How about Mr. Skinner and my Jared?"

"Not yet, but I suppose we'll hear them at the door any minute now."

Nellie Rokker took a deep breath and leaned back, closing her eyes. Dola put an arm on her shoulder.

"I'm terribly embarrassed about the way I behaved last night," Mrs. Rokker offered.

"Don't you think another thing of it. That was a horrible ordeal to go through. We had a tornado hit our place near Guthrie, Oklahoma. When we came up out of the cellar, there was nothing left. Picked the house clean and left the barn intact."

"What did you do?"

"We lived in the barn until we could leave for California."

"I don't want to move again. I don't want to sleep in a tent. I don't want to see my children starve. I already lost . . ."

Dola clutched the woman's shoulder. "Nellie, as long as I run a restaurant, not one of your children will ever be hungry. Now put that thought out of your mind. When the men get home, they can roof and side your house. In the meantime, you'll stay right here with us."

Nellie Rokker shook her head. "I don't know why you do this for us. We don't deserve it."

"Nellie, don't you start in with that again. Life isn't about getting what we deserve. That's what heaven and hell are for. Life is enjoying the gracious surprises the Lord has in store for us. All good gifts come down from above."

Caitlynn came over and sat on her mother's narrow lap. "I've never met anyone like you Skinners," Nellie murmured.

Dola patted the woman's bony shoulder. "You must have been nappin' because there are plenty more like us."

"I'd like to be nappin'. I'm very tired."

"Go on up and help yourself. Stella, do you mind taking Punky up with you? Rita Ann and I want to walk over and take a look at your house."

Stella reached out her hand. "Come on, little Punky."

He toddled over and grabbed onto Stella. "I'm medium," he insisted.

Dola let out a big sigh as she watched all of them troop up the stairs. *I wouldn't mind a nap myself. I will not sleep on the stairs tonight. I don't know what arrangements we can make. Perhaps we can round up some cots and . . . I'll check with Lucky Jack.*

No. Not Lucky Jack. I do believe I've leaned on him enough. I'll ask Omega to have Lucian LaPorte round up some cots. If there are any in town, he will know where they are. Of course, I will not ask him where they came from.

She stared around at the empty dining hall.

Rita Ann, where did you . . . oh, yes . . . Mr.
Hudson Frazier.

Dola marched into the kitchen. The young mechanic stared at a pile of ham mounded up on the plate in front of him.

Rita Ann leaned over his shoulder.

"What are you doing, young lady?"

Rita Ann pulled back. "I was just seeing if he liked the ham."

"I suggest you give him room to open his mouth and move his fork."

Mr. Frazier looked up with a sheepish grin. "This is surely a generous portion."

"Yes, well, you might be gettin' the special kitchen edition. Regular meals are not quite that generous, but we often have seconds. I try to make sure everyone is happy when they leave."

"I wasn't expectin' all this and pie too," he mumbled.

Dola raised her eyebrows. "Pie?"

"You know, Mama, there was some extra peach cobbler."

"We were saving that for Daddy and —"

"Oh, I saved Daddy his bowl."

"And Jared?" Dola pressed.

"Is Jared your brother?" Hudson Frazier asked.

"He's sort of like a brother," Rita Ann replied.

Frazier pushed the bowl of cobbler back. "Maybe you ought to save this pie for him."

"Jared's gone. He went to find his daddy. He might not even come over. It would be a shame to have to throw it out," Rita Ann insisted.

Hud Frazier gave a wide, dimpled grin. "Well, we sure don't want to waste it."

Dola shook her head. *Oh, my . . . look at that smile.*

"Oh, good. Can I get you some more biscuits?"

"Eh, yes, Miss Rita Ann."

"And some butter?"

"Surely."

"Would you like plum preserves?"

Dola cleared her throat. "Rita Ann."

"Mama, I thought you were going to look at the Rokkers' house."

"And I thought you were going with me."

"I'm sort of busy right now. You go ahead."

"Rita Ann, I'd like to talk to you in the dining room!"

"In a minute. I need to —"

"Right now, Rita Ann!"

Rita Ann sighed and trudged to the door.

Dola led her by the hand to the middle of the dining room. "Young lady, what do you think you're doing in there?"

"I'm feeding a hungry man, just like Jesus would want me to."

"Do you think the Lord wants you to fawn over him like that?"

"Fawn over him? Is that what I'm doin'? I never fawned over anyone before."

"Rita Ann, I'm your mother. Don't try to be coy with me."

"Okay, Mama, I might be fawning over him a little bit."

"How much?"

"A whole lot! Isn't he the most handsome boy on the face of the earth? Did you see his dimples when he smiles. I thought my heart would stop beating. 'Mine eye and heart are at a mortal war. How to divide the conquest of thy sight.' "

"You keep this up, and you'll be at war with your mama. That man is ten years older than you."

"Daddy's almost ten years older than you."

"That's entirely different," Dola proclaimed.

"But you knew you loved him when you were thirteen. You told me that," Rita Ann reminded her.

"You are not thirteen."

"I will be January 1st."

"Rita Ann, I will not have you acting like a fool in front of that young man. Now I want you to walk with me across town to the Rokker home. We'll discuss this on the way."

"But — but what if Hud wants something else to eat?"

"Mr. Frazier has enough food piled on his plate to last until midnight. And I'm sure he will still be there when we return."

"I'll go check on him and then catch up with you."

"You will walk out the front door right now." Dola went back and stuck her head into the kitchen. "Mr. Frazier, we have to step out for a few minutes. Just leave the dishes there when you're through. You can use the back door if you want to look at the motor car."

"Thank you, ma'am." Dimples exploded to frame his smile.

"You're welcome," Rita Ann called out as she peeked around her mother.

Tugging her twelve-year-old by the arm, Dola stormed out to the front door. They had just reached the porch when a thunderous explosion rocked the building and the street. Dola staggered and grabbed a porch post.

"What was that?" Rita Ann cried.

People ran out into the middle of the street in fear and confusion.

"I don't know . . . but I think it came from over there. Look at that smoke. It must be a fire!" Dola pointed straight west.

"Either that or dirt," Rita Ann murmured.

O.T. and Jared gawked at the great cloud of dust as neighbors and strangers rushed to their side. By the time the yellowish brown fog lifted, the entire yard was encircled with men, women, children, dogs . . . but no one said a word.

They just stared.

"It's — it's — it's all gone, Mr. Skinner!" Jared finally cried out. "The earth done opened up and swallowed our whole house!"

O.T. rubbed his mustache and then his dirty, unshaved chin. He shook his head. He opened his mouth. He pointed with his hand. But he couldn't find any words.

"What are we going to do, Mr. Skinner?" Jared sobbed. "What are we going to do? Ever'thing is gone!"

Lord, I've never . . . I mean, he's right. . . . It's all gone. Just like in the Old Testament. 'And the earth opened her mouth, and swallowed them up, and their houses, and all the men that appertained unto Korah and all their goods.' But that was because of disobedience. . . . This . . . Why . . .

A strong hand grabbed O.T.'s arm, and he spun around. A big black man in suit and tie, sweat rolling down his face, was trying to catch his breath. "Sweet mercy, what happened here, O.T.?"

"Lucian! Would you look at this? A sinkhole opened up, and a whole house collapsed into it. I've never seen anything like this."

"Anybody in there?"

O.T. stood and stared.

LaPorte shook his shoulder. "I said, is anyone down there?"

"Eh . . . no, it was empty. Just me and the boy were there. We made it out. Barely," O.T. mumbled.

"I've got to get down there and pack out our goods." Jared started toward the hole.

"No!" O.T. grabbed the boy's shoulder. "It's too dangerous, Jared. It's all gone, son."

"But that's our stuff!" he sobbed.

"It's ruined now, boy," Lucian added. "O.T.'s right. You cain't go down there. It's too risky. Let it go."

"But — but that's our house!" Jared wailed. "It ain't fair!"

"No, it ain't fair," O.T. said.

"Life ain't always fair," LaPorte observed. "Boy, I should know it ain't fair. But there's nothin' down there but rocks and sticks. Even them ain't stable."

Jared tried to pull away. "But it's all we got!"

O.T. kept his hand clamped on young Rokker's shoulder. "It's over, son. It's gone. It's just a big grave, and ever'thing is buried. Praise the Lord no one was in it. No one got hurt. The sandstorm had ruined about ever'thing anyway. Remember? We didn't see much worth savin'. It's time to tip our hats and walk away."

"No!" Jared yanked against O.T.'s grip, but Skinner held him tighter. "Let me go! It ain't your stuff down there — it's mine!" he screamed.

"Jared . . . listen to me. The dust storm ruined everything. There's nothing of value left."

"But . . . what will Mama do? . . . And what will Daddy say?"

Holding both of Jared's shoulders, O.T. spun him around and looked in his tear-filled eyes. "He'll say he should have been here instead of you. They will both be very happy you're safe. That's the important thing. You still got that locket?"

Jared slowly opened his clenched fist to reveal the locket.

"See, you did save somethin' — the important thing," O.T. said.

The boy threw his arms around O.T.'s neck and wept.

O.T. hugged him back. "It's okay, son. . . . Go ahead and cry."

"But I ain't supposed to cry," he sobbed.

Lucian LaPorte patted the boy on the back. "You wouldn't be human if you didn't cry. Some things is worth cryin' over."

"Don't tell my mama. . . . Don't tell Rita Ann that I cried."

"I won't tell 'em, but I won't lie if they ask. I don't reckon it does any good to fight the way the Lord made us."

A tall, thin man with a filthy face and a battered round lunch bucket scooted through the noisy crowd and up to O.T.'s side.

"This your place, mister?" he asked.

"It belonged to the boy's family. They are friends of mine," O.T. reported, still hugging Jared Rokker.

"Anyone get hurt?"

"Nope."

"That's a miracle from God." A pink tongue darted in the mouth framed by miner's dust.

O.T. nodded. "I reckon it is."

"It's the July Extension, you know," the man said.

"What do you mean?" O.T. asked.

175

Jared pulled back to stare at the man.

"I work at the July Extension Mine. It's right below here. They've been followin' a lead too close to the surface, and they knowed it. They stopped diggin' last week, but when the electricity went out last night, the pump shut down, and that shaft flooded with water. We built a dam down there to keep the water from flooding the other shafts. Must have backed up and eaten away at the dirt under the house."

"Are you sayin' it's negligence?" Lucian pressed.

"I cain't say that aloud." The man's voice was barely above a whisper. "I need my job. They'd fire me if I say anything. My family is countin' on me. But I'm tellin' you, it was negligence, all right." The man turned and slipped back into the crowd that was now boisterous in their appraisal of the situation.

Jared looked up at O.T. "What am I going to do, Mr. Skinner? What am I going to do?"

"First thing, we got to go find your mama and let her know you're all right." O.T. led Jared back through the crowd toward Ada and Ida, being held by an old gray-bearded man with a cane. "Your mama will be worried sick."

"She'll hide under the covers when she finds out what happened to our house. But all the covers are down there!" He pointed back to the deep conical hole in the ground.

"Come on, Jared, we got to take Ida and Ada back to the livery and get over to café and —"

"I'll take the mules back. Take my hack," Lucian offered. "Just park it at the café. I'll pick it up there."

"How are we going to tell Mama?" Jared wailed.

"We'll just have to think of something between here and there." *I hope You have some good ideas, Lord, because I surely can't think of any.*

When they rounded the corner onto Columbia Street, there was a crowd on the front porch of the restaurant. Dola held Punky's hand. A dirty-faced Tommy-Blue and Danny Rokker slumped on the steps. Stella and Caitlynn both shaded their eyes with their hands. There was Nellie Rokker, thin, gaunt, but standing and alive. Rita Ann stood next to a strong-shouldered young man with curly blond hair.

I don't know that man. I was gone overnight, and I don't know who that young man is. Maybe he's just early for supper or late for breakfast.

"Daddy!" Corrie hollered as she ran out to the carriage. "Daddy, I missed you. You found Jared. Hi, Jared! Did you see your house? There's nothing left but the framing. Where's Fergus? Didn't he come back with you? Did you know Mama hired a mechanic to fix the auto car? Look at this necklace. Mrs. Marsh gave it to me. Isn't it pretty? There's some kind of mine explosion, but nobody knows what happened."

O.T. stopped the carriage, let Corrie crawl up in his lap, and then drove the final twenty feet to the front of the hotel. Jared jumped out and ran to his mother.

"You're a dirty mess," she greeted him.

"Yes, ma'am."

"I want you to clean up before supper."

"Yes, ma'am. Has Daddy made it back?" Jared asked.

"I suppose you saw that shell of a house?"

O.T. glanced at his wife and then back at Nellie Rokker. "Eh, we need to talk to you about that."

"Dola said you could reroof, but I don't believe it's worth saving," she said.

"Mama, it's gone," Jared said gently. "Our house is totally and completely gone!"

She put her hand on his cheek. "I was over this mornin'. I know, Jared. Everything blew away."

"No! Tell her, Mr. Skinner! The earth done opened and swallowed it up."

Dola scooted next to Nellie Rokker. "What's this about, Orion? And what's the commotion down there?"

O.T. surveyed all their faces. "It seems that a flooded mine shaft collapsed at the July Extension Mine."

"Was anyone down there?" Dola asked.

"Not that I could hear, but it really shook the ground and —"

"And swallowed our house!" Jared blurted

178

out. "It's gone, Mama, and I couldn't do nothin' about it . . . except save your locket." He shoved the locket into his mother's bony hand.

"Orion?" Dola quizzed.

"It looks like the shaft collapsed somewhere under the Rokkers' house. The earth gave way deep down, and a sinkhole formed, sucking what was left of the Rokkers' into the ground."

"Oh, no!" Dola gasped.

"You mean our house plumb disappeared?" Stella asked.

"It's just a pile of splinters at the bottom of a hole," Jared reported.

"But . . . houses don't just disappear," Rita Ann protested.

"One time I seen a dairy barn and six milk cows get picked up and blown clean into the next county," the curly-haired young man proclaimed.

O.T. looked back at the young man. *Am I supposed to know who this is?*

Tommy-Blue tugged his arm away from Corrie. "Can me and Danny go get an ore sample? On top of the July Extension? I'll bet we'd get $600 a ton."

Punky squirmed down to the porch and ran to O.T. "Carry me, Daddy!"

"Is it really all gone . . . everything?" Dola pressed.

"When we got there, the frame was still standing. Then we heard a rumble, and the ground shook, and something exploded. We ran, and it sucked ever'thing into the ground," Jared declared.

Dola put her arm around Mrs. Rokker.

Then with a voice so deep and strong that Dola flinched, Nellie Rokker declared, "It was a horrid place to live. Good riddance, I say. Good riddance!"

Dola stared at Mrs. Rokker. *Last night this woman was hiding under her covers in a sandstorm. Now she says, "Good riddance"?*

"What are we going to do, Mama? Where will we live?" Stella moaned.

"We will load up our wagon and push on out after your father. He will have found us a place by now."

"We don't have a wagon, Mama," Danny objected.

"Don't sass me. Jared will get us a wagon."

"You mustn't leave," Dola blurted out. "Stay with us until —"

"Until Elias gets back. He's on his way now, I'm sure. If you left, you could miss him," O.T. cautioned.

"Yes, you're right. We will wait until Elias arrives and then depart from Goldfield. It was a simply horrid house. I'm glad I never have to live in it again."

Walking up the boardwalk toward the café, Lucian LaPorte covered three feet with each step. "You tell them?" he called out.

"Yes. Though it still sounds crazy to say it."

"Mr. LaPorte, would you be so kind as to transport my children and me to our former home. They need to see what it looks like, and I do have several boxes of things to pick up at the neighbors," Nellie requested.

He tipped his bowler at Mrs. Rokker. "Yes, ma'am, I can do that."

"Nellie, would you like me to come along?" Dola asked.

"What on earth for? You have your own family to take care of. We will be fine. Come along, children." With chin held high and narrow eyes flashing, Nellie Rokker led Caitlynn to the waiting rig.

"Danny, don't take any ore samples without me," Tommy-Blue pleaded.

Lucian LaPorte climbed up into his rig and waited for the Rokker family to crowd in. "O.T., the livery man was askin' about young Rokker's mule."

"Fergus took it."

"And you go home after you deliver the Rokkers, Mr. LaPorte," Dola directed. "Your Omega is waiting for you."

He grinned and waved his hat. "Yes, ma'am, I reckon she is!"

As the carriage pulled away, Corrie tugged on O.T.'s shirtsleeve. "You're a mess, Daddy."

"You're right, honey."

"But not as bad as Jared. What happened to him?" Rita Ann asked.

"He got stuck in a snake hole."

"Really?" Tommy-Blue shouted. "How come I never have any fun like that?"

Dola slipped her arm into O.T.'s.

"I can't believe Mrs. Rokker's taking it so well," O.T. said. "I figured she'd go right off the deep end. So did Jared. He was scared to death to have to tell her."

"It was last night that she went off the deep end," Dola reported.

"Tell me about it while I clean up, Mrs. Skinner."

"I would be happy to, Mr. Skinner. Shall I roll out the tub in the kitchen and boil some water?"

"I'll need to soak two weeks to get this dirt off."

"You'll get about half an hour," she said. It was almost a giggle. Her neck muscles loosened, and her shoulders relaxed. She could feel the wrinkles in her forehead melt away.

"All right, kids, I need you to —"

"Can we go over to the sinkhole?" Tommy-Blue asked. "Please, Mama, it would be very educational. I ain't never seen one before."

" 'I ain't'? Yes, I can see where you need some education all right," Dola concurred.

Rita Ann glanced at Hud Frazier. "I think I'll stay here."

"I was hoping you'd say that," Dola said. "You take Punky up and read him a story and try to get him to nap. Tommy-Blue, you can go, but you and Corrie have to stick together.

Do you understand?"

"All right!" Tommy-Blue raced down the boardwalk, stopped, and then ran back. "Aren't you coming, Corrie?"

"Yes, but I'm not going to run."

Tommy-Blue sulked as he moved toward Corrie with his hands in his pockets. As soon as he got even with her, she shoved him back, and he tripped. He sat down hard on the wooden bench in front of the restaurant. Corrie took off on a dead run west.

Tommy-Blue struggled to his feet and took after her screaming, "That ain't fair!"

O.T. held the door open for Dola, Punky, and Rita Ann, and then put up his arm to block the door. "Sorry, son, the restaurant is closed until supper."

"Daddy, this is Hudson Frazier. Mama hired him to fix our motor car," Rita Ann explained.

"Oh?"

"Actually I'm tradin' an hour's worth of work for each meal," the young man reported.

"You don't say."

"He's a very good mechanic, Daddy," Rita Ann advised.

"Well, unless things have changed overnight, the auto car is in the alley, not the restaurant. You can go around there."

"Yes, sir." Hud turned back toward the porch.

"It's quicker if he goes through the kitchen, Daddy," Rita Ann insisted.

"I'm not in that big a hurry to get it fixed. He can walk around," O.T. replied.

"Daddy!"

"Rita Ann, your mama needs you to take Punky upstairs."

O.T. shut the door behind his daughter and turned back to the young man on the porch. "Son, do you really know about auto cars, or are you just bummin' a meal or two?"

"I can fix it, Mr. Skinner. I truly can."

"Good. I trust you, son. Now step down here on the street for a minute."

Hudson Frazier followed O.T. off the boardwalk.

In the dirt O.T. drew an X with his boot. Then he took two long steps away from the X and drew a large circle around the X. "Now the X is my daughter Rita Ann, and the circle is the fire line," O.T. explained.

Hud Frazier scratched his neck. "Fire line?"

"Yep. The minute you get closer to my daughter than that line, you're fired."

"Rita Ann?" Hud grinned. "You're joking."

O.T. stared into the young man's eyes. "Try me."

"But — but Rita Ann's just a kid," Frazier sputtered.

O.T. put his hand on the young man's shoulder. "And that, son, is exactly my point."

Six

O.T. lounged on the balcony overlooking Columbia Street. He buttoned up a clean white collarless shirt. The freight wagons lumbered slowly beneath him, raising a fog of dirt and sand, but it hovered only a foot above the ground. In the distance a woman shouted, "Leroy." O.T. wondered if she was calling her son, a dog, or her husband. In any case, Leroy didn't respond. She kept calling.

Dola stepped out on the balcony.

"Mr. Tolavitch gave me a few days off without pay to go see if I can find Rokker," he reported. "You think we can afford it, what with you hirin' a serving girl and a mechanic?" O.T. tucked his shirt in and hitched up his denim jeans.

Dola glanced back at the big one-room apartment. "Orion, you have to go look for him. If you don't, who will?"

O.T. stared west over the top of Goldfield at the Malpais Mesa. "I know, but the chances of findin' him ain't very good, Dola Mae. If Rokker's alive, he'll come back here when he can."

"Or abandon his family. You remember poor Mabel Kipper back in Guthrie with those six children and all?"

185

"Well, if Rokker isn't comin' back, I certainly won't find him."

Dola slipped her arm into his. "He could be dead. That was a terrible storm to be caught in all alone without provisions."

"In that case I probably won't find him either."

"Are you goin' to swing by the Wilkinses' mine and get Fergus?" she asked.

O.T. patted her hand. "Yep. Wouldn't try it without him. He knows this desert as well as anyone, except ol' Tom Fisherman, and he's too busy findin' more gold. I thought about takin' Jared. But I'm wonderin' if he should stay and take care of Nellie and the kids."

"I doubt if she'll let him out of her sight for a while, but she is doin' much better than I could have imagined."

O.T. glanced back at the apartment and lowered his voice. "That can change in a flash."

"I know," Dola whispered. "But I'll enjoy it while it lasts. I've never known a woman who had more physical, mental, and family strains. It's like she's a lightning rod for crisis."

"You could have a rough week while I'm gone."

"I have a whole bunch helping me." She let her hand drop off his sleeve. "What direction are you headed?"

He waved his arm straight over the balcony. "We'll go west on one trail to this place called Don Fernando's and then take another trail home."

"A whole week? I'll be worried sick."

"Fergus said it wasn't quite so far anymore, what with more roads and ranches. I figure we can make it there and back in five days. You going to get along all right with all the Rokkers bunked here?"

Dola took a deep breath and let it out slowly. "We'll endure. What choice do we have, O.T.?"

O.T. brushed his graying mustache with his fingertips. "Well, we could just load the kids and our meager belongin's into the wagon and head to Dinuba, California. We could be there in a week if we didn't have any breakdowns."

"And if we had something to eat."

"Course, I never cottoned up to the idea of arrivin' at Pearl and Pegasus's place penniless and hungry."

"You still dreamin' of drivin' that auto car to California?" she teased.

O.T. leaned on the rail and watched an old man trudge by alongside a donkey piled high with coyote pelts. "You did say that boy who's eyein' our Rita Ann can fix it?"

She raised her eyebrows. "That's what he claims. But I can assure you, the attention is the other way around."

"If he gets that auto car fixed, maybe we'll move to California before Christmas . . . if we save up enough for gasoline."

Dola crossed her arms and hugged herself. "Wouldn't that be wonderful?"

"We could plow the ground." His eyes

danced with every word. "They say you can plow in February in California. And we'd set out the vines in the spring."

Dola grinned. "You still thinking about growing raisin grapes?"

"That's where the good money is, Dola Mae." His voice was no longer tired. It bounced on each word. "Pegasus says that we could make $500 an acre on raisin grapes."

"Yes, and it was Pegasus who got us to move to west Texas and try to raise cotton." The smile lessened.

"It would have worked if we hadn't had the worst drought in twenty-seven years."

"I know." She reached over and stroked his gray hair. "Why are we talking like this? We're not going to move in December. Goldfield is this horrid desert town that needs us. As long as we're needed, neither of us will leave."

"Well, right now I need to go get supplies and grease some axles on the wagon," he asserted.

"And I have seventy-five hungry mouths to feed . . . once more."

He slipped his rough, callused hand in hers. "You think we'll ever have time for each other again?"

Her voice was soft, melodic, like a lullaby. "Just you and me?"

"Yes, ma'am."

She raised his fingers to her lips and kissed them. "Orion Tower Skinner, are you flirting with me?"

"It's been so long you can't tell?"

She rubbed his hand against her cheek. "I can tell. Believe me, Mr. Skinner, I can tell."

Corrie dashed out on the balcony and slipped her fingers into O.T.'s free hand. "Daddy, are you going to find Mr. Rokker?"

"I'm goin' to go look for him, darlin'. I'll be gone for a few days, and I'm expecting you to help Mama and Rita Ann."

"Why can't I go with you, Daddy? Rita Ann has Haylee to help her now."

O.T. felt something sticky on the palm of her warm hand. "Because you need to look after little brother when Mama and Rita Ann are working."

"Why can't Tommy-Blue take care of Punky? And all the Rokkers are here. One person less wouldn't make any difference. There would be more room to sleep, and Mama wouldn't have to sleep on the stairs."

"That's enough of that, Corrie Lou Skinner," Dola scolded.

"I don't know why I can't go with my daddy," Corrie grumbled.

"Mama's right." O.T. squeezed her hand. "It's not open for debatin'."

Corrie puffed out her cheeks and blew air through her pouting lips.

O.T. ran his hands through his daughter's short, brown, very thick hair. "When I get back, darlin', I'll have a lot of work to catch up with. Maybe you can help me make some of my rounds."

189

"Can I drive the wagon?"

"I reckon you could."

The spark returned to Corrie's blue eyes. "I'll pray for you while you're gone, Daddy!"

"Thank you, darlin'. I'm countin' on it."

Rita Ann stuck her head in the doorway and shouted across the apartment, "Mama, Haylee's here to work."

Dola glanced around for a clock that wasn't there. "Is it that late?"

"I think she's early."

Dola scurried back into the apartment. She rubbed the bridge of her nose and then her forehead. "Let's see . . . have her start peeling the potatoes. You help her."

"I was sort of, you know, helping Hud."

"What do you mean, 'helpin' Hud'?" O.T. asked, coming into the room.

Rita Ann rocked back on her heels and flopped her head from shoulder to shoulder. "Well, actually I was just watching him."

"Watchin' him what?" O.T. snapped.

"Fix the auto car, Daddy!" she retorted.

His voice was terse and his words chopped. "I don't want you out there."

"Why?"

"Because . . . eh," O.T. muttered. Corrie dropped his hand and meandered over to where Punky sat playing with green spools.

"Because," Dola interjected, "it's difficult for a young man to concentrate on his work with a pretty, young girl standing around. He might make a mistake and hurt himself."

"I never thought of that." Rita Ann took a deep breath. "Perhaps I better go apologize to him!"

"Rita Ann, you are going to peel potatoes and not leave the kitchen. Is that understood?"

"Yes, Mama." Rita Ann sulked out the door mumbling, " 'Like an unperfect actor on the stage, who with his fear is put besides his part . . .' " She turned at the doorway. "Mr. LaPorte came by to see you, Daddy."

"He's downstairs now?"

"Yes."

"Daddy, carry me!" Punky demanded as he waddled across the room.

With fresh shirt tucked in and barefoot, O.T. toted Punky down the stairs. Lucian LaPorte lingered near the coffeepot in the kitchen while Rita Ann and Haylee Cox squatted with giggles at the potato bin.

"Hi!" Punky called out.

"Howdy, li'l Skinner!" Lucian greeted him. "You want a cup of coffee?"

"No!" Punky replied. He squirmed down out of O.T.'s arms and sprinted to the girls. "Haylee-Haylee-Haylee!"

Haylee Cox just had time to turn around to catch the leaping two-year-old.

Lucian took a sip of coffee. "You headin' out to look for Rokker?"

"First thing in the mornin'. I got it cleared with Tolavitch."

LaPorte's white-toothed grin was wider than the coffee cup. "Wish I was goin' with you."

O.T. examined an empty cup. "You're invited, partner." Then he poured the cup full.

"Got to keep my hack goin'. Talk is that Sinclair and Mosburg are going to start using an auto car for a hack. That will be tough to compete with." LaPorte rubbed his clean-shaven chin.

"If that kid out there gets that Thomas auto car goin', you can use it for a hack," O.T. offered. "At least until we leave for California."

Lucian shoved his bowler to the back of his head. "You still plannin' on goin' to California?"

"Someday. Aren't you?"

"I aim to go to California and to heaven, but I don't know which will be first. Nobody wants to spend their life in Goldfield. At least, not on purpose."

O.T. took a gulp of coffee. It burned all the way down his throat. "I was serious about the auto car. We wouldn't need it much. Of course, I don't know if they will have any gasoline in town."

"I might take you up on that, O.T."

"Are you going with us to find Rokker?"

"Nah, just wishful thinkin'. I got a business to run. Besides, some man has to stick around and look after the womenfolk and kids."

"You're right about that." O.T. stared down at his bare toes. "Seems like I've been gone at all the wrong times. But between you and Lucky Jack Gately, ever'one's been looked after. That's when a man can tell his real friends."

Lucian plunked down the coffee cup. "I had me a talk with the folks at July Extension this afternoon."

"I thought this was the time of the day you slept," O.T. declared.

"I'll catch up some other day. I wanted to talk to them about the Rokker house. They claim its collapse had nothing to do with their mine shaft. Said it was just a shoddily built house."

O.T. took another gulp of coffee. This one didn't burn half as bad. "Lucian, it was a poor excuse for a house, but we've got a sinkhole twenty-five feet deep."

LaPorte ran his fingers through his black curly hair. "That's what I tried to explain to them."

"What did they say?"

"Said if I wanted to pursue it any further, I should speak with their lawyers."

O.T. stared across the kitchen as Punky rolled a potato over the floor. "Did you talk to their lawyers?"

LaPorte stared into O.T.'s eyes. "The clerk said they had no intention of speaking to a — a hack driver about a mining lease."

O.T. stared right back. "They don't like hack drivers?"

"Not a black one that pokes around askin' embarrassin' questions. I was told very clearly not to come back."

"I reckon your questions were a little too close to the target. This is startin' to rile me. They shouldn't treat the Rokkers that way. And they shouldn't treat you that way."

"O.T., you and Dola Mae are about the only color-blind white folks I've ever met. But I've gone through a lot worse things, so it don't bother me. However, they shouldn't ignore the Rokkers like that. Maybe you ought to check it out, O.T. They might listen to the famous Wall Walker."

"That would get me two minutes with the miners but not a second with the mine owners. They didn't need free city water. But I will check it out when I get back. Elias ought to go there with me. They owe him an explanation."

"They owe more than an explanation. You better load up on water and feed for you and those mules. Ain't much out on that desert, I hear," Lucian urged.

"I know. I can't figure out how Rokker's getting along out there. He thought he was only going to be gone for an afternoon. I'm hopin' he's on his way back now that the storm is over. Seems like the roads are opening up."

"Did you hear that ol' Wyatt Earp is in town?" LaPorte announced.

"No, I didn't. Are you sure?"

"I ain't seen him, but someone said they saw

an old Arizona gunman down at the stock exchange. Who else could it be?"

"Earp was the one in Dodge City, right? Or was he in Deadwood?"

"It was that ruckus down in Tombstone," LaPorte corrected him. "You know, him and Doc Holiday."

"Was Holiday the one who was gunned down in El Paso?" O.T. inquired.

"That was Hardin. John Wesley Hardin."

"Don't reckon I recall anything about Tombstone. Didn't hear much news when I was a youngster, but I think I've heard the kids mention something. Is he sellin' autographs?"

"Earp? How would I know? I ain't seen him. But he don't sound like the type to sell autographs."

"Rita Ann paid fifty cents for Frank James's autograph back in Guthrie," O.T. said. "At least, the old man claimed to be Frank James."

"I'll nose around and find out who he is for sure," LaPorte offered. "But if you're gone, you might miss him."

"If it really is someone famous, make sure Rita Ann gets to see him, Lucian. She's the one something like that would mean the world to. She'll want his autograph."

"If you ain't back in a week, Skinner, I'll come lookin' for you." LaPorte flashed his large, white, straight teeth.

O.T. stared into the black man's dark eyes. "I'm countin' on that, Lucian."

Only a couple of tables full of men were left in the restaurant when Dola reentered the room with coffee for the breakfast stragglers.

Jared Rokker came down the stairs, his face and neck scrubbed pink. "Mama wants to know if we can take our breakfast upstairs. She feels funny about facin' everyone and havin' to explain about our house. I'll tote everything, Mrs. Skinner."

"That's fine, Jared. Stella's helping in the kitchen. Have her dish up whatever you want. I presume Tommy-Blue and Danny went prospecting already?"

"They said they was going to work the alley behind the Northern Saloon."

"They told me they were going behind the Nevada Stock Exchange."

"Same thing. Just depends on how you look at it." Jared shrugged. "Mornin', Miss Rita Ann," he called out as she scooted in with an empty pan to gather up dirty dishes.

"Mama, do we have any plum preserves left?" Rita Ann asked.

"Young Mr. Rokker spoke to you," Dola reminded her.

"Oh, hi, Jared. I'm sorry. Mama, I need the plum preserves. They're Hud's favorite."

Dola glanced over her shoulder. "He's in the kitchen?"

Rita Ann pinched her narrow lips together. "No, of course not. But he might be stopping

196

any moment now."

"Rita Ann, you go help Jared put together some breakfast for his mama and the others upstairs."

"Mother, I'm looking for the plum preserves."

"They are in the crock on the shelf above the bread box."

"Really?"

"Trust me. Now go help Jared."

"Who's going to clear the tables?"

"You and Haylee, as soon as everyone is through eating."

Punky scooted down the stairs on his bottom, wearing only underwear and dragging a small knitted black-and-red afghan. "Mama!" he called out. "I'm here!"

"Yes, you are, darlin'. And where are your clothes? Why didn't Corrie dress you?"

"I'm not naked," he declared.

"That's fine. You wait there. Let me give Mr. Gately and the boys some coffee."

The lanky blond man with strong shoulders opened his arms toward the toddler. "Come see me, Punky!"

"Lucky-Lucky-Lucky!" he hollered as he ran across the room, sweeping the floor with the afghan.

"You should call him Mr. Gately," she corrected.

"Not today, Mrs. Skinner. This is our lucky day," Lucky Jack informed her.

"You boys hit pay dirt?"

"Yep. You were so busy earlier I couldn't tell you. The graveyard shift punched into a rich vein at 800 feet about midnight," Charlie Fred reported.

"You really hit it?"

"We've been down there all night. It's the real thing, Mrs. Skinner," Wasco added.

"Oh, boys, that's wonderful — for you . . . for Mrs. Marsh . . . for everyone. Have you told her yet?"

"Yep. Woke her up in the middle of the night. I knew she'd want to know."

Dola brushed her hair back. "All that time she guarded that mineshaft, she really had a treasure down there."

"Yep," Charlie Fred said. "Her husband was right."

Lucky Jack Gately bounced Punky on his knee. "She's planning on moving to San Francisco, you know."

"I didn't know that." Dola glanced up as Jared Rokker lugged a tray full of food up the stairs. Stella Rokker followed him with a coffeepot. *We not only have houseguests, but they want breakfast in bed.* "I knew if you hit a rich vein in her mine, she would certainly move from Goldfield, but I didn't know where. Corrie will miss her. They've gotten close. She goes over there every day."

Punky reached up and grabbed Lucky Jack's mustache. "Whoa, li'l pard." Lucky Jack liberated his mustache. "I figured that's where she was headin' this morning."

"Who?"

"Your Corrie."

"My Corrie?"

"She was scootin' down the alley when we came up from Fremont Street," Charlie Fred reported.

"She most certainly was not. She's upstairs," Dola huffed.

Rita Ann burst out of the kitchen and came straight to her mother. "It's horrible, Mama. You've got to do something!"

"Wait a minute." She waved Rita Ann still. "What's this about Corrie?"

"Mother, you have to do something quick!"

She turned to Rita Ann. "Did someone get hurt in the kitchen?"

"Yes!" Rita Ann wailed.

Lucky Jack jumped to his feet and handed Punky to Dola. "What happened, darlin'?"

"My heart's broken!" Rita Ann sighed.

Lucky Jack plopped back down and winked at the toddler in his mother's arms. "Your sister has a broken heart, little brother."

The two-year-old's eyes widened. "Punky didn't do it!"

Rita Ann bit on her quivering lower lip. "Mother, you have to fire Haylee."

"What are you talkin' about?"

"I just can't work with her anymore."

"But you and Haylee were laughing and carrying on this morning serving meals."

Rita Ann stomped her foot. "Everything is changed!"

"What happened?"

"Hud came to the back door!" Tears streamed down Rita Ann's face.

Dola set the coffeepot on the table. "And?"

"And he asked to speak to Haylee."

"Then what?"

"That's it!" she wailed.

"He asked to speak to Haylee, and you want me to fire her?"

"Don't you see, Mama? Don't you see?"

Punky, still riding Dola's left hip, reached up and pulled her hair down out of her comb and over her ear. "Rita Ann, are you telling me you're jealous of Haylee and want her fired because of that?"

"Yes!" Rita Ann sobbed. "You have to do it!"

"That's the most absurd thing I ever heard of. I will do no such thing. He isn't talking to you because your father threatened to fire him the minute he came within three feet of you."

Rita Ann laced her fingers under her chin. "Daddy didn't mean that."

"Well, young Mr. Frazier certainly believes your daddy meant it."

"But it's not fair! She's — she's so . . ."

"Wait a minute," Lucky Jack cautioned. "Never be satisfied with second best, Rita Ann."

She brushed her tears off her cheeks. "Second best?"

Charlie Fred scratched his thick black neck. "The boy obviously has bad eyesight if he's chosen her over you."

"And his lack of wisdom is appallin'," Wasco chimed in. "Don't you go chasin' someone that dumb."

"Add to that the fact that he doesn't know *Hamlet* from *The Merchant of Venice*. You can do better than that!" Lucky Jack insisted.

"But — but — but he has those cute dimples when he smiles," Rita Ann blurted out. Then she covered her mouth.

"So does your mama, darlin," Lucky Jack replied. "And you don't see me chasin' after her."

Dola felt her face flush.

"But Mama's married!"

"And do you think your daddy married her just because of her dimpled smile?"

"My mama's purdy," Punky announced.

"Daddy always teases and says he married Mama because of her biscuits and gravy," Rita Ann offered.

"See? It takes more than dimples," Lucky Jack laughed. "My point is, the good Lord will lead you to someone that has more than just a dimpled smile. That's only part of it. Ain't that right, Mama?"

Dola turned away and headed for the stairs. "Rita Ann, clean up after the men. Tell Omega I'll be down as soon as I get Punky dressed and wake up Corrie."

"Corrie went bye-bye!" Punky declared.

Dola stopped on the first step and spun back to the table where the men sat. "What did you start to say about Corrie?"

"She was traipsin' in the alley downtown when we came in. We thought she might be goin' to see Mrs. Marsh," Lucky Jack explained.

"And I said you must be mistaken because my Corrie is upstairs!" she replied.

"I reckon we could have been mistaken," Charlie Fred mumbled.

"I should say so." *Corrie would never go anywhere without telling me. Or telling Orion. But he left before daylight. Well, there was that time she got on the trolley car and rode across Denver, but . . . Corrie Lou Skinner, you had better be here!*

Dola pushed open the door to the apartment. The Rokker family, minus Danny, gathered around the table. "Good morning," Nellie Rokker offered. "I see Mr. Skinner has left to go find my husband."

Dola surveyed the room. "Yes, he left about daylight."

"There is one advantage of having no belongings whatever. We are packed and ready to go at a moment's notice. I suppose if he doesn't come back until late, we'll wait and leave in the morning."

"Mama, we can't leave. We don't have a wagon or supplies," Stella reminded her.

"Nonsense. Your father will take care of that. We just need to be ready," Mrs. Rokker insisted.

Dola glanced out at the empty balcony. "Have any of you seen Corrie? I need her to do some chores."

"Corrie went bye-bye," Punky repeated.

"She was gone when I got up, Mrs. Skinner," Stella declared.

Dola stepped over next to the table. "When was that?"

"About daylight, I reckon. I heard Rita Ann get up and figured I could help in the kitchen too."

Dola stormed across the room toward the balcony.

"Uh, oh!" Punky gasped. "Punky get down!"

Dola set him on the bed and marched out to the balcony overlooking Columbia Street. *I can't believe that my daughter would wander off so early in the morning without telling me. Did she tell me? Did she say something, and I didn't hear? It's been so hectic.*

She leaned on her hands on the rough wood railing of the balcony and studied the street as if expecting to spot Corrie at any moment. *Lord, I really don't need this. I have plenty to worry about, plenty to do, plenty of crises to deal with. Help me figure this out quickly. There's got to be an explanation here.*

Dola spun around and marched back through the apartment. "Punky, you stay here," she ordered. "Nellie, can you watch little darlin' for a few minutes?"

"Certainly. I'm sure we won't be leavin' until tomorrow."

Dear Nellie, there are sometimes when I think you've already left.

The restaurant was empty when she returned. Haylee and Rita Ann were clearing tables.

"Rita Ann, have you seen Corrie?"

"Isn't she upstairs?"

"Obviously not, or I wouldn't have had to ask you. Lucky Jack seems to think he saw her heading down the alley about daybreak."

"Why would she do that?"

"That's what I'd like to know."

Dola stepped over to the sixteen-year-old. "Haylee, have you seen Corrie?"

"No, Mrs. Skinner. But thanks for talkin' to me." Haylee glanced around the room. "That's more than some people will do."

"Rita Ann!" The words chucked out of Dola's mouth like a spear.

Rita Ann turned her back. "I have nothing to say to her. I'm just not in a talkative mood."

"Young lady," Dola scolded, folding her arms across her chest, "I have quite enough on my mind without your childish games!"

Rita Ann burst into tears and ran back to the kitchen.

"Rita Ann!" Dola hollered. "You get back in here right now!" Dola stalked toward the kitchen. "You're acting just like —"

"Like a twelve-year-old?" Haylee finished.

Dola watched the swinging kitchen door rock back and forth. "I suppose so," she mumbled.

Haylee started toward the kitchen. "Let me go talk to her."

"You're the one she's mad at," Dola called out.

"I know." Haylee stopped near the door and turned back. "But I'm also the one who can still remember what it's like to be twelve."

Haylee Cox scooted into the kitchen.

I shouldn't have snapped at Rita Ann so. Lord, I'm just very concerned about Corrie. Haylee's right. Rita Ann's only acting her age.

Tommy-Blue ran in. "Mama, he's here, and I seen him!"

"Who's here?"

"Mr. Brannon. Mr. Stuart Brannon. I seen him in front of the stock exchange."

Dola pulled off her white cotton apron. "Mr. Brannon is here in Goldfield?"

"Danny said it was Wyatt Earp, but it was Mr. Brannon. I ought to know. We met him that one time in Gallup, New Mexico Territory."

"Did you invite him over for breakfast?"

"I didn't talk to him!"

Dola walked him back to the open front double doors. "Where did you say he was?"

"At the stock exchange, but he was walkin' south."

"Tommy-Blue, where is Corrie?"

"I ain't seen her, Mama. Are you goin' to come talk to Mr. Brannon?"

"I'd like to, but I can't go barging all over town looking for a man."

"Why not?"

"It's just not proper."

"You mean, we got to do things proper?"

"Right now I need to find Corrie. Would you run over to the hotel and ask Mrs. Marsh if she's seen her?"

The nine-year-old shifted his weight from one foot to the other. "But, Mama, what about Mr. Brannon?"

"I only have attention for one emergency at a time. Go see if your sister is at Mrs. Marsh's. And if you see Mr. Brannon, tell him you are Dola Mae Davis Skinner's son, that we met him once in Gallup, and that my uncle was his friend Everett Davis. Then tell him that your mother would love to have a visit but is tied up at the restaurant right now."

His eyes widened, and his mouth dropped open. "Mama, I couldn't tell him all that! What if he's packin' a gun?"

"What difference would that make?" Dola neatly folded her apron and set it on a table near the door.

"What if he's chasin' outlaws?"

"He's not a lawman anymore."

"What if there's outlaws chasin' him? Remember the book *Stuart Brannon, Ambush at Outlaw Cave?*"

"I seem to have forgotten that one." Dola shoved him out the door. "Go find your sister and get her back here. She's in real trouble."

Tommy-Blue stalled on the boardwalk, calling back into the restaurant, "That's the one where Mr. Brannon hides in the back of the cave down in Mexico while Trevor and them highwaymen are squattin' in the front of the cave talkin' about a plot to hold up the bank. Brannon pounces on them, and there's a big gunfight inside the cave. He kills ever' one of them and only has a slight wound to his non-shootin' arm. Then he discovers that the rico-cheting bullets uncovered a gold vein in the side of the cave. He tells that poor Mexican family about the gold 'cause him bein' a for-eigner, he can't have it. They go mine the gold and become quite wealthy and buy a large haci-enda just across the border from Douglas and decide to raise white-faced Herefords."

"Tommy-Blue!" She glared down her narrow nose at him.

"I know, I know, go find Corrie Lou."

"Thank you."

"And I'll tell Mr. Brannon that my mama wants to see him real, real bad."

"You don't have to put it . . ."

Tommy-Blue raced out of sight.

Dola watched him dash west. *Lord, I have never been in a place that strained my emotions more than Goldfield. From crisis to jubilee to crisis.* She rubbed her eyes with her fingertips and could feel the permanent wrinkles at the corners. *But my children . . . I must know where my children are. Maybe this is how Nellie felt when Jared was lost out in the sandstorm. Maybe it's how she feels now with her husband missing. It's an anxious, desperate feeling. Something is very wrong and won't be right until Corrie is accounted for. I'm going to have to hug her and whip her, and I don't know which to do first . . . Oh, Lord, keep her safe! I just want to hug her.*

She plucked up the folded apron and hurried toward the kitchen. She tried to push her hair back up into her combs. *I'm glad there's no mirror in the dining room. My hair must be getting grayer by the minute.*

She heard giggles in the corner that immediately stopped when she walked through the door. Haylee and Rita Ann were huddled near Omega LaPorte. "It sounds like you are all having fun now. That's good. What were you talking about?"

"Oh, nothin', Mama," Rita Ann replied. Then she broke into giggles again, her face blushing.

"Omega, what were you telling these girls?"

"Now don't you fret, Mama. I was just telling them the difference between men and women."

"You what?"

"It was really funny, Mrs. Skinner," Haylee reported.

Dola put her hands on her hips. "Omega?"

"Mama wouldn't think it was funny," Rita Ann cautioned. Then she burst out laughing again.

"Is anyone going to tell me what's going on?"

"Nope. I don't think so." Omega winked at Rita Ann.

"Well, this is quite annoying to come in here and find you all with secrets behind my back."

"They ain't secrets behind your back. They are secrets right out in front of you. Listen, would you rather come in here and discover these two fightin' like cats and dogs?" Omega LaPorte challenged.

Dola's voice softened. "I suppose not."

"Well, there you have it."

"But I can't imagine why you won't . . ."

"I was tellin' them about certain features of the male personality," Omega explained.

"I trust you were not telling these young ladies any lies."

"Believe me, honey, ever' last word was the gospel truth!" Omega insisted.

Haylee and Rita Ann glanced at each other and burst out laughing again.

"This is a fine situation. I have one daughter missing and one acting like a silly goose!"

"Which one am I, Mama?" Rita Ann retorted.

"I'm sorry I can't join in your amusement, but Corrie Lou has wandered off without asking me, and I'm quite distraught."

"Maybe she went over to Mrs. Marsh's," Rita Ann suggested.

"I sent Tommy-Blue to check."

Omega put her arm around Dola. "Honey, go find that little rascal girl of yours. We'll clean up the kitchen."

"Go on, Mama. Omega can finish her stories!" Rita Ann snickered.

Dola pointed a long, thin finger at the black woman. "I trust the stories are as clean as this kitchen, Omega LaPorte."

"I ain't goin' to tell these girls anything but the truth."

"The moral, biblical truth?" Dola pressed.

"Yes, ma'am," Omega snapped back. "Of course, there is sin in the Bible!"

"Omega!"

"Go find your girl. We'll be fine."

Dola stopped at the back door and looked in the small mirror. *Dola Mae, you look forty if you look a day. That's one thing that's so wonderfully romantic about Orion Tower Skinner. That gray-haired man actually thinks I'm beautiful. Oh, sometimes I wish I could see myself in his eyes.*

Dola hurried out into the alley.

"Good morning, Mrs. Skinner," a man's voice rasped out.

Dola's eyes searched the alley, but she could see no one.

The man's voice seemed to radiate up from the dirt beneath her feet. "I'm under the auto car."

She spied two denim-covered legs and worn brown boots poking out to one side. "Hud, is that you?"

"Yes, ma'am."

"What are you doing under there?"

His boots scrunched around some in the dirt. "I'm trying to get my wrench. It dropped down here and got stuck. Oooh!"

"Are you all right?"

"I banged my knuckles."

"Please be careful." Dola stood up straight. "Mr. Frazier, have you seen my Corrie this morning?"

"No, ma'am. I ain't seen her, but I seen your oldest . . . briefly."

"I imagine you have."

"Ever' time I stick my head in the kitchen door to ask a question or beg a biscuit, them girls and that colored lady start gigglin' at me. Do you know why that is, Mrs. Skinner?"

Dola studied the dirt-covered leather seats of the touring car. "I have no idea, Mr. Frazier."

"I was wonderin', Mrs. Skinner, do you know what I could do to keep them from doin' that?"

She looked down at the worn brown boots. "Hud, I suppose you could refrain from sticking your head in the doorway."

"I never thought of that. Thanks, Mrs. Skinner."

"You're welcome, Hud."

"Oh, no!" he groaned.

"What's the matter?"

"I got my hand stuck!"

"Oh my, what can I do?"

"Oops . . . there, I got it free."

"I'm going on to find Corrie if you'll be all right."

"Don't worry about me, Mrs. Skinner. I know what I'm doin'."

Somehow, Mr. Hudson Frazier, that doesn't seem to encourage me much. Dola scurried down the alley toward the street. *I don't believe I've ever carried on a conversation with a pair of boots and denim pant legs before.*

Most of the buildings on both sides of the alley were two-story. That kept Dola in the shadows. When she reached the street, she went west to Columbia Street. Then she worked her way down the crowded boardwalk toward the center of town.

Soon she spied Tommy-Blue's thick dark brown hair bouncing as he sprinted her way. From a block away he began to call out, "Mama! Good news!"

Dola quickened her pace but refused to yell across the crowded boardwalk. *I'm glad you found her, but I would be happier if you had waited and walked her home.*

Tommy-Blue waved his hand above the crowd. "Mama, we found it!"

You mean you found her. Do not call your sister an it.

When Tommy-Blue reached her side, he was breathless, with one suspender hanging down his arm. "Mama, your worries are over!"

"So your sister was at Mrs. Marsh's?"

"Better than that, Mama, we found color in the alley behind the Northern Saloon." He opened a clenched fist full of dirt. "Look! And there's plenty of it. One man said we should go file a claim on the alley. Will you do that for us, Mama? It only costs $2, and we can pay you back from our diggin's."

"Tommy-Blue Skinner!" She grabbed his shoulder so hard he dropped the dirt on the boardwalk. "I do not care a twit about dirt in the alley behind the Nevada Stock Exchange. Did you find Corrie?"

He stared down at the dirt pile by his shoe. "Nope."

She didn't lessen her grip. "Did you even go to the hotel?"

"Oh, yeah. The man at the desk said Mrs. Marsh left early this morning on a stage to Tonopah. She was goin' to catch a train to Reno and San Francisco."

"She left town?"

"Yes, he said she was going to go look for a house in San Francisco," he reported.

She rubbed her temples with her fingertips. "So soon?"

"And that ain't all. He said Mrs. Marsh carried a big bag, and a little girl was with her carryin' a little bag." Tommy-Blue squatted down and tried to scoop the dirt back into his hand.

"My daughter did not go to San Francisco!" she asserted.

Tommy-Blue stood up with the dirt clutched in his hand. "Nah. She probably just went down to the depot to say good-bye."

"But the stage left at daylight." Dola scowled at Tommy-Blue. "Young man, just what has your sister been doing since then?"

His eyes grew wide. "You ain't mad at me, are you?"

She laid her hand on his shoulder. He clutched the dirt tighter this time. "No . . . no, darlin'. I just don't know where Corrie is, and your father's gone. I'm extremely worried. I'm sorry for snapping at you." She let out a deep sigh.

"It's all right, Mama. The Lord will lead you."

She ran her finger through his hair. "Thanks, honey. I know you're right. I'll go to the stage office and see what I can find out."

He stepped back. "Do I have to go with you?"

"No, you go on."

"I'm going to have Mr. Tolavitch assay this for us."

"Well, don't pester him. I want you home by noon. I don't want two children wandering around town."

Tommy-Blue spun around and ran straight back down the boardwalk. Dola watched until he was out of sight. *Lord, it must be a wonderful feeling to never lose sight of your children. I worry about them enough when I can see them.* She waited for two freight wagons to pass and then crossed the street.

The sign on the counter at the express office read: Harold Blankenship, Manager.

A woman with full lips and a frown greeted Dola. "What do you want?"

Dola cleared her throat. "I need to know if my daughter was on the morning stage to Tonopah."

"You can't keep track of your own kids?"

Dola squeezed her hands together. "How I raise my children is not what we're discussing. I would like to look at your passenger list for this morning to see if my daughter was on the stage, please."

The woman looked past Dola. "I can't do that."

Dola turned and glanced out at the street but could not see anything. "You can't do what?"

"Let you look at the passenger list. Only Mr. Blankenship can allow that."

Dola could feel her face begin to flush. "Then let me talk to Mr. Blankenship."

The woman scratched her head and then examined the contents of her fingernails. "He won't talk to you today."

"What do you mean? I demand to talk to him." Dola's voice was rising.

"Demand all you want. He was on that stage to Tonopah and won't be back until tomorrow.

Unless you want to buy a ticket or ship something, I have work to do in the back room."

Dola could barely keep from shouting. "This is absurd. My daughter's safety is at stake, and you won't let me see the passenger list?"

"Don't go hollerin' at me. Company rules is company rules."

Dola leaned over the counter. "Do you have children of your own?"

The woman refused to look her in the eyes. "Nope. I'm not married."

"I can see why," Dola mumbled. "I can't impress upon you enough how important this is." Dola pressed her fingertips on her temples and tried to force herself to relax. "Let's try this from another direction. If I gave you my daughter's name, could you please look and see if that name is on your list? That way, I will never see nor touch the list."

The woman glanced around the room as if expecting to find Mr. Blankenship spying on her. "I reckon I could do that."

"Her name is Corrie Lou Skinner."

"Are you Mrs. Skinner?"

"Yes."

"The Wall Walker's wife?"

"Yes, I am. Now may I see the list?" Dola reached out her hand.

"Nope." The woman pulled the list back. "But I can tell you, there ain't no Corrie Lou Skinner on the list."

"Is Mrs. Marsh's name on your list?"

The woman studied the invoice. "Yep."

"Would it be possible for you to read the name immediately before and after Mrs. Marsh's? Perhaps my daughter used an alias."

"Why would she do that?"

"She likes pretending."

"The name right above Mrs. Marsh is Mr. Cypriot Ortiz."

"How about the one below Mrs. Marsh?"

"Eh . . . it looks like Ada Guthrie."

"That's it. That's my daughter!"

"Ada Guthrie is your daughter?"

"Yes. Ada is the name of one of our mules. And we're moving to California from Guthrie, Oklahoma. That's my daughter."

"Are you sure?"

"Yes, yes." Dola glanced around the room. "But why would she go to Tonopah? I don't understand," she mumbled.

The clerk lowered her voice and leaned over the counter. "Can I ask you a personal question?"

"I suppose so." Dola smelled peppermint on the woman's breath.

"Does she make very good money workin' in the cribs?"

Dola jerked back. "What?"

The big woman pursed her lips. "Just wonderin' what them girls made. I sold the ticket to Miss Guthrie. She was a little taller than you and about half again as heavy."

"My daughter is ten years old!" Dola fumed.

"Then this ain't her. This gal looked twenty going on forty."

Dola rubbed her forehead. "Then Corrie Lou didn't take the stage! Where could she be?"

"Maybe she's home by now, and you missed her."

Dola noticed that the woman's eyes looked much softer and less defiant than before.

"Maybe you're right. Thank you for the help."

Dola walked slowly back to the restaurant. She didn't notice the wagons in the street, the people on the crowded boardwalk, nor the hot, bright desert sun above.

She didn't hear the yelps of dogs, the curses of teamsters, or the shouts of saloon hangers-on. She didn't see a hefty woman tow a young boy by the ear, the lady in the black dress hanging laundry out the window of her second-story room, nor the old Indian in handcuffs being marched toward the jail.

The entire world could have marched up the street, but all Dola could see was the happy, round face of Corrie Lou.

O.T. marveled at the quiet, motionless desert that stretched out in front of Ada and Ida. Their hooves hardly made a sound in the soft dirt that covered the road to the Weepah Hills. There was a slight squeak in the wheels of the wagons, but the axle grease seemed to mute that. The air had a hint of coolness, tasted fresh, and smelled like sage. However, he could not see sage for a mile in any direction.

For several hours he had rolled northwest of Goldfield without seeing another person on the trail. The sun rose slowly, and the air warmed. The shadows from the wagon shortened. The mules' gait settled into a steady routine. He continually surveyed the eastern horizon in hopes of spying someone or something that might be Elias Rokker.

The bench of the old farm wagon had a familiar feel to his backside. The leather lead lines laced between his fingers slipped into a natural groove. O.T. appreciated the clean socks wrapped around clean toes. There was no sand in his boots, no silt at the back of his knees, no grime on his neck, no sting in his eyes.

Lord, there's a quiet, desolate beauty in this empty land. The sandstorm wiped it clean and covered most of the traces of man. When You were here on earth, You used to get away to lonely places and pray. I wonder if this was the kind of place.

O.T. glanced back at the wagon. A brown canvas tarp covered two twenty-gallon kegs of water, a 100-pound sack of oats, an old wooden box of cooking utensils, and two flour sacks full of supplies. *That looks like plenty unless Fergus eats us bare the first day or two. Don't know how one man can eat so much, be hungry all the time, and still look so thin. He's a funny, old man. He*

219

began life early in one century, will end life in another, and in between how his world has changed . . . How all of our worlds have changed.

In the distance he spotted the first sign of the buildings at the Wilkinses' mine. The rough, unpainted wood seemed to have aged in just the few days since he had last been there.

If Fergus is gone . . . well, he can't be gone because he was comin' to town after the dividends were issued. And I didn't see him on the road. But if he's gone, I'll just set out after Rokker on my own. I couldn't look myself in the eye if I didn't try.

But I hope Fergus is here because I surely don't like to think of travelin' out here alone. Perhaps I should have insisted Jared come along. At least I would have someone to talk to.

Ace Wilkins swung the gate open as O.T. approached the cluster of buildings and mine headworks.

"Didn't expect to see you, Skinner," Ace called out.

"Just came to pick up that ol' Paiute junior partner of yours. I need him to help me."

"Fergus went to town yesterday evenin'," Ace reported.

"To Goldfield?" O.T. quizzed.

"He left here at dark on that short mule of his. Said he likes travelin' at night. Claims he gets more sleep that way."

O.T. pulled off his hat and ran his fingers through his gray hair. "Don't that beat all? I was countin' on him goin' with me to look for Elias Rokker."

"Desert's no place to go it alone. Are you headin' out all by yourself?" Ace quizzed.

"I reckon so," O.T. mumbled.

"No, he isn't." The voice was muted under the brown canvas tarp in the back of the wagon. But it was young, feminine . . . and familiar.

O.T. felt every muscle in his body tense.

Seven

Rita Ann was lugging Punky on her thin twelve-year-old hip when Dola returned.

"Didn't you find Corrie, Mama?"

Dola searched the anxious eyes of her oldest child. *I am not going to cry. I am not going to break down. I'm the mother. I'm supposed to know what to do.* "Not yet, darlin', I did —"

"Mama-Mama-Mama!" Punky called out. He squirmed out of Rita Ann's arms and clutched his mother's brown dress.

Dola rested a hand on his head. "Hi, baby." She turned back to Rita Ann. "I did find out that Corrie slipped down to the hotel to see Mrs. Marsh off. Apparently that lode Lucky Jack's crew discovered is truly rich. Mrs. Marsh is going to San Francisco to look for a house already."

Rita Ann tugged at the lace collar of her pale blue dress. "Where did Corrie go after that?"

"That's what I need to figure out." Dola took Punky's hand and led him and Rita Ann inside the empty restaurant. "Who does she visit in town besides Mrs. Marsh and the Rokkers? And the Rokkers are all upstairs."

Rita Ann retied the perfectly tied white lace bow at her waist. "They're not here anymore."

"What do you mean?" Dola glanced up the

stairway as if expecting to see all the Rokkers standing in line.

Rita Ann picked up her Shakespeare book as she and her mother strolled toward the center of the room. "Mrs. Rokker cleaned them all up, got Danny to come home, left Punky with me, and then took them all to the office of the July Extension. Said she would wait in the lobby with the whole family until they talked to her about what happened to their house."

"Well . . . good for her. If I wasn't worried sick about Corrie, I'd march down there and sit in the office with her. They have to provide some kind of compensation for the Rokkers. It's the right thing to do."

Rita Ann chewed on her lower lip. "What are we going to do about Corrie, Mama?"

"Where's Tommy-Blue?"

The twelve-year-old scrunched her nose. "He's in the kitchen looking for something to eat."

Punky tossed a round wad of paper across the floor. He kicked it out in front of him and then chased it. Then he kicked it back.

Dola slowly followed after him. "Have Haylee and Omega finished up in the kitchen?"

"Haylee's through." Rita Ann strolled step for step with her mother to the doorway. "But she's probably out back. She and Hud seem to have an awful lot to talk about."

Dola paused in her pursuit of Punky. "That doesn't bother you now?"

Rita Ann raised her hand and slowly spun around on one foot. " 'When, in disgrace with fortune and men's eyes, I all alone beweep my outcast state.' "

When Dola grinned, she realized it was her first smile in hours. "That sounds ominous."

"Mama, Haylee's a really fun person, and Hud . . . well, he does seem a bit dull. So I decided if I could only have one of them as a friend, it should be Haylee."

"Darlin', you're soundin' a whole lot older than twelve."

Rita Ann walked out onto the porch. "Yes, but I still look twelve."

They reached Punky, who had picked up the wad of paper. "My ball!"

"I see it, baby. . . . That's nice." Dola turned back to Rita Ann. "Yes, you do look twelve. And I'm glad of it. Just remember, every woman looked twelve at one time."

"Even Haylee?"

"Yes, even Haylee." Dola latched onto Punky's hand. *Of course, Haylee was probably eight years old when she looked twelve!*

Rita Ann wrinkled her nose. "What are we going to do about Corrie?"

Dola stared down Columbia Street. "We've got to find her."

Tommy-Blue meandered onto the porch with a big biscuit half stuck out of his mouth and one in each hand. "Mmrhmmphaa," he mumbled.

"Tommyblue-Tommyblue-Tommyblue!" Punky ran to his brother and yanked a biscuit out of his hand. He crammed it halfway into his mouth and tottered down the boardwalk.

"You see what kind of influence you have?" Dola scolded.

Tommy-Blue bit the biscuit in half and held the rest in his free hand. With a big gulp he swallowed the bite. "Sorry, Mama. Did you find Corrie?"

"No, and we need to look for her," Dola instructed. "I want you and Rita Ann to go together. I'll take Punky with me." She glanced down the boardwalk. "Li'l darlin," she shouted, "come back here!"

Punky spun around, dropping the biscuit to the boardwalk. He reached down for it.

"No!" Dola hollered.

Immediately he stood up and crammed the dirty biscuit back into his mouth.

Dola threw up her hands. "Come on, grubby, I'll wash your face." She picked him up but left the biscuit in his mouth. The rolled-up wad of paper was still clutched in his hand. "Rita Ann, you and Tommy-Blue go up and down Main Street. I want you to peek in every store and ask if they've seen Corrie Lou Skinner, the Wall Walker's daughter."

"Do we have to say Wall Walker?" Rita Ann pressed.

"Yes, because there are a number of people who remember what your father did last month. It might motivate them to look more closely."

"Ever' store, Mama? Even the saloons and the cat houses?"

Dola felt her back stiffen. "Tommy-Blue! Don't you talk that way."

He stared down at his shoes. His voice was barely audible. "I was jist askin'."

"I don't want you to go to lower Main Street, and please stay out of all the saloons. You can ask anyone in front of the saloons though. But you two stay together. Do you understand?"

Tommy-Blue's eyes widened. "We don't have to hold hands, do we?"

"I have no intention of holding your sticky, dirty hand!" Rita Ann declared.

Tommy-Blue licked off a smear of butter lodged between his fingers. "My hands ain't all that dirty," he declared.

"You don't have to hold hands," Dola said, "but you do have to take care of each other."

"Where are you and Punky going to look?"

The two-year-old crammed the entire dirty biscuit into his mouth, then coughed, and sprayed crumbs clear across the boardwalk.

"We have to cover the rest of town."

"All of Goldfield?" Tommy-Blue questioned.

"And Columbia, if need be. She has to be somewhere."

"That will take you a long time," Rita declared.

"Yes." When Dola picked up the two-year-old, she felt a sudden sharp pain in her back. "After you finish, come back to the restaurant and wait. She might just decide to come home, and someone should be here. If I'm late for starting supper, tell Omega to go ahead. She'll know what to do."

"Do I have to stay at the restaurant after we're done?" Tommy-Blue quizzed.

"Yes, because if Corrie shows up, I want you to come find me."

Tommy-Blue picked his teeth with his thumbnail. "I won't know where you are."

Dola pointed across Goldfield. "Go up and down every street."

"Oh, yeah, and I could make preliminary surveys of potential diggin's!" Tommy-Blue exclaimed.

"You will come look for me straightway. Is that clear?"

"Yes, Mama." He looped his thumbs in his suspenders. "Shall we start now?"

Dola looked at him from head to toe. "Not until —"

"— you wash your hands," Rita Ann concluded.

"It's like havin' two mamas!" Tommy-Blue moaned as he trudged back into the kitchen.

Dola washed up Punky, pulled a mostly clean pair of worn canvas bib overalls on him, and then added white socks and laced up his shoes. "Punky, I'm not going to carry you all over town. I know it's a long walk, but we don't have any choice."

"Punky can run."

"But Mama isn't going to run. You will hold my hand and walk beside me."

He rubbed his nose with the palm of his hand. "Punky can run!"

I don't know why I'm attempting this, but I know I must, Lord. As long as I don't know where she is, I have to look. "I'll carry you down the stairs, but that's all!" When she reached over to pick him up, he snatched something off the floor. "Put that trash paper back," she instructed.

"Punky's ball!" he announced.

"It's a wadded-up piece of paper."

He clutched it to his chest. "Punky's ball!"

"Are you going to carry that all day?" she quizzed.

He nodded his little, round head up and down.

"Well," she sighed, "I suppose it's better than carrying a dirty biscuit."

"Punky's hungry!"

"No, Punky is not hungry," she chided. She started down the stairs.

"My mama's purdy!" he declared.

"Don't you try to sweet-talk me, young man. I'm not giving you another biscuit."

Dola and Punky walked hand in hand.
For one block.
Then she relented and lifted him to her hip.
A pain shot down her left shoulder to the small

of her back. She tried to stand straighter and ease the pain. His little right arm was wrapped around her, and his left hand clutched his paper ball. He greeted everyone on the sidewalk the same.

"Hi, I'm Punky!"

"Baby, you don't have to talk to everyone," Dola cautioned as they strolled in front of two bearded men passed out on a bench in front of the Little Red Saloon.

A woman with her dress hem a good foot off the ground sashayed by.

"Hi, I'm Punky!"

"Well, li'l darlin', I'm Gracie Lil." She glanced over at Dola's frown. "I don't think your mama wants you talkin' to me."

Dola looked away. "I didn't say —"

"Oh, you said it with your eyes, Mama. That's okay. Most fellas I talk to, their mamas wouldn't approve either!" Her laugh was deep, guttural, and loud as she flounced on down the boardwalk.

"She's purdy," Punky announced.

Dola used her free hand to brush hair off her forehead. *Lord, Goldfield is a difficult town to raise children in. It would be nice if You moved us to Dinuba.* "Yes, darlin', but you think all women are purdy!"

A man in a three-piece light wool suit, black silk bow tie, and bowler hat scurried by them.

"My mama's purdy!" Punky announced to the man.

The man spun around and stared at Dola. She could feel her face heat up.

The man tipped his hat and scooted on past them.

"Punkin, you're going to embarrass your mama to death. Now don't say things like that. Just say, 'Hi, I'm Punky.' Okay?"

They worked down the south side of Columbia Street and crossed over to the north side. The first store was Janni-Rae's Emporium, which had a canvas banner reading: "Miracle Medicines and Other Exotic Remedies for the Modern Woman."

An aroma of scented candles or incense wafted from the half-open door. Dola didn't bother looking inside. She took advantage of a white wooden bench with ivy leaves painted on it. She set Punky beside her.

"Mama needs to rest, baby."

"I'm not a baby. I'm medium!"

"You're getting bigger by the minute!" Dola tried to stretch her back and rub her shoulders.

I can't cover town like this, Lord. Who am I kidding? I will be lucky to tote this lump of sugar back to the restaurant, let alone any farther. I've got to have some help. O.T., I wish you weren't so busy finding others that you could help me find your daughter. She's doing this on purpose. She's mad at us for not letting her go with you, so she's playing hooky! Well, her little, round bottom will have to answer for this.

Dola reached up and brushed tears off her cheeks.

And if I'm so angry at her, why do I keep crying?

She stood and took Punky's hand. "You walk for a while. Mama's back hurts."

"Mama's purdy!" he announced.

"Darlin', it don't even sound good from your lips anymore. Your mama is old, tired, stoop-shouldered, and worried sick. That's what she is."

The street held a steady stream of wagons, carriages, and an occasional car. The noise of axles, horses, mules, and conversations dulled into a steady drone. She kept Punky walking close to the edge of the sidewalk so those in a hurry could scoot past them. Half the buildings had raised wooden boardwalks. Most of those had awnings or balconies that shaded them.

By the time they were in front of the Yukon Saloon, she was carrying Punky on her right hip. This time the pain started in the small of her back and shot down her right leg.

An older man with a long gray beard and tattered straw hat sat on a bench and smoked a long-stemmed clay pipe. "Afternoon, Mrs. Skinner."

She paused to look him over. "I don't believe I recall your name." She moved the toddler around in front and held him with both hands.

"Wentworth Jones," he announced as he waved the stem of his pipe like a pointer. "Ate

231

breakfast at your place this mornin'."

"Excuse me for not recognizing you, Mr. Jones."

"Ain't no problem." When he smiled, she noticed how tobacco-stained his teeth were. "I reckon I'll be back for supper as well."

"That's good, Mr. Jones. I'm glad you enjoy our restaurant." She shifted Punky to her left hip and rubbed the bridge of her nose.

The old man took a long, slow drag on his pipe and let the smoke curl slowly from his mouth. "What are you two doin' way down at this end of town?"

Dola stepped aside to let two women in tight satin dresses rustle between them. "I'm looking for a daughter of mine who's playing hooky. Have you seen a little, round-faced girl with short, thick brown hair? She is wearing a green dress."

"No, ma'am. But I've jist been sittin' here a minute or two. Let me ask inside." He pointed to the door of the Yukon.

"I would appreciate it."

He pulled himself off the bench. "What's your girl's name?"

"I'm Punky!"

"How do you do, young man."

"My daughter's name is Corrie Lou Skinner."

"This is my ball!" Punky held out the wad of paper.

The old man sauntered over to the tall,

narrow white doors, swung them open, and shouted, "Anyone here seen a little girl named Corrie Lou Skinner around town today? Her mama is out here lookin' for her."

"Dola Mae!" a voice bellowed from deep inside the saloon. "Dola Mae, are you out there?"

She stiffened and carried Punky farther away from the door.

Wentworth Jones motioned to her. "Someone's callin' you."

Dola Mae steadied her jaw. "I'm not going to talk to some man in a saloon."

"Dola Mae, wait!" the slurred voice from inside sounded closer, louder.

I don't think I want to see this, Lord. I don't want to know who it is. I don't even want to be here.

Dola spun around and tromped toward the shoe store next door.

"Dola Mae, darlin' . . . wait!"

The voice was now only a few feet behind her. Punky looked back at the man and shouted, "Lucky Jack!"

Dola's heart sank. Her neck muscles stiffened. She took another step toward the shoe shop. A hand grabbed her shoulder. She stopped but didn't look back. "Do not touch me, Mr. Gately!"

His hand pulled back. "You still lookin' for Corrie, Dola Mae?"

"Mr. Gately, I must insist that you address me as Mrs. Skinner," she snapped.

233

"You aren't goin' to turn around and even look at me?"

"Mr. Gately, you have been a dear friend to me on several occasions. I am extremely grateful for every act of kindness you have shown me, my family, and my friends. However, as a friend, I will not condone your drunkenness."

"Just a little celebration on hittin' the big time in the mine." His voice was clear and very loud.

"Sin is always excusable in our eyes, but never in the eyes of the Lord."

"Why ain't you turnin' around?" he demanded. Several people on the sidewalk stopped and stared.

"Because I like having you for a friend, a sober friend. I don't want to see you drunk. I do not want that image of my friend Lucky Jack Gately to be forever locked in my mind. Goodbye, Mr. Gately."

She could hear him walk behind her.

"You need help findin' Corrie Lou?"

"Not from a drunk."

"You only want perfect people to help you find her?" he pressed.

Dola spun around. Lucky Jack's curly blond hair was disheveled. The top button on his white shirt was missing. The shirt was half tucked into his trousers. His eyes were red, almost squinted shut. He propped himself up by leaning on the building.

"No, I'm not looking for perfect people. I'm looking for my daughter. You are right. I need help, and I would accept any offer, short of the devil himself, to find my daughter."

"Mrs. Skinner, you surely know how to sober a man up in a hurry."

"I expected better from you, Mr. Gately. But that's my fault. I shouldn't blame you for my misplaced confidence. If you or anyone else sees or hears anything about Corrie, I would be most grateful to learn of it." She turned and began to walk away.

"Bye, Lucky Jack!" Punky called out.

"Bye, li'l punk," he called back. "Take care of your mama."

"My mama's purdy!"

"Hush," she scolded the two-year-old.

"And mad!" Punky squealed.

Dola Mae Skinner stormed along the boardwalk with a two-year-old on her hip, peering into every store, and speaking to no one.

This is a horrid town, Lord. No one should live here. It's filled with greedy people hoping to make it rich in a hurry. Women sell their virtue as if it were a block of cheese. Men spend their money getting drunk and gambling. Explosions devour houses. Sand can blow for days on end, blinding eyes and blasting everything in sight. It's a place where people you trust turn out to be rascals. It's a place where children can wander off and get lost.

I want to gather my family all up and be gone! If

Corrie and Orion are home when I get there, we are getting in the wagon tonight and leaving.

Dola fought to hold back the tears. *I will not cry. You can't make me cry anymore, Goldfield. You are not my home. I'm not going to stay here. I'm going to a better place. Any place outside of Hades is better than this!*

Building after building.

Clerk after clerk.

Time after time.

"Have you seen a ten-year-old girl with a thick mop of brown hair whose name is Corrie Lou Skinner?"

Over and over.

The question was always the same.

And the answers were identical.

"No."

Dola was only a block away from the restaurant when she put Punky down and tried to straighten her back. *I'm very tired, Lord. Tired of packing a heavy boy. Tired of packing the worry about Corrie. Tired of packing the guilt that nags at me that if I were a better mother, I would know where my children are. Tired of cooking for men who get drunk by noon. Tired of a husband who's not here when I need him most.*

Dola clutched Punky's hand and began to sob. *Oh, Lord God, I didn't mean that. You know how I love that man. I made him go look for Mr. Rokker. I would have nagged him until he left. But he will be gone for a week and not even know his daughter is missing. This is not good, Lord. It's not a good situation. It's not a good life. I want to go home. Not to my home, but Your home, Lord. Send me a chariot like You did for Elijah. Send me an angel to lead me home. Oh, Lord, the burden is too heavy!*

Punky tugged at her hand. "Hi," he called out. "This is my ball!" He held out the other hand with the wadded-up piece of paper.

Dola looked up to see whom he was talking to. Lucian LaPorte sat in the driver's seat of his black leather hack, his long-legged black horse standing proudly in front.

"Lucian!" Her voice cracked as she spoke.

"Yes, ma'am, were you expecting someone else?"

She pulled a cotton handkerchief out of the sleeve of her dress and began to wipe her cheeks. "I, eh . . ."

"You got a little dust in your eyes?"

"Mommy was cryin'!" Punky reported. "This is my ball!"

LaPorte motioned to the empty seat behind him. "How about you and your mommy and your ball goin' for a ride with me?"

Dola shaded her eyes. "Where are we going?"

"We are going up and down every street in Goldfield lookin' for a delinquent young lady named Corrie."

"Corrie Lou went bye-bye," Punky announced. "This is my ball."

Dola stepped closer to the edge of the sidewalk. "Are you serious about giving us a ride?"

"Come on." Lucian reached down and offered them a hand.

Dola transferred Punky up to him.

"You sit up front so your mama can ride back there like the queen."

"My mama's purdy," Punky insisted.

"Here's a young man who is wise beyond his age." Lucian reached his big, strong arm down to help Dola step up into the carriage.

"That young man was drilled by his father to say that one line over and over and over. It was the first sentence ever spoken by that li'l darlin'."

LaPorte's grin was as wide as his jaw. "I predict he will go far in life."

Punky held up the wad of paper. "This is my ball."

"But maybe he shouldn't try to be a baseball player."

"It seems to be his toy of the day."

"Where to, Mama?" LaPorte asked.

"Let me check the restaurant. Then we will hit every street in town except Columbia and Main."

"Sounds like a good plan."

"Lucian, while wallowing in self-pity back there, I asked the Lord to send a chariot from heaven with an angel driving it to take me home."

"Hah! The Lord played a joke on you, Dola Mae. He sent an old hack and a big black man instead."

"No, he sent a chariot driven by an angel," she insisted.

"Now don't puff me up too much. I was hired for this job, sort of."

She leaned forward, her hand on the back of the front carriage seat. "Hired? By whom?"

He waited for a two-horse surrey to trot past and then pulled the carriage out into the middle of Columbia Street. "Actually I agreed to donate half the cost myself, so I'm only half hired by a friend of yours."

"Lucian LaPorte, who hired you?" she demanded.

"My mama's mad," Punky declared.

Lucian patted the toddler on the head. "I reckon you're right about that, Punky."

"I'm not mad," she barked. "Who hired you?"

"Lucky Jack Gately."

Dola flopped back against the sun-warmed leather seat. "What?"

"He came over to the house and beat on the door until I came out. Said he'd pay me double fare all afternoon if I'd take the job." LaPorte loosened his tie and unfastened the top button of his white shirt. "I said, sure. Then he said he wanted me to chauffeur you around until Corrie was found. I told him I didn't need to be paid, but he said it was important to him that he pay me. I argued him down from double fare to just regular fare. So I'm gettin' paid well — just not as much as I could have been gettin'."

Dola gripped her fingers tightly and stared down at them. "Was Mr. Gately still drunk?" Her voice was so low she wasn't sure that Lucian heard her.

"No, ma'am. At least not bad drunk. He was totin' a cup of coffee when he came to the door. But I could smell the liquor on him."

"I can't let him pay for this."

"He said you'd protest, but he said to tell you that he ain't the devil, and you'd have to accept the help."

She stared across the street at two freight wagons being unloaded. Her thoughts were on a drunken Lucky Jack Gately — his disheveled hair, untucked shirt, bloodshot eyes.

"Did you hear me, Dola Mae?" LaPorte said.

"Mr. Gately is right. He's not the devil. I'll accept the generosity of you both. Let's go by the restaurant. If Rita Ann and Tommy-Blue are home by now, I'll leave this little punkin with them."

"This is my ball," Punky announced again.

Corrie stood in the wagon and hugged her father's neck. "Do you love me, Daddy?"

Sweat rolled down O.T.'s forehead and burned the corners of his eyes. The desert sun blasted straight down, compressing the ground heat like a heavy blanket. He leaned his head back and kissed her round, dusty cheek. It was soft and very warm. "You know I do, darlin'."

Her grip on his neck never lessened. "Do you love me the most?"

The desert road was flat, the fog of alkali dust suppressed, the rhythm of the wagon monotonous.

"What do you mean, do I love you the most?"

Her little, round mouth was only a few inches behind his ear. "Do you love me more than you love Rita Ann?"

"Now, Corrie . . . don't you . . ."

"You love Mama more than you love me, don't you?"

"I love you with 100 percent of my Corrie-Lou love."

"What do you mean, Daddy?"

"Well, when I first saw your mama, the Lord gave me a whole heart full of love just for her. It was Dola-Mae-Davis love. I couldn't use it on anyone else. But I could be stingy and hold some back. But I never have. She gets the entire supply of Dola-Mae love."

"And you don't have room for any others?"

"Now just wait. Then when I first saw Rita Ann, the Lord gave me a big supply of Rita-Ann love. It doesn't compete with Dola-Mae love. That's different. I can't use Rita-Ann love on anyone else. I could hold some back, but I never do."

"How about me, Daddy?" She squeezed his neck tighter.

"Well, when I saw you, oh, my, the Lord gave

241

me a whole supply of Corrie-Lou love. Now I can't use it on Mama. I can't use it on Rita Ann. It's just made for Corrie Lou, that's all. I could hold some back, I suppose, but I never have. I want you to know I love you with every once of Corrie-Lou love the Lord gave me!"

She leaned forward until her chin rested on his shoulder. "I like that, Daddy."

He reached back and patted her shoulder. "Now why are you askin' all of this, darlin'?"

" 'Cause you don't ever whip Mama or Rita Ann," she replied.

He brushed some of the road dust out of his mustache with his fingers. "Rita Ann got spanked when she was little."

"She did?" Corrie stood up straighter. "Right on the behind?"

"Yes, she did."

"Did you love me less when you spanked me, Daddy? After what I did?"

He leaned back so that his right arm could circle her waist. "Darlin', I didn't spank you because I love you less. I spanked you because I love you so much."

Her round lower lip curled. "It don't seem like it when you're spankin' me. I don't reckon I'll be able to sit down for a week."

"Darlin', in this life we have to receive the consequences for our actions. It's a very serious thing to disobey your mama and daddy. That has consequences."

"You don't have to take me back to Goldfield. Wouldn't you just please take me with you? You could spank me ever' day," she pleaded.

O.T. took a deep breath. Then he leaned back and kissed her cheek again. "Darlin', I'm not goin' to spank you again for that. You received your punishment. I forgive you, and I won't bring it up again."

The rumble of the wagon kept her bouncing softly against his back. "Mama's goin' to bring it up again." Her arms were still around his neck, her hands locked under his chin.

"I imagine she will. But I'll tell her you already received your just deserts."

"Ain't nothin' like dessert," she complained. "But I didn't cry in front of Mr. Wilkins. Did you notice that, Daddy? I'm gettin' bigger 'cause this time I didn't cry."

O.T. felt a tear roll down his cheek into his mustache. He kept his head forward, and yet he reached back and hugged her. "I noticed, darlin'." Each word seemed to catch in his throat. "It's okay to cry when you hurt, darlin'."

She leaned forward and ran her soft, warm hand along his cheek. "Are you hurtin', Daddy? Is that why you're cryin'?"

"I'm hurtin' on the inside, darlin', on the inside."

"Why, Daddy? Did I hurt you on the inside?"

O.T. took another deep breath. "Corrie, I don't like havin' to spank you. It grieves me. I'd rather hug you and kiss you and never

243

have to spank you again."

"I'll be good, Daddy. I won't run off and hide in your wagon ever again. I promise I'll be good."

He kept hugging her. " Corrie Lou Skinner, did you run off and hide in my wagon? Why, I must have forgotten all about that already."

"Daddy!"

"It's all over with, baby. I won't bring it up again."

"I love you, Daddy."

He kissed her cheek again. "And I love you, darlin'. I'm glad you wrote Mama a note tellin' her where you went. I wouldn't want her worryin'."

"I told her I couldn't help myself, but I had to go with my daddy, and that I prayed that she would one day forgive me."

"That's what you said in your note?"

"Sort of like that. But I almost didn't get to the livery in time. I didn't know Mrs. Marsh was leavin' for a trip, and I helped her to the depot. Then I ran over to the livery, and you were harnessing Ada and Ida, so I just dove underneath the tarp. I thought if we made it to the Wilkins brothers' mine, you wouldn't turn back."

The empty dirt road stretched perfectly straight ahead of them on a long, gradual incline with no vegetation in sight at all.

"You were wrong, weren't you?"

"I reckon so. But if Fergus had been at the

mine, would you still have turned back?"

"There's no way of knowin' that, darlin'. Maybe not. As long as Mama knows you're with me, I reckon I'd have just kept you."

"Would you have to spank me ever' day?"

"What for, darlin'? Did you do somethin' naughty? I plumb forgot."

She leaned forward and kissed his cheek. Then she pulled straight back. "Eooh, Daddy, you need to shave!"

"Now you're sounding like your mama," he laughed.

"Does Mama kiss you on the cheek? I thought she only kissed you on the lips."

"On occasion she kisses me on the cheek. For variety's sake, I reckon."

"I like kissin' on the cheek better. Kissin' the lips is too slobbery," Corrie declared.

"I might regret askin' this, darlin', but how do you know that?"

" 'Cause Punky always wants to kiss me on the lips, and he slobbers all over!"

O.T. laughed.

"Daddy, do I have to kiss Aunt Pearl when we get to California?"

"I suppose so. She's just that way."

"She always smells funny. All I remember about her is them big mooshy lips and a funny smell."

"Aunt Pearl does like her lilac perfume."

"I like Uncle Pegasus," she declared.

"That's nice."

"He sort of looks like you — only old."

"Thank you, darlin'. Some days I feel older too."

"How do you feel today, Daddy?"

"Well, back there when I had to spank you, I was feelin' mighty old. But right now, with your arms around my neck, I feel like a young man of forty!"

"You are forty, Daddy!"

"See there!"

"You're being silly."

"Is that all right with you?"

She hugged his neck. "Yep."

He pushed his hat to the back of his head. "You want to drive this rig?"

"How can I? I don't think I can sit down."

"You can come around here and stand between my knees."

"Drive a rig standing up?"

"Sure. I seen them gals in the wild west show do the same thing one time. Come on, you're as good a horse lady as any of them and twice as purdy."

"Now you're bein' very silly." Corrie climbed over the wagon seat and stood between her father's knees. He helped her get braced and then laced the lead lines in her small hands.

"It's all yours, darlin'. Drive us home."

Without turning around she called out, "I love you, Daddy!"

O.T. murmured in a soft, choked whisper, "I know, darlin'. I know."

Every bone and every muscle in her body ached when Dola crawled back into Lucian LaPorte's carriage. She flopped down in the backseat and sighed.

"No luck?" he asked.

"No one has seen her except the hotel clerk when she was with Mrs. Marsh at daybreak."

"Maybe she did go to San Francisco. Kids don't always have a perspective on time or distance," he suggested.

She fanned her face with her hands. "I just can't believe that. But knowing that she was on her way to San Francisco would be better than not knowing anything. This is about to kill me. If I wasn't so tired, I know I'd be bawling." She rubbed her neck. The high collar of her dress was completely drenched.

Lucian LaPorte pulled out a white handkerchief and mopped his face. "Where to now, Mrs. Skinner? We've covered every street, store, and tent in sight."

She waved her hand to the northeast. "Take me back to my other children, Lucian. I'm going to hug them all night. Besides, I have a supper to serve."

"I reckon Omega and them others can fill in for one meal. I'll help 'em if they need it. You need the rest."

"You're an angel — you really are. There will be rewards in heaven for you, Lucian LaPorte."

"If there are any rewards for me in heaven, it

will be by the grace of God."

Dola leaned her head back on the leather carriage seat and closed her eyes. "I reckon that's true for all of us."

It was almost 4:00 P.M. when they returned to the restaurant. The streets were nearly empty. On the boardwalks people hovered in the shade.

"Looks like they mounted your new sign." Lucian pointed to the large white sign with black-and-red lettering. "The Newcomers' Café. I like that."

"So do I, but today everything feels old." She sat up and brushed her hair back over her ears with her fingers.

When they pulled up to the front steps, Tommy-Blue and Danny Rokker scampered out.

"Mama, guess who's here!" Tommy-Blue shouted.

"Corrie?" Dola's heart quickened as she climbed out of the carriage.

"No." Tommy-Blue's chin dropped. "Didn't you find her?"

Dola shook her head and stepped on the boardwalk.

"I'll check back later," Lucian said as he tipped his black hat.

"I can't thank you enough, Lucian."

"Your eyes just did," he insisted. "You might want to thank Lucky Jack as well."

She stood on the porch and watched him drive away.

Tommy-Blue tugged on her arm. "You didn't guess who's inside!"

"It's Wyatt Earp!" Danny shouted.

"No!" Tommy-Blue corrected. "It's Stuart Brannon!"

"That's what I meant," Danny mumbled.

Dola peeked through the open restaurant door. "Mr. Brannon is here?"

"He's been waitin' almost an hour to see you," Tommy-Blue explained.

She hurried to the door. "I trust you've entertained him."

"He's been listenin' to Mama tell all about our house bein' swallowed up," Danny reported.

Although there was still plenty of light from the descending sun, electric lights were on when Dola entered the café. An aroma of roast, soapy water, and alkali dust hung in the air. At the biggest table near the kitchen door sat an older gray-haired man in an ill-fitting three-piece wool suit. His white shirt was buttoned at the neck, but he wore no tie. His battered Stetson was shoved back on his head. His clean-shaven face was square-jawed, deeply tanned, and highly wrinkled. His eyebrows were a thick, bushy gray.

Sitting around the table were Nellie, Jared, and Caitlynn Rokker, plus Rita Ann. She had a notebook and pencil in front of her. Omega LaPorte and Haylee Cox lingered at the kitchen doorway. Punky sat on the old man's

249

knee, still clutching his wadded ball of paper.

"Mama-Mama-Mama-Mama!" Punky shouted as he squirmed to the floor and shot across the room.

The old man with slightly stooped shoulders stood and pulled off his hat. His gray hair was almost white but still thick. "Mrs. Skinner, it's nice to see you again."

She held out her hand. "Mr. Brannon, it's indeed a pleasure to have you here." She was surprised at his strong grip. "Please call me Dola Mae. Uncle Everett always did."

Brannon nodded and grinned, cracking the wrinkles on his face. "Only if all of you call me Pop. That's what ever'one in Arizona calls me."

"He ain't even totin' a .44, Mama," Tommy-Blue reported.

"You know," the Arizona legend replied, "Tommy-Blue is a mighty fine name. Your Great-uncle Everett was a true partner of mine, one of the best I ever had. He would have liked that name too." Brannon stared across the room as if looking across decades.

"How come you don't wear a six-gun anymore, Mr. Brannon?" Tommy-Blue pressed.

He motioned for the boy to come over and then put his arm on Tommy-Blue's shoulder. "A few years back I started readin' all those dime novels that Mr. Hawthorne Miller's been writin' about me. I guess I got to believin' them so much, I realized that I had personally shot and killed ever' bad man, sneak thief, footpad,

250

highwayman, train robber, and piggy bank snatcher in North and South America and parts of Europe. Then I finally figured it out. There just isn't anyone left to shoot! So I don't have any reason to pack a revolver anymore. Course I do carry one in my satchel — for emergencies."

Tommy-Blue's eyes widened. "Wow, really? Did you really shoot them all?"

Rita Ann sat up and adjusted her glasses. "He was using a hyperbole."

"Is that better than a Colt .44?" Tommy-Blue pressed.

"Sometimes," Brannon grinned. He let his arm drop off the boy's shoulder.

"Mr. Brannon has been listening to the ordeal of our house," Nellie Rokker reported.

"Yep." Brannon nodded. "That isn't right, Dola Mae. The July Extension Mine is liable for that house. I don't know what kind of courts you got down here. I wish my good friend, Judge Kingston from Carson City, was still alive. Good man. He wouldn't let this kind of thing happen," Brannon declared.

Dola glanced over at Nellie Rokker and was surprised how collected and at ease the frail woman looked. "I take it you didn't have much luck with the July Extension people?" she asked her.

Nellie Rokker's hands were folded together on the table in front of her. "We sat in that office for six hours, and no one would talk to us."

Dola could feel the dampness of the back of her dress pressing against her. "They didn't even talk to you? I can't believe that."

"I can," Omega called out from the doorway. "They wouldn't speak to Lucian neither. They don't think they have to listen to anyone."

"I hear you have a missing daughter," Brannon commented.

Dola rubbed her forehead. "I'm beginning to think she ran off with a lady friend of ours to San Francisco. I don't know. I'm worried sick over it."

"Sometimes the Lord can surprise us," Brannon encouraged her.

Dola studied the kind eyes of the old man. "I know, Pop. But at the moment I have a tough time trusting Him."

"O.T. is out of town, I hear," Brannon continued.

"Yes, and he'll be quite disappointed at missing you. Are you going to be here long?"

Pop Brannon slowly pulled off his wool suit coat. "No, I'm headed on up to Tonopah to catch the train to Carson City. I'm goin' antelope huntin' up in the Black Desert with an old friend of mine." He folded the coat and laid it across his knee. "He's givin' a speech in Carson City tomorrow. Then we'll go huntin' for a few days. He's been kind of busy recently, and it's our first huntin' trip in a few years."

"Where's your friend from, Mr. Brannon?" Rita Ann asked.

"He's originally from New York, but he lives in Washington, D.C., right now. Doesn't get out west too often anymore."

"What's his name? Maybe I've heard of him. I try to read up on current news," Rita Ann inquired. "I read every newspaper we get hold of. Don't I, Mama?"

"She's a very good reader, all right," Dola said.

A sly smile crept across the old man's face. "His name is Theodore, but I call him Teddy." Brannon winked.

"Theodore?" Rita Ann gasped. "You mean . . . you mean, you're going hunting with President Roosevelt?"

The old man chuckled and rocked back in his chair. "Like I said, I just call him Teddy. And he calls me Brannon."

Rita Ann's face turned red. She pointed across the table. "He — he — he knows the President of the United States!"

"Take some deep breaths, darlin'. You'll be fine," Dola said.

"But — but . . . 'Oh, how I faint when I of you do write,' " Rita Ann blurted out. Then she covered her face with her hands.

"Number 80 or 81?" Brannon inquired.

Rita Ann peeked around her fingers. "What?"

"Was that Shakespeare's 80th or 81st sonnet?" Brannon pressed.

Rita Ann dropped her hands. "It was the 80th!"

Stuart Brannon winked at her. "Even an old man likes to read somethin' in addition to his Bible."

"Can you stay for supper?" Dola asked.

"I'm sorry, but I've got a stage to catch in an hour and a couple more people to talk to," he reported.

"Well, thank you for stopping by."

"Dola Mae, your uncle was one of the best partners I ever had in my life. I've grieved his death for almost thirty years now. You folks feel like family to me. I was serious about you stoppin' down at the Triple-B Ranch some-time."

"This is my ball!" Punky toddled over to Stuart Brannon and held up the now-frayed paper wad.

Brannon held out his hand. "Shall we play catch?"

Punky threw the ball high over Pop's head. Dola was amazed at the old man's quick hands. He reached up and snatched the ball out of the air. Then he examined the paper wad. "Where did you get this fine ball, Punky?"

The toddler's eyes lit up. "Corrie gave it to me this mornin'!"

"What?" Dola exclaimed.

"My ball." Punky held out his hands. "Throw!"

Brannon tossed the round wad of paper un-derhanded to the two-year-old. But it was Dola's long fingers that reached over and plucked it out of the air. "Let me see Corrie's ball," she murmured.

She slowly unwrapped the white paper and recognized the familiar uneven scrawl. Her heart raced as words and then a sentence came into view: "Dear Mama, forgive me. I went with my daddy. My heart would break if he left without me. Don't hate me forever. I love you. Your less-than-perfect daughter, Corrie Lou Skinner."

Tears clouded Dola's eyes so quickly the final words blurred. She sat down hard on the bench behind her, her hands holding her cheeks.

"Mama, what is it?" Tommy-Blue asked.

"It's okay," she sobbed. "It's okay now. Corrie's with Daddy. . . . Everything is okay."

Eight

Corrie Skinner was still standing between her father's knees when they reached Goldfield. She held the leather lead lines between her short, little fingers as the old farm wagon rattled and squeaked its way up Main Street. Her head was high, chin out, nose slightly upturned.

She didn't glance to the left or right. Her jaw was set, her face frosted with road dust. Her thick, short bangs bounced across her forehead.

"Maybe you ought to drive now, Daddy," she suggested.

O.T. patted her arm. "You're doin' fine."

"You see that boy over there in the brown suit?" she asked. "Don't turn and look."

O.T. gazed south out of the corner of his eye. "The one with the tight shirt collar?"

"Yeah. That's Colin Maddison, the third, with two d's."

O.T. leaned close to her ear. "I bet he's impressed with your drivin'."

"I really couldn't care less," she asserted. Then she peeked at the boy wearing the suit. "You want me to drive to the livery or to the restaurant?"

"Which do you want to do?"

"I think Mama's going to be mad at me. Let's go to the livery first."

O.T. waved his hand to the east. "Then turn at the next corner."

She leaned back against his chest. "Thanks for letting me drive, Daddy."

He slipped his arms around her waist and hugged her. "You're welcome, darlin'. As soon as I find Fergus, I'll figure out when we're headin' back out to look for Mr. Rokker. You'll have to stay home, young lady."

"I know, Daddy. I will. I promise I'll never, ever do anything to cause you to spank me again!"

O.T. watched a black carriage pulled by matching white horses scurry by.

"I can't ever be good like Rita Ann, but I can be Corrie-Lou good," she continued.

When they got to the livery, she yanked back on the lead lines and shouted, "Whoa, mules!"

"Darlin', that's all you're ever goin' to have to be. Park out here by the stock tank. I'll have the livery man water and grain the mules. I think I'll leave them hitched until I find that ol' Paiute. Maybe we'll head back out to the desert tonight."

O.T. had just climbed down and reached back up for Corrie when a twelve-year-old boy wandered out of the barn. "Hi, Mr. Skinner!"

O.T. pushed his hat back. "Chester, how are you doin'?"

"Wow, Miss Corrie, did you drive the wagon

all the way from Tonopah?"

Corrie tried brushing some of the road dust off her long dress. "We weren't in Tonopah. We were out toward Alkali."

The boy grabbed Ada's rigging and led the mules to the water trough. "Well, my daddy don't let me drive standin' up."

She glanced at her father.

"Corrie likes to feel the wind blowin' in her face," O.T. explained. "Where is your daddy, Chester?"

With both mules drinking, the boy walked back to O.T. "Still over at the jail, I reckon."

O.T. glanced down the dirt street at the two-story block building that loomed on the horizon. "What's he doin' there?"

Chester ducked into the barn and came out carrying two feed bags. "They caught that Indian who stole our mule."

O.T. pulled off his hat. "What Indian?"

"That old Paiute." The boy slipped a canvas bag over Ada's nose.

"Fergus?" Corrie called out. "They arrested Fergus?"

"Yeah, that's the one. He stole our little mule, and the sheriff done arrested him and tossed him in the hoosegow." Chester slipped a feed bag on Ida.

O.T. paced in front of the wagon. "He didn't steal that mule."

"He didn't?" The boy jammed his hands into his back pockets.

"Young Jared Rokker rented the mule. Then I sent Lucian LaPorte to tell your dad that Fergus wanted to rent him, and I would stand good for it."

"I don't know nothin' about that. That was the day the Rokker house was swallowed. Folks were runnin' all over as if the whole town would be destroyed like Sodom and Gomorrah. That black man came in here sayin' somethin' about an Indian had our little mule. That's all I remember. Daddy said the old Indian stole that mule. You want me to unhitch your team?"

"Leave them hitched, but rub them down the best you can. I might need to leave again this afternoon."

"Yes, sir."

Corrie tugged on O.T.'s arm. "What about Fergus, Daddy?"

"I reckon you and me better go do somethin' about this, don't you?"

"Yeah." She nodded. "Will we need the shotgun?"

He ran his fingers through her hair. "I don't think so."

O.T. and Corrie waited on the boardwalk across the street from the Esmeralda County Jail while the Tonopah stage rumbled by.

"Daddy, when they finish the railroad from the north, will they quit runnin' the stage to Tonopah?" Corrie asked.

"I suppose so. Hold my hand while we cross the street."

Corrie scurried to keep up with him. "I like stagecoaches. They look so adventurous."

"Well, darlin', things change, and we learn to accept new ideas."

"Did you ever drive a stagecoach, Daddy?"

"Nope. Never did."

"I'd like to drive a stagecoach," she declared.

"A six-up team is tougher than two old mules," he explained.

"I bet I could do it," she boasted.

An explosion behind them caused both of them to spin around. They watched a car putt-putt down the street. "A stagecoach might be easier than drivin' one of them," O.T. remarked.

There were sixteen steps up to the sheriff's office. Corrie hopped on one foot all the way to the top.

It took five minutes of explanation and five dollars to settle with the livery to get Fergus released. Corrie walked between her father and the Paiute, holding each of their hands out on the sidewalk.

"Why don't we just get in the wagon and go look for Mr. Rokker? I can go with you. I'll be the cook," she declared.

"Not this trip." His tone was crisp but not harsh. "I think we've discussed that. I'm takin' you home, and we can all get some supper."

"You're coming with us, aren't you, Fergus?" Corrie asked. "I can sit right between you and . . . Well, perhaps I'll stand."

"I never turn down an invitation to eat. But I have to go to the bank first," the Indian announced.

"You got bankin' to do?" O.T. quizzed.

"Yep. Got to deposit my 10 percent."

"You have it on you?"

The old Indian pulled a folded piece of paper from the flannel shirt pocket. "$2,624.55!" he announced.

"You had that in your pocket all this time? You could have paid the fine," O.T. charged.

"But I didn't steal the mule."

"You could have bought the mule!" Corrie exclaimed.

"I could have bought the livery." The old man grinned. "But I didn't like the mule."

O.T. pulled off his hat and ran his fingers through his hair. "Well, partner, no matter how rich you are, I still need your help findin' Elias Rokker."

"I know." There was a wry smile on the wrinkled, leather-tough face. "You can't get along without me!"

"What if I wouldn't have come to town?" O.T. stopped walking and stared at the Indian's dark eyes. "How long were you plannin' on stayin' in jail?"

Fergus's reply was a monotone. "Until supper, but I knew you would come."

"I was clear out at the Wilkinses. If I hadn't had a girl to bring home, I might have gone after Rokker on my own."

"But you didn't. I will be at the restaurant soon."

"Don't get into any more trouble," O.T. chided.

"I believe I might buy myself some new boots," Fergus said. "Or perhaps I will buy a boot store."

O.T. dragged two chairs out of the apartment and onto the balcony. Dola plopped down in one. As soon as Orion sat in the other, she lifted her bare feet into his lap, and he began to knead them with his thumbs and fingers.

"You've had a long day," he said.

"So have you."

"Yes, but I wasn't worried about where my daughter was."

"The strange thing is, Punky carried that wadded-up note all day, and it wasn't until Mr. Brannon unrolled it that I knew she was with you," Dola said.

O.T. rubbed his unshaven chin. "I'm sorry I missed Pop."

"He said he'd try to stop back by after his hunting trip with the President." Dola scrunched down in the chair and leaned her head back.

O.T. continued to massage her feet. "This is the first time I ever knew someone who knew the President."

"Rita Ann was in heaven," Dola declared. "She wanted to go with him to Carson City."

O.T. stared out into the Goldfield night. "You think I was too hard on her?"

"Rita Ann?"

"No, Corrie."

"Orion, quit frettin' over giving your daughter a spanking. She needed it. And I can assure you, she doesn't love you any less." Dola nodded toward the apartment behind her. "Look back in there. What is your youngest daughter doing?"

"Looks like she's drawin' a picture."

"It's a picture of her standing next to her daddy and driving an old farm wagon. She told me that this has been just about the best day of her life. Does that sound like she hates you for it?"

"'Just about' the best day?"

Dola grinned, her eyes still closed. "Also notice she is drawing standing up."

He rubbed her foot, her ankle, and a few inches up past her ankle. Dola kept her eyes closed. *Lord, what wonderful surprises You had for me today. I thought I wouldn't see Orion for a week. I thought I might not ever see my daughter again. And here I am, with both of them home, my feet propped up, and my man rubbing them. This might be a perfect evening. No, a perfect evening would be for all the kids to be in bed asleep . . . in separate rooms. Orion Tower Skinner, I do believe I'm lusting after you.*

"Daddy, you let me drive the team all the way from Alkali, didn't you?" Corrie called out.

O.T. turned his head toward the open doorway. "Yep, that's right."

"See there!" Corrie called out.

"Daddy, when do I get to drive the team that far?" Tommy-Blue hollered.

O.T. glanced over at Dola, who opened one eye. "When you're Corrie's age."

"I'm already as big as her."

"You won't be my age for nine more months!" Corrie taunted.

"I'm bigger than you now," Tommy-Blue insisted.

"I'm taller," she argued.

"No, you aren't," he countered.

Corrie laid down her pencil. "Yes, I am. Ask Mama."

"Mama!" Tommy-Blue yelled.

"You two settle down!" O.T. hollered.

Dola reached over and patted his shoulder. "Welcome home, Daddy."

"At least, there's only one family in the apartment tonight."

"Yes, we were quite shocked when the man from July Extension showed up and offered to put the Rokkers in the hotel for the night."

"I suppose Nellie's camping out at their office did some good. But only one night? That hardly seems fair."

Dola slid her feet down. Even the wooden balcony floor felt warm to her touch. "Nellie said they wouldn't even talk to her. So I'm not sure what helped them change their minds."

"Mama, Punky peed in his bathwater!" Rita Ann called out.

"Pull him out."

"I'm not going to reach in there!" Rita Ann squealed.

Dola slowly stood up. Muscles tightened in her thighs and calves. "So much for a quiet moment on the balcony, Mr. Skinner."

"Can I help, Mrs. Skinner?"

"You stay here and rest for both of us." She reached down and squeezed his hand. "I'm glad you and Fergus decided to wait until morning. I don't much like the thought of you going out on the desert at night."

"I'm glad you were thinkin' of my safety." He wouldn't let go of her fingers. "For a minute I thought you wanted me back for some other reason."

She began to rub the palm of his hand. "Oh? What in the world ever gave you that idea?"

"You've been holding on a lot tonight."

"You're my treasure, Orion Tower Skinner. Of course I hold onto you."

"An old buried treasure," he laughed.

"You aren't buried yet." She bent over, kissed his ear, and whispered, "I'll be back, Mr. Skinner. Don't go away."

Dola sauntered back into the apartment.

"Mr. Skinner?" a voice called out from the boardwalk below.

O.T. stood and walked to the railing. In the night shadows he could see someone, but he couldn't make out who it was. "Yes, what can I do for you?"

"I understand the Rokkers are staying with you. Is Mr. or Mrs. Rokker there? I'm Kelsey McDonald from the July Extension Mine."

"The Rokkers are not here, Mr. McDonald. Mr. Rokker is out of town, and Mrs. Rokker is over at the hotel."

"Which hotel is that?" McDonald asked.

"The one where you rented a room for her family."

"Eh, we didn't rent a room for them, but I did want to give them some good news."

"What do you mean, you didn't rent a room for them? I was here when a man from the Grand Union Hotel came and said a room had been rented for them."

"We didn't do it," McDonald repeated.

"Who did?"

"I have no idea. But we do have rather good news. The board of directors has a two-story house over on Sixth Avenue. We have decided to provide it free of charge to the Rokkers for a year. We want to help them during their time of great need."

"That's suddenly generous of you," O.T. said. "I'm glad to see it. It's the right thing to do. But I didn't know there was a house available in town."

"It was, eh, built for one of our directors, but he decided just a short while ago to continue to live in Tonopah instead."

"I'm glad to hear that," O.T. called down.

Corrie wandered out on the balcony. "Who are you talkin' to, Daddy?"

"Mr. McDonald from the July Extension Mine."

"Mr. Skinner, I understand you know Mr. Stuart Brannon. Is that correct?"

Corrie peeked over the railing. "I don't see no one."

"Yes, he's a family friend," O.T. called down. Then he put his arm on her shoulder. "Yes, well, it's sort of like talkin' to the Lord. You can't see Him, but you know He's there."

McDonald's voice grew a little louder. "Do you know how I can contact him in Carson City?"

Corrie meandered back into the apartment.

O.T. stared west at the electric street lamps. "No, sir, I don't. I heard that he's goin' huntin' with —"

"With President Roosevelt?" McDonald asked.

"Who's Daddy talkin' to?" O.T. heard Tommy-Blue's voice.

"Someone like the Lord," Corrie replied.

O.T. fastened the top button on his shirt. "That's what I heard."

"Daddy and the Lord are probably talkin' about you, Corrie," Rita Ann remarked.

"No, they aren't! Me and Daddy already talked to the Lord about that, and they both forgave me."

McDonald continued, "Well, if you hear from Brannon, would you tell him about the July Extension providing the house for the Rokkers?"

"Yes, but I don't understand," O.T. replied.

"Any chance you can come down? This is quite confidential."

The well-dressed man was sitting on a bench on the boardwalk in front of the restaurant when the stocking-clad O.T. Skinner reached the front door. "Did you want to come in, Mr. McDonald?"

"No, this will just take a minute."

O.T. walked out on the darkened boardwalk and sat down on the other end of the bench.

"Let me be quite candid, Mr. Skinner. The July Extension is not in the business of supplying houses to people. We owned the ground the Rokker shack was on. We deemed the house uninhabitable and didn't even know the Rokkers had moved in until the sinkhole opened up."

"Then what made you change your mind?" O.T. questioned.

"Mr. Stuart Brannon," McDonald declared.

"What did he have to do with this?"

"He strolled into my boss's office unannounced late this afternoon, laid a six-gun on the desk, and sat down. He said something to the effect, 'My name is Stuart Brannon from Arizona. Perhaps you've heard of me. I'm on my way up to Carson City to hunt antelope with President Roosevelt. He asked me to bring him a report on how things were going in Goldfield. Now what is this rumor that you blew up some folks' house and heartlessly refuse to replace it?'"

O.T. stretched his jeans-covered legs out in front of him. "Pop Brannon said that?"

"Stuart Brannon, the notorious Arizona gunman, with a Colt single-action army revolver within reach, said that."

"And how did your boss respond, Mr. Mc-Donald?"

"His eyes grew big, and sweat popped out on his forehead. The jist of it is," McDonald continued, "the Rokkers get the house, and we want Mr. Brannon to know that before he meets with the President."

"Perhaps a telegram sent to the governor's office will reach him," O.T. suggested.

"I certainly hope so. We don't need a bad report on the Goldfield mines. There is difficulty enough now with the miners' union." McDonald stood up. "Now I need to go talk to the Rokkers."

"They will be delighted, I'm sure."

"In which hotel are they staying?"

"The Grand Union, I heard," O.T. said.

"I didn't think they had any rooms available for months."

"Well, someone got them one."

O.T. watched the short man in the three-piece suit, white shirt, and black tie disappear into the night. *An old, white-haired man with a Colt .44. Maybe the Old West hasn't been completely tamed. Oh, my, I would have liked to have seen that mine director's face! It would've had more chagrin than the devil's when Jesus walked out of the tomb!*

O.T. lay on top of the comforter in the pitch-black wearing jeans.

No shirt.

No socks.

Just jeans.

His right arm cradled Dola's shoulders.

He could feel the warmth of her body and the beat of her heart through the thin flannel nightshirt she wore. He stared at the dark ceiling.

Her lips were only an inch from his ear. "What's the matter, honey?" she whispered.

His voice was low, peaceful. "Can't sleep, darlin'."

"You worried about Mr. Rokker?"

"Yeah, I'm worried that he's missin' out on everything. He wasn't here for the storm, for Nellie's collapse, for the house being ripped apart, for it sinking into the ground, and he's not here when the July Extension gives them a free house for a year. It's strange he's not a part of any of his family's most important happenings."

"What can you do about it?"

"I'm thinkin' I need to take care of my own

job and my own family."

Dola propped herself up on her elbow. "You mean, you aren't going to go look for him?"

"I'll go. But I don't feel motivated to be gone a whole week. Just a day or so out and a day or so back, unless I find some lead that makes me want to press on. The storm has been over for two days. If he died in it, I'll never find him. If he didn't . . . then he can find his way back. I have no reason to think he's in trouble. It's 1906. He's not goin' to get ambushed by Indians."

"But you'll take Fergus, won't you?" she asked.

"Yep."

Dola flopped her head back down on the pillow.

"Why don't you come with me?" he whispered.

"What?" she croaked.

He kissed her cheek and put his lips to her ear. "Let Fergus stay with the kids, and you and I go for a trip."

"Nice dream, old man. I have a family to raise and a job to take care of."

"So do I," he replied.

Her eyes were wide open. "Then why all this talk about us going someplace?"

O.T. let his hand drift to hers, and he laced his callused fingers into her callused fingers. "I just don't feel like leavin' all of you. We've been on the road together for so many months that I just don't want to go anywhere without you."

She raised his hand to her lips and brushed a kiss across it. "Maybe you should take one of the kids."

"I'll go, Daddy!" Corrie called out. "I'll be very good and cook and —"

"Corrie can't cook as well as I can," Rita Ann declared. "Let me go, Daddy!"

"Cook? Daddy can cook," Tommy-Blue hollered from the dark. "I should go and collect ore samples. I bet there's a whole 'nother Goldfield waitin' to be discovered!"

"That's a gruesome thought," O.T. murmured.

Dola rolled over on her back, O.T.'s arm still under her neck. "Well, so much for a private conversation. It's a wonder little brother didn't volunteer to go."

"My mama's purdy!" Punky called out.

"Can I go, Daddy?" Corrie pleaded. "Please! I promise to be good!"

"You girls need to stay and help Mama with the restaurant," O.T. insisted.

"Then I'll go," Tommy-Blue shouted.

"That's not fair, Daddy!" Rita Ann whined. "Just because he's a boy is no reason he should —"

"I'll take you all," O.T. boomed.

Dola sat straight up in bed. "What?"

"If you can hire another girl to help out, I'll take the whole passel," he offered.

"Yeah!" Corrie yelled.

"You've been out in the desert heat too long, old man," Dola chided.

"You don't mean Punky too, do you?" Rita Ann called out.

"My mama's purdy," Punky squealed.

Dola flopped back down. "We're getting carried away."

"I'm serious," O.T. insisted. "I'll take the kids. You'll have a busy Saturday. Then Sunday you'll have to yourself. When's the last time you had a day to yourself?"

"I've . . . I've never in my life had a day to myself."

"Well, you got one now. We're goin' campin'."

"We've been camping ever since we left Oklahoma," she reminded him.

"Yes, but we won't need the tent. We'll just sleep under the stars."

"I ain't goin' to sleep in no snake hole like Jared," Tommy-Blue announced.

"You kids can sleep in the wagon."

"You better plan on leavin' little punkin with me," Dola said.

"Oh, no, I insist on taking him," O.T. declared.

"Okay," she concurred.

"What?" he said.

"I said, okay. You can take him too."

O.T. rubbed his unshaven cheeks. "Just like that?"

"You aren't bluffing me, Orion Tower Skinner, are you?"

"No, ma'am."

"Do I have to watch Punky?" Rita Ann groaned.

"I'll watch him, Daddy!" Corrie volunteered.

"Can I drive, Daddy? I bet I can drive our wagon as good as Corrie," Tommy-Blue boasted.

"We'll see," O.T. said.

"Tell me again how long you'll be gone," Dola requested.

"We'll probably be home by Monday night."

"When are we going to leave?" Rita Ann asked.

"As soon as Mama hires another girl in the mornin'."

"What if Mr. Rokker comes home tonight?" Tommy-Blue asked. "Can we go look for him anyway?"

"If he's home, we'll still go."

"And leave Mama?" Corrie added.

"My mama's purdy," Punky chirped.

"We'll go and give Mama a day off, no matter what," O.T. maintained.

Dola snuggled up in his arm. "I love you, Orion Tower Skinner."

"Are you two going to kiss and stuff?" Rita Ann challenged from the dark.

"What kind of stuff?" Corrie probed.

"Never mind," Rita Ann said.

"Does anyone in this room mind if I kiss my wife?" O.T. announced.

"On the lips?" Tommy-Blue asked.

"Mama, you'd better kiss Daddy on the lips

because he needs to shave, and his cheek scratches," Corrie advised.

"Is there any other advice I should have before I kiss this man?" Dola asked.

"Don't slobber. He doesn't like slobbery kisses on the lips," Corrie suggested.

"Thank you all," Dola laughed.

"Well?" Rita Ann pressed.

"Well, what?" Dola replied.

"Did you kiss him yet?"

"Yes, several times."

"Really? Wow, Mama's fast!" Tommy-Blue declared.

"Are we really going in the morning, Daddy?" Corrie asked.

"Yep. Now that's enough talk. I want everyone to go back to sleep."

Dola rolled to her side and laid her head on his chest. "You have got to be kidding, Mr. Skinner. None of us will be able to sleep now!"

"My mama's purrrrrr . . ." Punky's voice faded to silence.

"Well," Dola whispered, "maybe one of us will sleep."

Dola stood on the front porch of the restaurant at daybreak. In the seat of the farm wagon sat O.T., Punky, and Fergus. Corrie stood behind her daddy, arms around his neck. Rita Ann and Tommy-Blue sat behind them on a recently attached wooden bench. In the back were stacked several bundles.

275

"I can't believe you are really going through with this," Dola said.

"And I can't believe a very sturdy girl named Lupe Martinez showed up at the kitchen looking for work before daylight," O.T. replied. "The Lord must have sent her."

"Omega says she doesn't speak much English but is a very good cook."

O.T. pushed his hat back. "Are you going to be all right?"

"Me?" Dola laughed. "Mr. Skinner, let me remind you that you have charge of four children. I am expecting you to bring four children home. No less, no more. All I have is seventy-five hungry men to feed, and I now have three capable helpers."

"I still think I have the better end of the deal."

Dola carefully surveyed the full wagon. "I'm sure you're right about that. Did you remember everything?"

"That is yet to be determined."

"Do you have the shotgun?"

"What do we need a shotgun for, Mama?" Tommy-Blue asked.

"To shoot snakes," she replied.

"I have my Shakespeare book," Rita Ann said.

"I have my gold pan," Tommy-Blue added.

"I have new boots." Fergus grinned.

"Punky has a ball!" The two-year-old held up a tattered wad of string.

"I have my daddy!" Corrie said.

Dola walked over to the edge of the unpainted farm wagon. "And what do you have, Mr. Skinner?"

"Treasures untold, Mrs. Skinner."

She reached up and grasped both girls' hands. "I will miss you all terribly. If you want to hurry home, that is quite all right with me!"

They waved.

And shouted.

And giggled.

And then were gone.

Dola stood on the porch until the wagon was completely out of sight.

It's like an era changing, Lord. I don't know what it's moving to or exactly where it's been . . . but seeing them roll away . . . something's changing. Is it possible that they can actually survive a few days without me? Is it possible that I can survive a few days without them? That seems more unlikely.

"Are you Mrs. Skinner?"

This is crazy, Lord. Who has ever heard of a woman with young children having time to herself? I believe I will take a long nap after breakfast.

"Excuse me, ma'am, I have a delivery for . . ."

And tonight I will fill the tub with steaming water and soak and soak and —

"Mrs. Skinner?"

She turned to see a gray-haired man on the bench of a one-horse paneled wagon. "Are you Mrs. Skinner?" he asked again.

"Yes, excuse me. My mind was elsewhere."

"That's good. For a minute I figured you was deaf."

"What can I do for you?"

"I have a delivery for the restaurant," he announced.

"All the kitchen deliveries are at the alley door." She motioned.

"This ain't food. It's for the dining room."

Dola brushed her hair back from her forehead and stepped closer to the wagon that smelled a little like perfume. "What is it?"

"Twenty-four red roses in them little tiny crystal vases. One for each table in the place," he declared.

She stared at the old man's steel-gray eyes. "I beg your pardon?"

"Yep," he grinned. "Them roses came in fresh last night on the train all the way from Burbank, California."

She folded her arms across her chest and could feel her ribs. "But I didn't order fresh roses!"

"Didn't say you did." The old man climbed down to the street and looped the lead lines around the long handle of the hand brake. "They are a gift."

"From whom?" she demanded.

"Don't know. I'm jist the delivery man. I reckon they wanted to surprise you. Somebody rich, no doubt. They sent 'em straight up from southern California. You don't know George

Wingfield, do you?"

"Eh, no, I don't."

"How about Colin Maddison, the second?"

"With two d's?"

"Yep, that's the one."

"No, I don't know him either, but I met his son."

"This ain't no kid. And them tiny vases ain't free," he continued. "No, ma'am, there's a big-time spender here. I was told to put one on ever' table in the restaurant. Shall I go ahead?"

"Yes, by all means." Dola stared to the east. *A big-time spender who knows how many tables we have in the restaurant? Lucky Jack! Never underestimate the remorse of a repentant rich man!*

O.T. turned the wagon west just past the cemetery. By the time he reached the flanks of the Montezuma Mountains to the west, Punky was asleep on top of the pile of blankets in the back of the wagon. Tommy-Blue was drawing a picture of each dry stream bed and arroyo, rating it for possible mining potential. Corrie continued to stand and clutch her father. Rita Ann recited sonnets to a dozing old Paiute.

" 'Alas, 'tis true, I have gone here and there, and made myself a motley to the view,' " she droned.

"Darlin', perhaps Fergus has had enough recitin'," O.T. cautioned.

With long gray braid hanging down his white-shirted back, his wide-brimmed black felt hat pulled low, Fergus opened one wrinkle-encased eye. "No, no. Let her go on. I enjoy each word."

"See!" Rita Ann rejoiced. "Fergus likes Shakespeare!"

"I can't understand a word you say," the old man replied, "but you say it so soft and sweet. The tone is like flute music. It is easy to sleep to."

O.T. smiled. "Well, see there. The ol' Bard of Avon is still good for something!"

" 'As a decrepit father takes delight to see his active child do deeds of youth —' "

"No more decrepit-father sonnets!" he complained.

Corrie held up her round, little face in triumph. "My daddy is not old!"

"Well, my daddy is!" Rita Ann stuck out her tongue at her sister.

"Can I drive the wagon?" Corrie asked.

"I get to drive first," Rita Ann demanded. "I'm the oldest."

"Corrie can drive first. She asked first," O.T. replied.

Corrie crawled around in front of O.T. and gingerly sat on his knee as he gave her the lead lines.

"Wow, Daddy, look over there!" Tommy-Blue pointed.

O.T. glanced to the north. With the sun still low in the east, shadows filled the deep arroyo. He looked for movement. For something out of place. For an animal. A man. Anything.

"Okay, son, I'm lookin', but I don't see anything."

"Can't you see the dirt?"

"Yep. I can see that."

"Don't it look like just about the best diggin' dirt you ever saw?"

"It sort of all looks the same to me, son. Always the same colors — buckskin, alkali, yellow, rust — that's all we can see in any direction."

Fergus opened one eye and then closed it. "There's nothin' over there," he mumbled.

"How do you know?" Tommy-Blue said.

"Tom Fisherman dug test holes in that arroyo."

Tommy-Blue scooted up to the front seat as the wagon pitched and rattled along. "You know Tom Fisherman?"

"He is a lousy shot," Fergus replied.

Tommy-Blue's mouth dropped open. "What do you mean?"

"He couldn't hit an antelope at 100 yards with a .45-70. That's why he has to keep findin' gold. He has to buy food."

"I still think we should stop and gather a sample. When are we going to stop for a nooner?" Tommy-Blue asked.

"How about noon?" O.T. suggested.

After a shadeless lunch stop, they continued to trek west. The sun was just touching the western horizon when they stopped next to a half-standing adobe wall. A lone Joshua tree stood guard about 100 yards down the draw.

Rita Ann and Corrie pulled out the blankets and food basket as O.T. washed off Punky's sweaty, dusty face.

Tommy-Blue ran around the short wall. "Did this used to be a town, Fergus?" he shouted.

"I don't remember this wall."

"Don't remember? You've never been here?"

"There is a bitter-water spring down by the Joshua tree. But there never used to be a wall."

"Well, someone built it," Tommy-Blue insisted.

"Yes. I wonder why I can't remember it." The old Paiute patted the top of the adobe. "My people did not build it. When I was young, we all lived in brush arbors. We did not build adobe houses."

"Perhaps it was the ancient ones, like over in Mesa Verde," Rita Ann suggested.

"It could have been the Spanish," Fergus added. "They had some kind of trail from the mines of California to Santa Fe."

"Like Don Fernando's gold?" O.T. asked.

"Yes. But the Don Fernando site is days away . . . I think. . . . I am not sure the Spanish trail was all that successful. I am not sure anyone made it across this northern route. Why have I never seen a wall only one day from Rabbit Springs?"

"Can I prospect while you set up camp? There ain't much daylight left," Tommy-Blue requested.

"Yes, but you have to fill in every hole you dig," O.T. instructed.

"I do? Nobody else does it," Tommy-Blue whined. "Why do I have to?"

O.T. put his hand on his son's shoulder. "Because nobody else does it."

Heat from the desert floor still radiated up through the brown wool blanket even after the sun went down.

"Daddy, Punky's face is dirty," Rita Ann reported.

"I just washed it," he maintained.

She pointed across the blanket at the two-year-old. "Well, look at it."

Punky's forehead, nose, and round chin were smeared with yellowish dirt. The toddler held a slice of apple in his hand. "I'm purdy!" he announced.

"That word has new meanin' when you use it, li'l brother," O.T. laughed. "Where's Tommy-Blue?"

"He's still diggin' his pretend mine on the other side of the adobe wall," Corrie replied.

Fergus studied the boiled egg in his hand as if it were a rare jewel. "He is the hardest-working boy I have ever known. He reminds me of my cousin's husband — you know, the one who used to live in Goldfield but has not come back."

"Does your cousin's husband look for gold?" Corrie asked.

"He looked for diamonds," Fergus said. He

slipped the entire peeled egg into his mouth.

"There aren't any diamonds in Nevada, are there?" Rita Ann asked.

"Mmhtphitrrrm."

"Don't talk with mouth full!" Punky instructed.

Fergus took a swig of water from the canteen, shoved the cork back in, and handed it to Corrie. "There are diamonds in Nevada. You just have to know where to look. My cousin's husband found lots of them."

"Where?" Rita Ann asked.

"In Carson City."

"There's a diamond mine in Carson City?" Rita Ann asked.

A wide, leathery smile broke across Fergus's face. "No. He found them at a jewelry store."

Rita Ann's hand went over her mouth. "Did he steal diamonds?"

"Yes, and now he's in the state prison, working very hard. I told you he was a hard-working fellow!" Fergus began to crack another boiled egg. "I wonder if my cousin went to see her husband in Carson City. Perhaps I should walk up there."

"Walk?" O.T. chided. "You have enough funds to take the stage and the train."

"Then my legs would feel neglected."

O.T. glanced back at the adobe wall and shouted, "Tommy-Blue, come eat your supper!"

A high-pitched reply filtered back over the

wall. "Ah, Daddy, the diggin' is gettin' easy!"

Fergus stood straight up. "That is not good."

"What is not good?" Rita Ann asked.

"Easy digging. This soil is packed tight, except for a layer of storm sand. There should not be any easy digging around here," Fergus declared.

O.T. stood, picked up Punky, and trooped after the old Indian. Rita Ann and Corrie followed.

On the back side of the adobe wall, a dirty-faced Tommy-Blue had a two-foot hole scooped out. "See how easy this is?"

"You should not dig there!" Fergus commanded.

Tommy-Blue stood up. Sweat and dirt smeared his forehead. "Why?"

"That looks like a grave," Fergus said.

Tommy-Blue jumped back. "Really!"

"And a fresh one . . . dug after the sandstorm. That soil has never had any rain on it," O.T. added. Punky squirmed his way down to the ground.

"But — but," Tommy-Blue stammered, "there ain't no tombstone or nothin'."

"Perhaps they don't want anyone to know it's a grave," Rita Ann suggested. "Maybe there has been a murder!" She wrung her hands. " 'Out! Out, brief candle —' "

"Rita Ann!" O.T. interrupted.

"Maybe it's an Indian grave," Corrie guessed.

"Not unless a white man killed him and

buried him," Fergus replied. "The grave runs north and south. Paiutes and Mojaves bury their dead east and west."

"Why is that?" Tommy-Blue asked.

"So they can see the rising sun," Fergus explained.

Tommy-Blue stared down at his hole. "What are we going to do, Daddy?"

"We will fill in the hole and go eat supper."

Fergus began to pace off the length of the loose dirt. Punky followed, trying to take long steps.

"What are you doing?" Corrie asked.

"The hole is over six feet long. A big person is buried here," Fergus asserted.

"May God have mercy on his soul. You children go eat. I'll fill in Tommy-Blue's hole." O.T. waved them off with a flip of his hand.

The underarms, collar, and back of O.T.'s white cotton shirt dripped with sweat when he finished covering the hole. The adobe wall kept the others partially out of sight. He leaned on the shovel and stared down.

A grave of a big man. Not an Indian. Someone out here who had no partner to tote him to town. Or no one who knew who he was. Someone hidden behind the wall. Out of sight.

Elias Rokker is a big man.

If it was just me and Fergus . . .

But it isn't.

Some things might be best left buried.

The dining room was scrubbed up by 10:30 A.M.

The kitchen by 11:00.

Omega, Haylee, and Lupe left soon afterward.

With the smell of peach pies cooling on the kitchen counter, Dola carried a cup of coffee up the stairs to the apartment. She propped the double doors open with red bricks and looked around.

Every square inch of this room reminds me of those who are not here. Rita's neatly made bed. Tommy-Blue's messy one. Orion's old hat and the smell of a sweaty jacket. There's Punky's stick bat and Corrie's picture of Dan Patch.

It's quiet.

She walked over to the sofa and picked up Tommy-Blue's dirty shirt.

I can't remember anything so quiet.

Dola dropped the shirt into the wicker basket and strolled along the foot of the tall featherbed.

Maybe that time before Rita Ann was born, and Orion and I were living in the barn at Guthrie trying to get our house built, and it got so still right before the sulfur storm hit that we could hear our hearts beat . . .

She sauntered to the double balcony doors and swung them open. A warm desert breeze rushed past her.

Course, we were young then.

She walked out on the balcony and laid her hands on the unpainted, rough pine railing.

With good ears.

She studied the busy, dusty street below.

And good hearts.

I have a feeling this will be the longest few days of my adult life. I will take a nap . . . in the middle of the day.

It sounds sinful, Lord. But all good gifts come down from above, and I will thank You for it.

Dola suddenly realized that a man in a dark brown three-piece suit, straddling a long-legged black horse parked in front of the restaurant, was looking up at her. The dimpled smile caught her eye.

"I hear you found Corrie Lou," he called up.

"Mr. Gately, you look very handsome today."

"Better than last time you saw me?"

"Well, yes, I don't believe you were at your best."

"My apologies, Mrs. Skinner." He tipped his wide-brimmed, black beaver felt hat. "I want you to know I'm not terribly proud of that moment."

"And I regret it if I sounded self-righteous. We are all sinners, saved by the same Jesus," she asserted.

"You had a right to expect better from me. Shoot, Dola Mae — I mean Mrs. Skinner, *I* expected better."

"Mr. Gately, any man so contrite may certainly call me Dola Mae."

"Thank you, ma'am."

"And I want to thank you for your kind acts as well. A truly contrite heart is evidenced by grace and generosity, is it not?"

"You mean, hirin' LaPorte to take you around town?"

"Yes, that was a great help, even though the little scamp had snuck off and hid in her father's wagon."

"And did the Rokkers enjoy the hotel room last night?"

"Lucky Jack, did you pay for that as well?"

"Charlie Fred and Wasco chipped in. We gave them our rooms, but I hear the Rokkers have a house now."

"That's my understanding as well," she replied. "I greatly appreciate your assistance. At times, you are certainly a prince."

"Dola Mae, bein' rich is sort of new to me. But if a man can't use his funds to help his friends and loved ones, well . . . what's the use in havin' them?"

"I trust I would feel the same should I ever have wealth," she remarked.

"Some figure the Skinners are the richest folks in Goldfield. Rich in blessings."

"Now just who thinks that, Lucky Jack?"

"Me, for one. I'd trade the gold mine in a flash for what O.T. has."

Dola could feel her face flush. "I don't think he would trade you."

"No, ma'am." Lucky Jack grinned. "Don't

blame him. He would be gettin' a raw deal."

"I missed seeing you and the boys at breakfast," she admitted.

"We spent the night at the mine and then came to town and bought ourselves some new clothes."

"I can see. You certainly look like a prosperous mine owner."

"Just a mine lease, but, my-o-my, it's a rich one!"

Dola brushed the hair back off her ear. *I should have at least combed my hair after breakfast. I must look rather . . . rather dull and frightful.* "Well, don't go spending all your money on roses, Mr. Gately. Although it was quite a lovely gesture, and I appreciate it greatly."

Gately rubbed his clean-shaven chin. "Roses?"

"Don't be coy, Mr. Gately. When all those roses and vases showed up this morning, I knew it was you who had sent them."

He pulled off his new hat and ran his long fingers through his neatly trimmed blond hair. "You got roses? That's a capital idea. I surely wish I had thought of it. But I have to be honest — it wasn't me."

Her shoulders and jaw sagged. "It wasn't?"

"No, ma'am. I doubt it was Charley Fred or Wasco either, but I'll check with them. Fresh roses, huh? I'll look forward to that tonight. I haven't sniffed a fresh rose since workin' in the warden's garden."

"Where?" she asked.

"Never mind. I'll visit later, Dola Mae." He tipped his hat and rode west.

Dola left the balcony doors open and returned to the apartment. She sat on the edge of the bed and tugged off her boots. Then she peeled the white stockings down slowly and rubbed between each toe.

Finally she unfastened the top button on the collar of her light green dress and lay on her back across the featherbed. The comforter felt soft and almost cool.

She stared at the cracking white paint on the ceiling.

Every time she closed her eyes, they seemed to swing open like a broken gate.

If Lucky Jack didn't send those roses . . .

Nine

A wagon.

Four kids.

Two mules.

Two men.

One twenty-foot-long, three-foot-high, two-foot-thick adobe wall.

No water.

The camp was primitive.

They abandoned the wall and moved down near the lone Joshua tree and a sandy indentation that Fergus claimed had once been a spring.

The sun set without a trace of wind, and the cool desert night settled on the hot earth like a heavy coat on a warm day. While it was still twilight, three bedrolls were laid out in the wagon and three underneath. O.T. rubbed down the mules.

"Daddy, I thought there was goin' to be water here," Tommy-Blue noted.

"The springs must have dried up for the summer," O.T. suggested.

Fergus rubbed his chin and stared up the arroyo at the adobe wall. "I haven't been here for a long time. A very long time. I wonder why that is? Perhaps there never was any water here. I don't even remember seeing that wall. It is strange."

"There had to be water here at one time. Why else was this house built?" Corrie reasoned.

"What house? There is only a solid wall — no doors, no windows, nothing!" Rita Ann retorted.

"Maybe it was a fort," Tommy-Blue offered. "They built it so they could hide back there and fight off the savage —" He glanced over at Fergus and swallowed hard. "Eh, Indians."

"Maybe they never got a chance to finish it," Corrie said. "Maybe they were all chased off."

"Or slaughtered," Fergus added.

"Or died of thirst!" Tommy-Blue ventured, licking his lips.

"We have enough water to drink," O.T. informed them. "But we don't have enough to swim in."

Rita Ann pushed her glasses up on her nose and tugged on her pigtails. "Daddy, where is Punky going to sleep? He's not going to be in the wagon with us, is he?"

"Little Punky's sleeping down here with me and Fergus."

"I'm medium," the toddler announced.

"Well, medium rare. You sleep at the ground level so you don't fall out of the wagon," O.T. instructed.

"I bet if we dug out that sanded-up spring, we could find water," Tommy-Blue asserted.

"You go diggin', and you'll only get more thirsty. We've got water for three days, and we'll have to make it last," O.T. maintained. He led them back over to the bedrolls and blankets at the fireless campsite.

"I ain't goin' to drink more than my share," Tommy-Blue said. "Maybe there's water jist one foot below the surface. Wouldn't that be somethin'?"

"If there was water within a foot, the soil would feel damp," Fergus remarked.

Tommy-Blue stamped the ground hard. "Maybe it's two feet down."

"Then the soil would smell like the air right before a rain," the old Paiute noted. "It doesn't."

They all sat down, except Punky and Tommy-Blue. "Maybe it's three feet down. Can I dig three feet, Daddy?"

"It's almost dark, Tommy-Blue," O.T. replied. "Big sis, you want to dig us out something for a snack?"

"I can still see," Tommy-Blue insisted. "I don't have to see much to dig."

"He is a very persistent fellow," Fergus observed.

"Well, stay away from the wall up there. Don't get your boots full of sand. And don't dig deeper than your belly button. This kind of soil will cave in on you."

Tommy-Blue's eyes widened. "But what if I find good color and need to go deeper?"

O.T. cleared his throat. "You heard me."

Tommy-Blue picked up the short-handled

shovel. "Okay, who wants to go help me dig?"

" 'How heavy do I journey on the way, when what I see, my weary travel's end . . . ,' " Rita Ann recited.

Tommy-Blue wrinkled his nose. "What does that mean?"

Rita Ann inspected a wedge of white cheese that she had pulled out of the cotton sack. "I'm not about to traipse over there in the dark and dig a hole in the ground."

Tommy-Blue circled the campsite. "What about you, Corrie?"

"I ain't diggin' nothin'. What if it's another grave?"

"It ain't a grave. It's a well. A spring. They don't dig graves in four-foot circles," Tommy-Blue contended.

"What if there are snakes in there?" she countered.

"Why would snakes be in an old sunken well?"

" 'Cause snakes get thirsty too."

"No, they don't. Snakes don't drink water, do they, Daddy?"

O.T. finished brushing Ada and strolled back to the wagon. "I imagine they do."

"I ain't never seen a snake get a drink."

Corrie rubbed her nose and wiped her hand on her dress. "There's a lot of things snakes do that you've never seen."

"Well, there ain't no snakes over there. Are you comin' with me, Corrie?" Tommy-Blue challenged.

"Nope. I'm stayin' with my daddy."

"Punky will help!" The toddler spoke up.

"I'd rather dig by myself." Tommy-Blue stomped across the camp. "Can I take the lantern?"

"No, we need it here. We only have one lantern," O.T. explained.

"But — but it will be pitch-black before I get three feet down."

"Maybe you should wait for mornin'," O.T. offered.

"I ain't waitin'. I'm goin' to dig. And if I find water, I'll name it Tommy-Blue Springs. And if I find gold, I won't have to share it with no one!"

"Stay within sight. I don't want to have to look for you," O.T. warned.

"If I had the lantern, I could watch for snakes," Tommy-Blue grumbled as he trudged off toward the sunken well.

"There goes the hardest-working boy in Nevada," Fergus declared. "Does he ever stop moving?"

O.T. wiped the blade of his pocketknife off on his dusty jeans and cut a thick slab of cheese. "Only when he's asleep."

"He don't stop movin' even then," Corrie commented.

"Look who's talking," Rita Ann snapped.

"You snore!" Corrie declared to her sister.

"I do not!" Rita Ann gasped. "Everyone knows it's Tommy-Blue who snores in our family."

"She snores, doesn't she, Daddy?" Corrie draped herself over O.T.'s knee.

"You wouldn't know. You're always asleep," Rita Ann said.

Corrie took a bite of cold biscuit. "Sometimes you snore," she murmured.

Rita Ann sat up with perfectly straight posture. "I do not! Sometimes my nose is stopped up, and I have difficulty breathing, but I do not snore!"

"Girls!" O.T. said. "There must be something else you can talk about. Pick another subject."

"All Rita Ann wants to talk about is boys," Corrie grumbled.

"That isn't true!" Rita Ann shot back.

"It is too!"

O.T. leaned back and laid his head on the blanket, staring at the stars. *Mama, I hope you're enjoying a peaceful, quiet evenin'.*

"Hey, ever'one, I found something!" Tommy-Blue shouted from the distant shadows.

O.T. sat up and peered through the twilight.

"Is it alive?" Rita Ann queried.

"No!" They could hear Tommy-Blue's laughter.

"Is it buried treasure?" Corrie called.

"No . . . it's sort of like a hat!"

"Bring it over here to the lantern and let us see it," O.T. instructed.

"I can't," Tommy-Blue hollered.

"Why not?" Rita Ann probed.

"I got my boot stuck."

"Stuck in what?" O.T. asked.

"In a hole."

O.T. stood and grabbed the lantern.

"Carry me, Daddy!" Punky called out.

"I believe I'll go see this buried hat." Fergus struggled to his feet.

"I'm goin' too." Corrie leaped to her feet.

"I'm certainly not going to stay here alone in the dark," Rita Ann declared.

Tommy-Blue stood at the bottom of a dirt basin not much bigger than a bathtub. It had been shoveled out about as deep as his knee in the middle of the hole. His left heel was crammed into an opening about the size of a large biscuit. The flickering lantern light reflected off his dirty face. "Is that a snake hole?" he asked.

"Did you say snake or stake?" Fergus grinned.

"Snake."

"No, I believe it is a stake hole," the Paiute explained.

"Stake hole?"

"Now I remember this place. There was a sign by the well that said Stinking Water. That must be the stake hole where the sign used to go. But I do not remember the short adobe wall. The sandstorm must have uncovered it."

"Stinking water?" Tommy-Blue jerked up his foot and scampered out of the hole. "Maybe this hole is deep enough. Ain't nothin' down here anyway."

The old Indian picked up the dirty brown felt bowler. "You found a nice hat. Except for the hole."

"Hole?" Tommy-Blue quizzed. "I didn't see a hole."

"It's a bullet hole!" Rita Ann exclaimed.

"Looks too big for a bullet," O.T. mused.

"It's a bowler," Corrie added. "Mr. Rokker was wearing a bowler when we saw him last."

O.T. glanced at Fergus.

The expressionless old Indian slowly nodded his head.

Punky was the first to fall asleep.

Rita Ann was the last.

At least, O.T. hoped she was asleep.

He stared east, waiting to see the moon rise under Venus and Capella. To the southeast he spotted Phoenix. In the west, Vega. He propped his hands under his head and studied the Little Dipper hanging down from Polaris. Straight above him Andromeda sparkled like a twinkling umbrella.

You went and named me Orion, Mama, and I've been gazin' at the stars ever since. Someday . . . someday they will roll back like a curtain . . . Oh, won't that be a sight to see, and the Lord'll come back ridin' that big white horse.

Now, Lord, I wouldn't mind it if You decided to come back tonight, 'cause I surely don't want to do what I know I have to do.

His hands were still propped under his head. Both were numb when the moon finally peeked over the eastern mountains and cast a pale glow across the desert. He waited half an hour and then sat up. Punky lay next to him. The toddler had kicked off his brown wool blanket and slept on his stomach, his overall-clad bottom pushed up in the air.

On the other side of the toddler, Fergus lay on his back. He was on top of the blankets, fully dressed, his hat perched on his face, his bony brown fingers laced together on his thin chest. O.T. rose to his feet slowly and peered over the sideboards of the wagon at three sleeping children.

Two sprawled across their blankets.

One looked as if she had not moved an inch since he had tucked her in and said prayers.

Another was definitely snoring.

He studied each sleeper for movement as he crept across the campsite and picked up the shovel. He slowly trudged out across the desert floor up toward the adobe wall. Halfway there, he turned to study the camp once more.

I have to do it, Lord. You know I have to do it. His family has a right to know if Elias Rokker is buried behind that wall.

The wall ran north and south. The moon cast a shadow where he needed to dig.

It will be an hour before I can see anything on this side of the wall. Didn't count on the shadow. I could go back and try to wake up again. Or I could sit here . . .

O.T. laid the shovel on the dirt and squatted down. He ran his fingers through the loose, dry soil.

I can dig down a couple feet in the dark. Tommy-Blue went about that far. I'll scoop it out and then wait for more light.

Within minutes he was sweating through his white cotton shirt. O.T. slipped off his suspenders and let them hang at his side. Each shovelful was slowly removed and carefully stacked to the west. He unfastened several buttons on his shirt.

Like a dim sundial, the wall shadow crept east as the moon rose over the desert. When the moon finally got straight above, it revealed a rectangular hole about six feet long and three feet wide, running parallel to the wall.

O.T. pulled out his bandanna and wiped his forehead. *I should have worn my hat just to keep the sweat out of my eyes.* He stared back down at the hole. *The next two feet are crucial. Relatives would bury a man six feet down, but no one wants to dig that deep for a stranger . . . or someone you murdered. Four feet would be the maximum.*

At three feet his back hurt, the muscles in his arms burned, and his legs felt stiff. Even in the slight coolness of the desert summer night, sweat dripped off his nose and chin.

There is nothin' here . . . no sign of anything . . . but it's been dug recently. Dug since the sandstorm.

Dug and filled in. And there isn't any real good reason to dig out here except to bury something out of sight.

Only Tommy-Blue would dig a test hole in such a site.

And no one would dig a big rectangular test hole.

He stooped down and ran his fingers straight down into the dirt. It was warm. Dry. Rough.

Lord, this ground is drier than our claim back in Guthrie. Nothing would rot. . . . Nothing would decompose. Nothing would spoil.

I hope.

The soil had not changed when the hole was waist deep. He crawled up out of the hole. The big moon was high above and lit the desert like a dying lantern. Standing next to the wall, he could sense a little air movement. O.T. stared down at the yawning black hole.

That's deep enough. Why on earth would anyone dig deeper?

Leaving the shovel propped against the adobe wall, O.T. trudged slowly back down toward camp. No one had changed position except Corrie. One arm flopped across her sister's legs.

He squatted down next to the crate and felt inside for a long iron bar they used to hold pots off the fire, if indeed they ever had enough wood for a fire. The iron rod felt cold in his callused hand as he pulled it out. He carried it at his side as he trudged back out in the moonlight to the adobe wall.

Staring down at the hole, he wiped his un-shaven chin and let out a slow, deep sigh. *Well . . . it's time to find out if I just worked myself into a sweat for nothin'.*

O.T. jumped into the hole with the shovel in one hand and the rod in the other. With both hands holding one end of the rod like a sword hilt, he stabbed the desert soil.

At one foot down, it hit something solid.

A cold chill rolled across each bead of sweat on his forehead.

He probed at both ends of the hole and found the same barricade at one foot below the surface.

It could be bedrock. This is the desert. It's dry. How much topsoil can there be? Maybe it's just a natural geological barrier.

And it could be something buried.

Or someone.

Tommy-Blue found Rokker's hat down at the well.

Or at least a hat like Rokker's.

And it did have a hole in it.

That doesn't mean . . . Lord, have mercy on the Rokkers.

O.T. dug straight down one more foot in the middle of the hole and struck something solid. He scooped the dirt off and could feel rough-cut, splintery wood.

Wood?

Rough wood?

A coffin maybe?

Who in the world would haul a coffin out here?

No one would murder Rokker and then bury him five feet deep in a coffin.

Maybe it's old wood.

Nothing would decompose in this hot, dry sand.

An old coffin?

But the dirt is freshly dug.

And I have to dig off all the dirt just to peek in.

It was almost an hour later when O.T. scraped off the last of the dirt and stared through the night shadows at the lid of the box at the bottom of the hole. He shouldered the shovel and wiped the sweat off his forehead.

I've been diggin' half the night to find out what's down here, and now I can't get up the nerve —

"Are you goin' to open that box or not?" The voice was deep, gravelly, old.

The sweat on O.T.'s neck felt as if it had turned to snow as he spun around. Fergus leaned over the adobe wall.

"Yeah, Daddy, we want to see."

He spied three sets of eyes peering over at him.

"What are you kids doing here?"

"What are you doing, Daddy?" Rita Ann asked.

"Well, I'm — I've got to — I just . . ."

"You're lookin' to see if Mr. Rokker is buried there, aren't you?" Corrie quizzed.

"Yep. I had to know."

"Why are you diggin' at night, Daddy?" Tommy-Blue asked.

"I didn't want you to have to see this."

"I'll close my eyes," Corrie offered.

"Where's Punky?" O.T. questioned.

"He's sleeping," Rita Ann reported.

O.T. stared through the moonlight at the wooden lid. "I'm not going to let any of you see something gruesome. So I want you to turn around and sit down in the dirt against the wall. Let me take a look in here first. Fergus, come around and help me pull this lid off."

"I do not like dead bodies," the Paiute returned. "I will stay with the children."

"I'll help you, Daddy," Tommy-Blue offered.

"No, no, you stay there. You sit down, all of you."

"We are sitting down," Fergus reported.

"What did you find, Daddy?" Corrie called out.

O.T. tugged on the lid at one end. "This looks like hand-cut rough cedar . . ."

"Not the box," Rita Ann scolded. "What's in the box?"

O.T. propped the lid to one side and stared inside the flat wooden box. "Well, I'll be . . ."

"Daddy, what's in the box?"

O.T. cleared his throat. "Nothin'. Absolutely nothin's in the box. The box is empty."

Dola Mae Skinner could not remember ever going to church by herself. Not when she was five. Nor fifteen. Nor twenty-five. There was always Mother and Daddy, sisters and brothers,

Grannie and Grandpa . . . and then Orion and the children.

The restaurant felt big and empty when she returned. Chairs were on the tables. The kitchen was orderly and spotless, and the upstairs living area was crammed with familiar things, but no people.

No sounds of dancing feet.

No whistles.

No songs.

No sonnets.

No giggles.

No whining.

No "My mama is purdy."

No "Dola Mae, darlin' . . ."

Still wearing her new green dress, Dola opened the doors to the balcony and stood gazing at the dusty street below.

Well, Lord, I've had my long bath . . . my quiet evenin'. . . . my sleeping in until daylight. I've read Your Word, sung Your praises, and been exhorted to live a holy life. Now . . .

Now I want them to come back!

She sauntered back into the apartment. *I must do something. I'll read . . . or sew. . . . I know there are things to mend, and perhaps I'll bake them a pie. I really must keep busy. I'll scrub the restaurant again.*

"What did you do on your day off, Dola Mae?"

"I scrubbed the floors!"

No! I simply won't. I will only do today what I could not do with all of them here. I will . . . I will

. . . wear my best hat and take a nice, long walk in the fresh air. Perhaps I'll stroll out to Rabbit Springs or the cemetery. I will stop and visit with anyone who wants to chat, and I will come home any time I please! And if the drugstore is open, I will march right up to the counter and — and buy myself an iced . . . I will buy myself an iced tea!

The sun was past halfway overhead, and the shadows now spread to the east as Dola strolled along Columbia Street. The street seemed quiet. The pious were tucked into dining rooms enjoying the relaxation of an after-church lunch. The impious were, for the most part, still asleep from a rowdy Saturday night. The saloons and gambling halls never closed. And Dola was sure that down in the crib district, business continued. Miners, clerks, and occasional cowboys perched on the row of benches that seemed to front every building.

Most tipped their hats her way.

Many spoke to her by name.

Lord, I've been in this town six weeks, and I know a couple hundred men and six women. I think if I added up all the men I knew by name in my whole life before we arrived, it would be about twenty, at the most.

I'm not sure how this all came about . . . or why. All I ever wanted to cook for is one man. One rustic, old farm boy with a heart of gold and a gentle touch.

I miss the kids, Lord. After a day and a half, I miss Rita Ann pushing her glasses up on her nose and reciting her beloved Shakespeare. I miss Corrie Lou's careless exuberance and love of life. I miss Tommy-Blue's energy. I miss my Punky, his innate sweetness. Someday they will grow up. Someday I'll go for a walk, and they will live somewhere else.

But I really, really miss Orion. Lord, I don't want any day to be without him. My children are the extra blessings you have lavished upon me in life. Orion is my life. For days . . . for months I haven't stopped long enough to realize it.

"Hey, Dola Mae, you want to go for a ride?"

Omega and Lucian LaPorte rolled up to the curb in their black leather buggy.

"Where are you two off to?"

"We're going to Tonopah and won't be home until very late!" Lucian reported.

"That's a long trip for one day."

"Fast horses," Lucian said.

"You're invited to join us," Omega added, tugging at the long sleeves of her bright red dress.

"Oh, no, I couldn't."

"Just why couldn't you? You have time. You ain't goin' back there and scrubbin' the floors again, are you?" Omega challenged.

"Well, you're right. I do have time. But I'm not going to go."

"There's an eight-piece orchestra in from Reno at The Mispah," Omega reported. "I intend to do some dancin'!"

"I didn't think you had on your red dress just for shopping."

"Ain't this dress somethin'?" Omega's bright white teeth contrasted with her black skin. "The color is almost sinful."

"It looks very good on you."

"If anyone ever complains about the dress, I just tell them Dola Mae Skinner gave it to me, and she's the most righteous woman in Goldfield."

Dola flushed. "Oh, my, that isn't true."

Lucian tipped his hat. "Of course it is, Dola Mae. But I'll admit, you don't have a lot of competition."

"Are you sure you won't join us?" Omega questioned.

"I'm enjoying a walk, thank you."

"Well, girl, don't get too red out in the sun," Omega called. "And if I ain't back by breakfast, it's because I'm still dancin'!"

Dola watched them drive away and then meandered along for another block. She folded up the small, green parasol and let it droop over her arm. She stood for several moments studying a row of sofas in the window of Fernley's Department Store.

It seems so out of place for a town like Goldfield to have a row of new sofas. I suppose someone will buy them, but everything here is so worn, so . . . so dusty . . . so temporary. That blue one is quite attractive. I've never owned a new sofa in my life. My goodness, who can afford those?

But that blue one is very nice.

I know, Lord — I shall not covet. But maybe You'll let me dream a little!

The porch swing in front of the Grand Union Hotel was occupied by two smiling young people.

"Hello, Mrs. Skinner!"

"Why, Mr. Frazier, you look very handsome in a suit and tie!"

"Doesn't he?" Haylee Cox replied. "You enjoying your day off, Mrs. Skinner?"

"Yes. Well . . . to tell you both the truth, I miss them all. Yet it's been a very peaceful day."

Haylee slipped her arm into Hud Frazier's as they continued to rock. "I miss Rita Ann," she offered. Then she glanced at Hud. "She's fun to visit with."

Hud shrugged. "I wouldn't know. She hasn't said ten words to me since the first day I started workin' on the Thomas auto car. That reminds me, Mrs. Skinner, I think I can have it runnin' by next week if I can only find the right part."

"That would be exciting. Do we have any gasoline?"

"Nope."

"That might be a problem."

Hud laced his hand into Haylee's. "Yeah, I haven't figured that one out yet. But I'm working on it."

Dola glanced at Haylee's dancing eyes. *Yes, young man, I would say you're working on it.*

"I hear there's a man on Wilcox Street that has five gallons of gasoline he will trade for a one-half interest in a mule, but I reckon that's kind of a steep price."

"That all depends on the mule, doesn't it?" Dola laughed.

"Mrs. Skinner, you have such a lovely smile," Haylee blurted out. "I don't reckon I've ever seen you laugh before."

"Oh, I'm sure you . . . It's not . . . Well, perhaps I've been too busy."

"You have cute dimples just like Corrie Lou!" Haylee added.

"Thank you, Haylee."

"You want to sit on the swing with us, Mrs. Skinner?" Hud asked. "Me and Haylee can scrunch up."

"Thank you, but I'm going on a little walk. But by all means, Mr. Frazier, go ahead and scrunch up."

"Yes, ma'am, I think I will."

The man in the creased suit and new bowler carried a polished walnut cane as he strolled out of the Banker's Club. Dola started to scoot by without even glancing up at him.

"I say, aren't you Mrs. Skinner?" he asked.

She stopped and studied the man, who looked about Orion's age. "Have we met?"

"I'm Mr. McDonald from the July Extension Mine. I talked to your husband on Friday. Is he at home now?"

"I'm afraid he's out of town for a few days. Is there anything I can do for you?"

"Tell him we did reach Mr. Brannon at the state capitol, and we let him know about the Rokkers' new home."

"I'm very happy for them."

"Quite the place too. Have you seen it?"

"No, but I was thinking of walking by there."

"I think you'll be pleased. You might show it to Mr. Brannon if he's ever back this way."

"I'll do that."

"By the way, when Brannon telegraphed back, he said to check with you to see if you got the gift from Soto's Nursery. Did he send you any trees or shrubs or flowers?"

"Oh . . . the roses!" she said.

McDonald pulled off his bowler and fanned his round face. "He sent you a rosebush?"

Dola tugged on the tight collar of her green dress. "No, he sent fresh roses for every table at the restaurant!"

"A thoughtful fellow. Well, good day, Mrs. Skinner."

Dola strolled slowly east along the awning-covered, raised boardwalk in front of the Liberty Saloon. An aroma of sweat, smoke, and whiskey rolled out from the open doors.

Pop Brannon sent the roses! How did he know there are twenty-four tables? What a thoughtful man. He goes hunting with the President, backs down the mine officials with a gun and a glance, and sends roses. You are a delightful man, Mr.

Brannon. I can't for the life of me understand how you could be a widower for the past thirty years!

Nehemiah's Drugstore was open, and Dola slipped inside, setting off the bell that hung above the door. She studied a rack of women's remedies. *Lord, I don't even know what these diseases are, let alone if this cures them. I would hate to know that much. It would worry me sick, even when I wasn't.*

She worked her way to the glass-topped oak counter near the back of the store. A boy who looked about Rita's age, wearing thick gold-framed glasses, smiled at her. "Can I help you, ma'am?"

She studied a list on the wall.

"Do you have iced drinks?"

"Yes, ma'am, what would you like?"

I would like to try a Coca-Cola. "Do you have freshly made iced tea today?" she asked.

"Yep."

"I will have an iced tea, please."

"Large or small?"

"Oh, I . . ."

"The small is this size." The boy held up an eight-ounce glass.

"She'll have a large Cola," a voice boomed behind her.

Dola spun around. "Mr. Gately! I — I better have an iced tea."

"Mrs. Skinner, there is not one drop of alcohol in a Cola. I should know, shouldn't I?"

"Well, yes, but I never —"

"It's a good time to try. I'm buyin'."

"Oh, I can't let you do that."

"Why is that, Mrs. Skinner?" Gately challenged. "How many times in the last month have you come back out to the dining room and given me and Charley Fred and Wasco an extra piece of pie and never once charged us for it?"

"But that's quite different."

"You mean, you're allowed to be generous, but I'm not?"

She shook her head, clamped her thin lips together, and grinned. "All right, Mr. Gately, your logic prevailed over my intuition."

"And I thought it was my devilishly good looks. Fix the lady one large Coca-Cola," he told the boy.

"Aren't you having one too, Mr. Gately?"

"I have to leave. The boys are outside waitin' for me. We have papers to sign and business to take care of in San Francisco."

"My goodness, the whole town is going to San Francisco."

"Only the ones with rich claims! You enjoy that Cola, Mrs. Skinner!"

Dola studied the dark liquid in the glass in front of her. She slowly lifted it to her lips. *Lord, if this is sinful, please give me a sign. I certainly don't want to . . .*

She hesitated as she watched the boy pour another Cola and gulp half of it down with one swallow.

Dola took a sip. It tingled her lip and buzzed in her mouth. *Oh, my . . . oh, my, that is tasty. I do trust it isn't habit-forming.* She took another sip.

"Ain't that Cola grand?" the boy beamed.

"It's quite different."

"I like it better than sarsaparilla or even root beer," he said.

She took another sip. "It does seem to have more . . . zip . . . or something." She slowly sipped until the glass was empty.

"You want another, ma'am?"

"Oh, no! That was very nice indeed." She set the empty glass down and turned to the door. For a moment she almost felt dizzy. *There is no alcohol in it, Dola Mae. Twelve-year-old boys drink it. Enjoy yourself.*

She looked both ways along the sidewalk as she exited the building to make sure no one was looking.

I will not tell Orion about this.

I should have had iced tea.

Flat, boring iced tea.

"Mrs. Skinner! I went to your house, and nobody's home!" Stella Rokker ran toward her. "Where did everyone go?"

"They sort of went campin' with their father."

"I thought Mr. Skinner went to look for Daddy."

"Oh, he did, but they decided to make an excursion out of it."

"And they left you here?"

"I needed to take care of the restaurant," Dola explained.

"But the restaurant is closed."

"It will be open tomorrow."

"Oh, yeah. . . . Well, it seems sort of funny," Stella said.

"What's that?"

"That our daddy's gone, and all of us are here . . . and that you're here, and your whole family's gone."

"They'll be back."

"And so will Daddy," Stella said.

"I'm sure he will."

"Mama sent me to get you."

Dola and Stella stepped aside as several lunch-bucket-toting miners tramped past them. "Is she having a bad spell again, honey?"

"No, she's having a good spell! She wants you to come see our new house. It's beautiful. It's like a castle. Did you know it has a fireplace upstairs and a fireplace downstairs?"

"My goodness, that is grand!"

"Mama cried because she was so happy! She said we could live there forever!" Stella grabbed Dola's hand as they walked together. The girl's hand was sticky and warm. Dola squeezed it.

The brand-new, two-story brick house on Sixth Street was meant to showcase the mine owner's prosperity. It boasted ornate Victorian trim, dormers and cupolas, a picket fence, and the only grass lawn in the city of Goldfield. At least, grass seed was planted, and tiny blades were trying to poke up through the desert dirt.

Nellie Rokker dragged Dola by the hand from one room to another, giggling and laughing as if she weren't thirty-five going on sixty . . . as if her husband weren't missing for days . . . as if she had the income to sustain the house's charm . . . as if the two-story house would solve all of life's problems.

Dola surveyed the brand-new furniture in each room. *Lord, I've never seen this much new furniture even in a store, let alone in a house. I don't want to be jealous. I don't want to covet. I'm happy for Nellie. . . . I'm happy for Nellie. . . . I'm trying not to be unhappy for Dola Mae!*

Dola finally waved good-bye to the Rokker family and strolled west of town. The late afternoon heat began to cool slightly from a steady drift of wind that slid down California's Sierra Nevadas and rolled across the desert. Her green cotton dress almost dragged the dirt as she tramped up the long driveway to the cemetery.

A rough wooden bench was propped up near the one Joshua tree, which provided the cemetery's only shade. She tried to brush some of the dust off the bench with her parasol. Then she sat down with her back to the sun and stared out across Goldfield.

Lord, for almost a month I've spent nearly every day in that café . . . in the kitchen . . . in the dining room . . . in the apartment above it. But I'm tired. That's not me. I need to be outside more. The truth is, I've loved our travels, our camping — loading up the wagon and feeling fresh air in my face and a strong man by my side.

I like concentrating on just my family. Sometimes this restaurant business spreads me too thin. Lord, I'm really not jealous of Nellie. I have prayed earnestly for you to take care of the Rokkers, and You have answered in wonderful ways! Beyond all my mind could even ask. But I, also, would love to have a place to live that is just my house. A place with no restaurant downstairs, no friends sleeping in the living room, no dirt floors or tent walls. Lord, I would love to have a place where I could grow my own garden and fruit trees! Then every day I could go out and water and hoe and prune and harvest and prepare delicious meals for my Orion and my Rita Ann and my Corrie Lou and my Tommy-Blue and "my-mama's-purdy" Punky.

Dola felt the tears slide down her cheeks.

This is absurd. They have only been gone thirty-two hours, and I'm blubbering like a five-year-old.

She stood up and brushed her dress down, wiped her cheeks, and took a deep breath. "Lord, there's Goldfield over there. It's filled with greedy, selfish, sinful, lawless people, and I don't know why in the world You even allow it to exist."

Dola opened the parasol and draped it over her shoulder as she surveyed the horizon. "And the truth of the matter is, it's just like every other town on the face of the earth. 'The Lord is not slack concerning his promise, as some men count slackness; but is longsuffering to us-ward, not willing that any should perish, but that all should come to repentance.' "

"I will stay in Goldfield. I won't complain anymore . . . as long as You're doing Your work in the lives of the people. I will do whatever You ask me to. But, Lord, I can't stay alone. Not for a year . . . not for a month . . . not for a week . . . not for another day."

She began to stroll slowly back down the incline toward town. *I don't know why I ever agreed to let them all go. A day off? A day of dreaded loneliness. Maybe that was why. Maybe that's what I needed to learn.*

She waited for a cloud of dust to settle after a stagecoach rattled by before she trekked back along the Goldfield road. She hiked well off the road to allow other rigs to roll on toward town. Her head was down, her eyes on the bare desert floor. *Lord, that was horrible self-pity. I'm ashamed I'm such a weak child of Yours. I do best when I'm too busy to feel sorry for myself. I will go back and mop the floor, wash the windows, scrub the kitchen walls and —*

"Hey, lady, you need a ride to town?"

A choir of angels proclaiming the Lord's return couldn't have thrilled her heart any more than those words. She spun around to a chorus of "Mamas!" and a tiny voice yelling, "Mama-Mama-Mama-Mama!"

Her hand went over her mouth. She fought

back tears. "Oh . . . my . . . oh!"

"Are you all right, darlin'?" O.T. called out.

Rita Ann stared at her from head to toe. "What are you doin' out here, Mama?"

"We came home early, Mama," Corrie shouted.

"Daddy dug up an empty box," Tommy-Blue blurted out.

Punky rubbed a fat, little hand across his filthy forehead. "My mama is purdy!"

"I don't know what you are all talking about," she offered, "but your voices are the most beautiful on earth."

Orion handed the lead lines to Corrie and stepped down from the wagon. He gave her his hand to help her up. "You on a walk to the cemetery?"

"Yes. Eh, did you find Mr. Rokker?" she asked.

"No."

"Are you going back out to look for him?"

"No."

"Where's Fergus?"

"He hiked back out to the Wilkins brothers' mine. He decided to go to Schurz and look for his cousin. The one who lived in Goldfield."

"But I — I don't understand."

O.T. assisted her to the wooden bench seat. "Well, climb aboard and I'll tell you."

By the time they reached downtown Gold-field, each family member had given an account of the trip and the digging. By the time they reached the restaurant, Dola had described the Rokkers' new house.

"What have you got there, Mama?" Tommy-Blue pointed to the wooden-awning-covered boardwalk in front of the closed restaurant.

She saw a whiskey barrel that had been cut in two, filled with dirt, and a small tree planted in it.

"Are you landscapin' the sidewalk?" O.T. laughed.

"I — I . . . It wasn't there when I started my walk," she stammered.

Corrie jumped out of the wagon and ran over to the tree. A small brown card was tied with green yarn to one of the tiny limbs. "It says, 'I thought you might enjoy this. Don't know if they'll grow in Goldfield, but it's the same variety of peaches I have down in Arizona. Best to all, Pop Brannon.' " Corrie stared at Dola. "Mr. Brannon sent us a peach tree!"

All the other children scampered down to view the tree.

All except Punky.

He crawled up in his mother's lap. "Punky's dirty," he announced.

"You are a dirt ball from head to toe!" she laughed and then hugged him and kissed his cheek. "And I couldn't care less. Let's go see that tree. Pop Brannon has got to be the most generous man on earth," she declared. "Do you know what else he did? He sent me twenty-four red roses so we could have a fresh rose on every table. Can you imagine that? I didn't think there was any man in Goldfield — besides you — who knew how many tables we had in the —" Dola caught a flash in O.T.'s blue-gray eyes. Her hand went over her mouth. "*You* sent the flowers!"

That rugged, sly smile that still tickled her throat and sent goose bumps down her back rolled across his face. She threw her arms around his neck, kissed him on the lips, and began to bawl.

"What's wrong with Mama?" Corrie asked.

"She's just happy," Rita Ann explained.

"Well, I ain't ever goin' to kiss no girl if they act that way," Tommy-Blue asserted.

O.T. saw Dola resting on the bench in front of the restaurant when he and Corrie hiked back from the livery stable. Sitting on the boardwalk in front of her was a round baked-enamel laundry tub half filled with water. And perched in the tub was a naked two-year-old trying to drown a dozen green wooden spools.

He studied Dola's face as he approached. *Lord, I've never known anyone who had a heart for her family like Dola Mae. She finds her greatest joy and contentment in taking care of all of us. And I find my deepest joy in takin' care of that woman. But I wish I could take care of her better. We need to save up a few dollars and move on to Dinuba. The desert can get cold in the winter. We'll move before Thanksgiving, spend the winter building a house, and plant the vineyard in the spring.*

Who am I kiddin', Lord? We'll spend the winter with Pegasus and Pearl and try to scratch out day jobs for beans and biscuits. We got jobs here, Lord, and a roof over our heads. To walk away would be ungrateful.

Corrie released her daddy's hand and ran toward the tub. "Mama, do I have to take my bath on the front porch?"

"No, you're too big for that. Everyone gets clean water tonight. You're all too dirty to share water."

"I'm medium!" Punky held his nose, closed his eyes, and ducked under the water. He came up coughing and giggling.

"Don't drink the water, darlin'," Dola cautioned.

O.T. sat down on the bench beside Dola. "Did you talk to the sheriff's office about Rokker's hat?" she asked.

"Yep."

"And the empty box?"

"Yep. He said he'd go out there personally at daybreak tomorrow."

"Tomorrow? Why not this evening?"

"I suppose he has other chores." O.T. leaned his back against the bench and slipped his arm around her shoulder. "How are you doin', Mrs. Skinner?"

"This might be the best day of my life, Mr. Skinner."

"That good?"

"I slept in. Went to church. Visited with friends. Had a nice walk. Then my man came home. My special treasures were with him. I have a dining room smelling of roses. I own my very own peach tree. My word, Orion, I can't imagine life any better than this!"

From a block away an auto car began to honk.

Dola stared.

O.T. sat up.

The naked two-year-old spat out a mouthful of water.

Tommy-Blue ran around the corner from the back alley.

Rita Ann flew out of the restaurant carrying her Shakespeare book.

And Corrie slid up next to her daddy and held his hand. "Is that our auto car?" she asked.

"Nah, Hud and Haylee are in the alley, and he's workin' on it," Tommy-Blue replied.

"On what?" Corrie asked.

"On our auto car," Tommy-Blue mumbled.

"It's the Rokkers!" Rita Ann called out.

"Mr. Rokker's driving!" Corrie yelled.

"He ain't very good at it," Tommy-Blue said as they watched the black touring car weave its way up the dusty Goldfield street.

"Look at our auto car!" Jared Rokker screamed above the rumble of the engine.

As Rita Ann, Corrie, and Tommy-Blue scampered around the car, O.T. scooped up a wet, naked toddler and led Dola out to the street.

"Welcome home, Elias! We've been worried about you!" O.T. said.

"Skinner, my Nellie told me all you done for them while I was in the desert. I cain't thank you and the missus enough."

"We're goin' to California!" Stella called out.

"I get a new dress and a new dolly and two pairs of shoes that nobody has ever worn before," Caitlynn declared.

Dola studied Nellie's eyes. They seemed to stare across the valley at Malpais Mesa. "It was a lovely home," she murmured.

"Elias, what happened?" O.T. called out above the roar of the engine.

"Don Fernando's gold!" he shouted. "I found it just like the map said."

"What?"

"Yep, it was buried next to an adobe wall in a box. I stumbled across it in the windstorm."

"But — but that site was supposed to be four days away."

"Four days from somewhere. Must have been a different Rabbit Springs. Anyway that wind blew the dirt off the wall, and I found it. Been up to Tonopah to deposit my money. Nearly $60,000."

O.T. shook his head and jiggled the naked toddler in his arm.

"We're going to buy a house in San Bernardino, California," Danny exulted.

"Daddy's cousin lives there," Jared added. "We each get our very own room."

"There were quite a number of rooms in the house on Sixth Street," Nellie said.

The big, bearded man leaned over the door of the open-topped car. "You should've seen me out there diggin' away. The wind was blowin', my eyes were squinted shut, my heart racin'. I'd just toss a shovelful up in the wind and let it blow all the way to Utah. My hat kept blowin' off. I had to pick it down."

"What do you mean, pick it down?"

"Slammed the pick straight through it into the ground. Then I got so excited I went off and left it. It probably blowed down a skunk hole. Don't matter. I done bought me these fine clothes in Tonopah. It took me and that mule a couple days to tote the gold."

"We all get to buy new clothes in San Bernardino," Danny declared.

"Are you going to leave now? I'd be happy to fix us all some supper," Dola offered.

"Can't do it. I don't know how to start this thing. Have to keep it runnin'," Rokker explained. "Say good-bye to ever'one, kids. You Skinners is good folks. We'd like you to come see us when you get to California."

"Yes, we'll do that," Dola said. "Nellie, I'm so happy for you."

"You're the best friend I ever had," Nellie Rokker mumbled.

"The Lord be with you, Nellie Rokker," Dola called.

"And with you, Dola Mae Skinner." There was a half-smile on Nellie's lips and terror in her eyes. "Promise you'll come check on me?"

"I promise."

Nellie Rokker did not release Dola's hand until the auto car began to roll. Dola stood back on the porch and waved as the Rokkers chugged down the street. A naked Punky climbed back into his tin tub but remained standing as the car drove out of sight.

"I can't believe he actually found buried treasure in that same hole that I was diggin'," Tommy-Blue snorted. "Three days earlier, and I would have been the one findin' that there gold."

"I can't believe a phony map led him there," O.T. added.

Rita Ann clutched her book to her chest. "I can't believe they would just up and leave like that. 'When I consider everything that grows, holds in perfection but a little moment . . .'"

"Daddy, do you think we'll ever find buried treasure?" Corrie asked.

"Nope."

"How come, Daddy?" she pressed.

He slipped his hand into Dola's. "'Cause when you have all you want in life, you don't go lookin' for buried treasure. Ain't that right, Dola Mae?"

She could feel the tension in her temples

melt. It seemed like a slow waterfall right down to her toes. O.T.'s hand felt strong, warm, loving in hers.

Lord, I've cried, pouted, coveted, and whined — no more. No more. "Daddy's right. We don't want to waste time lookin' for buried treasure."

"Some treasure you carry in your pocket, and some you carry in your heart," O.T. philosophized.

"We have the heart kind, don't we, Daddy?" Corrie exclaimed.

"Yep, darlin', and it don't ever wear out . . . or git stuck in the desert sand."

"I like our kind of treasure best," Rita Ann sighed. "We don't have to worry about losing it."

"Besides, we already have us an auto car," Tommy-Blue put in.

"Well, let's go into the kitchen and fix some supper," Dola suggested. She reached down and scooped the dripping toddler out of the tin tub. "Come on, Punky, you look like a pretty, little pink prune."

"My mama's purdy," he declared.

Dola Mae took a big, deep breath. "You're right, little Punky. I might just be the purdiest woman on earth!"